MW00927965

The Two-Timing Corpse

Other books by dusty bunker:

Numerology And The Divine Triangle (With Faith Javane)

Numerology And Your Future

Numerology, Astrology And Dreams

Birthday Numerology(With Victoria Knowles)

Quintiles And Tredeciles: The Geometry Of The Goddess

Dream Cycles

One Deadly Rhyme: The Number Mysteries

The Two-Timing Corpse

The Number Mysteries

dusty bunker

Mystery and Suspense Press
San Jose New York Lincoln Shanghai

The Two-Timing Corpse
The Number Mysteries

All Rights Reserved © 2002 by dusty bunker

No part of this book may be reproduced or transmitted in any form or by any means, graphic, electronic, or mechanical, including photocopying, recording, taping, or by any information storage retrieval system, without the permission in writing from the publisher.

Mystery and Suspense Press
an imprint of iUniverse, Inc.

For information address:
iUniverse, Inc.
5220 S. 16th St., Suite 200
Lincoln, NE 68512
www.iuniverse.com

Illustrations from the Rider-Waite Tarot Deck, known also as the Rider Tarot and the Waite Tarot, reproduced by permission of U.S. Games Systems, Inc., Stamford, CT 06902 USA. Copyright 1971 by U.S. Games Systems, Inc. Futher reproduction prohibited. The Rider-Waite Tarot Deck is a registered trademark of U.S. Games Systems, Inc.
Any resemblance to persons living or dead is purely coincidental.

ISBN: 0-595-21621-8

Printed in the United States of America

For Joan Hansen, Sandy Bouras and Dottie Limont.
Thank you for your eagle eyes and your friendship.

Acknowledgements

Thanks go to Col. George L. Iverson, Ret., of the New Hampshire State Police, and Lt. David L. Roy of the Brentwood Police Department, for their valued assistance. Any errors are mine since I tend to take liberties with the law (just on paper, of course!).

Also, a big thank you to editors Nancy Marple and Bonnie Corso. What would a writer do without such magical creatures?

And a final thank you to my breakfast companions, Skip and Matthew. Getting through breakfast without splattering a mouthful of food over the table because of their humorous exchanges is a chore, but I have persevered. A number of their repartees are sprinkled through-out this book. It's okay. They're family.

One wonders if it is "…always good
When a man has two irons in the fire."

The Faithful Friends [c. 1608]
Francis Beaumont and John Fletcher

WHEEL OF FORTUNE.

QUEEN OF PENTACLES

THE LOVERS.

KING OF PENTACLES.

DEATH.

THE DEVIL.

THE TOWER.

Prologue

The Tarot was the perfect touch.

Eleven cards had been carefully selected. They were neatly spread in the ancient Keltic cross: four cards surrounding the central three, a vertical line of four more to the right. The final outcome—Key 10: The Wheel of Fortune.

How appropriate.

But it was the Eight of Swords that had been deliberately chosen as representative of the man on the floor. That symbolic card was in position five—something that may happen.

Well, it had happened alright!

A laugh echoed in the cavernous building.

In a wash of blood on the cold cement floor lay the body of a man bound with heavy rope, the blindfold unnecessary over eyes that would never see again.

The black shrouded figure slipped the knife into a plastic bag, closed the door, and melted into midnight.

CHAPTER 1

"That's when I decided to kill my husband."

Katherine Vandalay tapped an unlit Newport against a slim gold case engraved with her initials. "And I need some advice."

Sam had seen thousands of clients, but never had been asked how to successfully exterminate a husband.

"You came highly recommended," the woman said as she crossed long shapely legs. "And I did look at one of your books. It was rather interesting. Your simple premise that our lives repeat in nine-year cycles made me think." She said it as if her literary tastes had gone slumming.

Sitting in her stuffed rocker opposite the woman, Sam practiced her Mona Lisa smile and waited for the other exquisitely clad foot to drop.

Sam figured Katherine Vandalay was around thirty years old. According to numerology, that was the age when major events happened. Killing one's husband certainly fit the criteria.

Samantha Blackwell, syndicated numerologist and author of acclaimed books on the subject, enjoyed her unhurried lifestyle in the town of Georgetown, nestled fifteen miles from the New Hampshire coastline. Whenever necessary, her recent introduction to the Internet put her in instant touch with the "outside world," as she called it—although she found, at age forty-nine, that she was more of a recluse than ever. Especially since the *incident* last year.

The deep velvety voice continued. "I thought you might be able to help me. You did solve those…" Katherine's slender fingers fluttered at the air "…what were they called? The Cowberry Necklace Murders?" A two-carat emerald-cut diamond flashed in the dim October sun.

Sam looked past the woman and out the window of her sun porch office, past the peeling white deck. She could see the maples blazing red and orange amongst thick pines in her back yard and waited for the 'flutterbys' in her stomach to alight. Sparrows darted in and out of the large house-shaped bird feeder. Georgetown was in the midst of tourist season, and this year, Sam was President of the Cowberry Festival Committee. It wouldn't do to slack off on this prime appointment from Agatha Beatrice Coldbath, owner and last remaining heir of the Coldbath Chutney fortune. How many times had the old dowager scolded her with the reminder that "since the days of King George III, my chutney has graced the delicate palates of royalty and heads of state?"

Sam was well aware that the town's year-round economy depended upon the square, squat jars labeled "Coldbath Cowberry Chutney— Chutney to the world since 1798." On the parchment-type labels, and beneath an artist's rendition of old King George's crown, was the large flourishing signature (digitally enhanced from the original) of the founder, William Hornblower Coldbath.

No mention was made that it was William's wife who had come up with the recipe, gave two jars to her ailing neighbor, who then sent one of the chutneys to a brother in England, who then gave it to his lady friend, a royal maid to King George III. No one was quite sure how the maid got the king's attention, but rumors were rampant.

Sam buried the fingers of one hand in her long fine hair and rubbed. Besides the Fair, she had clients to see and her weekly column to write. She didn't want to get mixed up in another homicide…if that's what this appointment was about.

Homicide.

She would never hear that word again without icy coils twisting around her spine.

She touched her left side as if she could feel the small scar beneath her sweatshirt. To Katherine, she said, "If you'd like to smoke, please step outside."

"What?" The woman frowned, then twisted a quarter turn to the right. She took a moment to examine the splintering white paint on the railings then faced Sam once again. A tiny spot at the corner of her left eye quivered as she looked down at the cigarette in her hand. "Oh. No, thank you. I don't smoke."

Really?

As the woman continued to tap the unlit cigarette, Sam was reminded of an early television commercial—a red Pall Mall cigarette box tap dancing on human legs to some jingle.

"It's a terrible habit," Katherine Vandalay added.

So's denial, Sam thought, *but hey, we all have our addictions.*

Sam took a deep breath. She had to admit she was envious of the can't-be-too-thin body encased in a creamy silk blouse and soft black suede skirt. The thick gold necklace at her throat matched her earrings. The woman smelled of Dior's *Hypnotic Poison* and reeked of money.

She looked down at her own belly bulge under her gray sweat pants, and was reminded of her daily struggle with Ring Dings and the bathroom scale. She vowed (again) to start exercising tomorrow and to get rid of the thirty extra pounds. But not before she got rid of Katherine Vandalay.

The cigarette tapping stopped. "Of course, I didn't kill my husband. Someone else did," the woman said. "I could never do such a thing. I loved Henry."

Sam tried to remain impassive. Again, her thoughts flipped back to last year. She closed her eyes for a moment as that terrifying scene roiled in her mind.

"But I'm afraid I'm a suspect," Katherine said. Shaking death from her mind, Sam fastened her attention on the woman before her. Katherine Vandalay's nostrils flared and the skin over perfect cheekbones grew taut as she continued. "Henry was thirty years older than I am, so naturally everyone thinks I was after his money."

Sam felt her insides shudder. She pondered the high-maintenance woman and wondered what really went on behind those violet eyes. Was this woman capable of killing another human being?

At some level, Sam thought, *everyone is capable. Even me, the animal-loving vegetarian, the one who stops at every little kid's lemonade stand, the first place winner in the Miss I-Can-Fix-It-For-You, Don't-You-Worry Contest.*

She let out a puff of air and wondered why she couldn't have an ordinary client—like the woman having an affair with the local priest or the crazed New Hampshirite plotting the downfall of Vermont. She didn't need to be reminded of the night that she shattered a man's skull with a fireplace poker.

"I'm a numerologist, not a detective or a lawyer," Sam said.

Katherine Vandalay sighed and, with the back of her cigarette hand, brushed at the spun gold hair that fell in folds to her shoulders. "Look. I have a lawyer, and private investigators can be troublesome. I want you."

The old World War II poster flashed through Sam's mind—a determined Uncle Sam pointing that finger of fate. Too many young people died in that war. Had fate singled her out to be involved in more death?

Katherine leaned forward. "I want you," she repeated.

Sam thought about that for a moment then said, "What do you think I can do for you?"

"Mrs. Blackwell, I'm desperate. I thought you could, um, see something?"

"See?"

"Yes. You know, like a psychic impression. Something that would clear me of my husband's murder." She floated back against the rocker cushion and resumed tapping the cigarette.

Sam took a deep breath as a wave of heat prickles washed over her upper torso. "First, my name is Samantha. Everyone calls me Sam. Secondly, I'm not a psychic."

Katherine Vandalay's penciled eyebrows rose. "Really? Oh, I thought…given what the newspapers said about you…"

"You can't believe everything you read in the newspapers, Mrs. Vandalay." That fact had been driven home after last year's fiasco.

The woman's fingers fell silent. "Please. Call me Katherine."

The heat was intense now, but Sam refused to flap the front of her sweatshirt in front of this woman who belonged on the cover of *Elle*.

How do they stay so thin? she wondered as she did when she stood in the supermarket check-out line surrounded by magazine covers with high-cheekboned, full-lipped, twenty-year-old faces gazing at her. She knew (if there were a just Creator in the Universe) that those impossible hairdos would fall flat as yesterday's birthday balloons as soon as the camera clicked and the fan stopped blowing.

To make matters worse, it seemed that every magazine promised the easy, super simple, last-one-you-will-ever-need, eat-all-you-want-and-lose-ten-pounds-a-week diet. Sam was an authority. She had tried them all and had come to the rather distasteful conclusion that the only thing that might work was sewing her lips shut for five months. But she hated needles.

Sweat beaded on her forehead. Instead of flapping her sweatshirt, she reached out to finger the ficus beside her, one of many plants in her jungle, as her daughters called the sun porch.

Katherine bit a tiny piece of her top lip as if considering her next move. Even beneath the makeup, dark half moons under her eyes attested to sleepless nights. Sam wondered if Katherine had been wrestling with incubi or flesh and blood demon lovers.

Be nice, she told herself. *A gorgeous young woman could be in love with an older wealthy man.* She smiled inside. *Sean Connery is a pretty sexy guy.*

Katherine pulled out her ammunition. "Charles Burrows told me about you. I'm his wife's second cousin, twice removed, sort of. Charles has a high regard for your problem-solving abilities. He agreed you could help me."

Sam tucked a wisp of hair behind her ear, then lowered her hand into her lap. "Really?"

She had a vague memory of Brun telling her about a distant relative who married into the Vandalay fortune. But she thought Brun had lost contact with that side of the family years ago. Even so, Katherine's connection complicated matters. Brun's husband, Chief of Police Charlie Burrows, was Sam's childhood friend. Sam realized she was going to have a hard time getting out of this one. She pulled on her right ear lobe. "I see."

Katherine settled back. Sam suspected that Katherine Vandalay was one of those women who always got what she wanted. One way or another.

"What were the circumstances surrounding your husband's death, Katherine?" Sam had read the papers and heard about the murder on the six o'clock news, but the devil was in the details. *Especially those Tarot cards.*

"Henry was in construction."

"Vandalay Enterprises," Sam acknowledged, stifling a crazy impulse to laugh as a vision of *Seinfeld's* George Costanza, the latex salesman for Vandalay Industries, popped into her mind.

"Yes. He owned Vandalay Enterprises. It seems everyone's building today."

Sam often passed the ten acres covered with metal buildings as she drove to Manchester on Route 101.

"How did he die?"

"Oh, yes, that," Katherine said. Her outlined melon lips pursed. She looked down at the still unlit cigarette between her fingers. "He, ah, he was found in the shop a week ago. Tied up with rope and wearing a blindfold." With her chin down, Katherine lifted her eyes. Long black lashes curled out from eyes that resembled dewy crocuses. "He had been stabbed. Many times."

A moment hung between them as Sam waited for Katherine to tell her about the cards. When the silence became prolonged, she said, "I see. Who found your husband?"

"Kenneth Ash, one of Henry's employees. He called me first, and of course, I went right over. As I pulled into the entrance, a car went tearing past me. Kenneth said it was a reporter. The man must have had his police scanner on and been in the area. I'm sure that's how the story got into the newspaper so quickly." She shook her head in disgust. "The police arrived right after I did. By then, there were half a dozen employees standing around. It was just awful." Her violet eyes lowered for a moment.

"Can you tell me more about that morning?" Sam said gently.

Katherine pursed her lips, then said, "Yes. Whoever did this terrible thing left Tarot cards beside Henry's body."

Finally. "Really?"

"Yes. Are you familiar with the Tarot?"

"Somewhat." Sam had written a series of columns a few years back on the subject.

"I didn't know what the cards were at first, but I did make notes," Katherine said.

Sam couldn't imagine having the presence of mind to take notes when standing over the murdered body of a beloved husband.

Katherine must have noticed her surprise because she added, "I was so distraught that I couldn't just stand there, so I went into the office for a piece of paper and sketched the design. I'm sorry I didn't get the numbers on the cards but they were laid out in some sort of a cross. I thought it might help me in the future to figure out who did this."

That could be helpful, Sam thought. *But wait a minute. I haven't agreed to take this case. Case?*

Now she was talking like Parker's Boston P.I., Spenser. She wasn't about to get involved again, so why did she find herself saying, "Did you bring that information with you?"

"Oh, no. I'm sorry. I should have. If you think it will be helpful, I will get it to you."

Sam blinked a few times as she wondered about the woman's inability to recognize important facts. Then she asked, "Why exactly did you want to kill your husband?"

Katherine tossed her head. "Oh, I would never have done it. I just wanted to plan it, to have the satisfaction of knowing I could do it. I had just decided I was going to *plan* to murder my husband when someone actually killed him."

Strange pastime, Sam thought, as she nodded. Plus, the word murder didn't seem to bother Katherine. She thought about her own horror and repulsion when the word had almost come home to roost. Again, she asked, "Why did you want to kill your husband?"

Katherine looked up at the Siamese wooden angel suspended from a gold hook on the ceiling above their heads, then out the window at the sparrows fighting for position on the bird feeder. After a moment, she looked back at Sam. "A number of reasons."

"Name three."

Katherine's smile revealed a row of perfect white teeth that, Sam figured, bought some orthodontist and his family a Caribbean cruise.

"I know there were other women. I often smelled perfume on his clothes, and it wasn't mine."

"And?"

"Isn't that reason enough?"

"Not for some women."

Katherine thought about that for a moment, then said, "There was his abuse."

Sam clenched her lips then said, "Did he beat you?"

Katherine laughed, a winged fluttery sound at odds with her throaty voice. "No, nothing like that. It was verbal abuse. He would rant and rave about how much money I spent on myself. As if he didn't like it. He was always showing me off like I was some kind of trophy."

"And the third?"

"Third what?"

"Reason."

Katherine didn't hesitate. "The absolute end was when he sold my silver Ferrari. We had a terrible fight, and the next day, my car was gone. He did it out of spite. He knew I loved that car. I will never forgive him for that."

Sam figured the man didn't need her absolution now. Tension bunched in the muscles behind her neck. Taking a deep breath, she placed a hand on each thigh and rolled her shoulders once, then focused on the woman before her. She wondered how many men found that dewy look irresistible. "Since I'm not a psychic, you want me to do what?"

"I want you to help me find the person who killed my husband."

"That can't be done through numerology."

Katherine shook her head. "No, of course not. Charles said you are very—what's the word he used? Oh yes. Intuitive."

"I see."

"And you're a woman. I knew you'd understand." She leaned forward again, the cigarette in one hand, the case in the other. "Please, Sam. I'll pay whatever you ask."

CHAPTER 2

At the Port Grande Hotel in Portsmouth, New Hampshire, private investigator Carl Gleason stared out his window at the mighty Piscataqua River and the red tugboats moored at the piers. Several seagulls rose and dove on the currents of the wind. The drawbridge on the aged Memorial Bridge that connected Portsmouth to Kittery, Maine, was raised. Lines of traffic in both directions waited while an oil tanker lumbered up the river.

If memory served Gleason, the Piscataqua River had one of the strongest currents in the world. The river separated Portsmouth from Kittery, Maine, site of the Portsmouth Naval Shipyard. Arguments had raged for years about the ownership of the yard: New Hampshire claimed that old deeds proved the shipyard sits on New Hampshire property; Maine strongly opposed the claims. Many tax dollars rode on the final judgement. The case stirred the same animosities as the donnybrook between the early colonial New Hampshirites and Vermonter Ethan Allan and his Green Mountain Boys.

But Carl Gleason couldn't stay focussed on the activity before him. He kept returning to that day—when was it? Six, seven weeks ago?—when the first contact was made.

Glenda had answered the phone.

Glenda. Carl smirked to himself. What a perfect name for a private eye's secretary. Like some dame in an old detective novel. And she looked the part. Generous breasts bulging seductively under tight sweaters, skirts above the knee. Legs without end. Curly black hair trailing down past her shoulders. But like many works of art, Glenda had a flaw: the woman never stopped talking. Gleason would have overlooked that if he could have gotten her into bed, but she wasn't interested. She thought of him as an old man. Yeah? Well, she didn't know what she was missing. Twenty years ago, she would have been panting after him like a dog in heat. The hell with her. There were plenty of other women in his little black book.

He shook off those thoughts. Once again, as he had so many times since that first strange telephone call with this client, Gleason replayed the scene.

Glenda leaned back in her chair, her hand over the phone's mouthpiece, and called to me. "Some guy wants to talk to you. He won't give me his name."

"Okay. I'll take it," I said. I picked up the phone, and said, "This is Carl Gleason. What can I do for you?"

"I'm looking for a woman."

"Aren't we all?" I said, laughing. After a minute, I realized levity wasn't his strong point. "Okay, then. Ah…can I have your name?"

The man's voice faltered, just for a moment, but I caught it. "John Smith," he said.

Right, I thought. I picked up my Mont Blanc pen, and began twiddling it. "Mr. Smith. Okay. Now, who is this woman you're looking for, and why do you need to find her?"

His voice was flat. "Why I need to find her is my business. You do your job, and you'll be rewarded. There'll be a big bonus check waiting for you when you've found her."

I suddenly had a vision of the proverbial carrot dangled in front of the horse. Inches away. But never quite within reach.

When I started to protest, the carrot planted itself before Michael's, the Shop for Discerning Men.

So I figured it was the client's business why he wanted this woman. If he didn't hire me, he'd call the next guy. I was hurting for cash at the moment, and there were those Italian shoes at Michael's I had my eye on.

"Alright, Mr. Smith," I said. "Let's get down to details."

And that was the gist of the ensuing conversations since that first contact six weeks ago. No hello, goodbye, or social niceties. Wham, bam, thank-you, ma'am.

Gleason didn't have a clue who his client was. He hadn't seen the guy, and didn't know where he was from. The envelopes sent to his office were postmarked from different cities along the eastern seaboard, and contained cash. There was no easy way to trace the client, even if Gleason wanted to. Which he didn't. He had been too busy rooting out this babe.

And now he was here in Portsmouth, ready to start canvassing the town. He'd ask discreet questions. He knew she was close by. And he knew he would find her.

Gleason didn't like dealing with a faceless client; this wasn't the way he worked. But the client had been paying on time from the beginning, with the promise of that big carrot when Gleason found the woman.

And the carrot had better be big, he thought, as he ran his hand over the front of his Armani suit. *I have my needs.*

CHAPTER 3

❀

Sam was pondering Katherine Vandalay's proposal.

She's willing to pay whatever I ask?

That was an offer Sam didn't want to refuse. She said to Katherine, "I'm not sure I can help you. The only reason I was involved in the Cowberry Necklace Murders is because my name was on the notes the killer left. I'm not a trained investigator."

"I understand. But you're a researcher. That much is obvious from your book. Please. I know you can help me."

Sam looked hard at Katherine Vandalay. She thought she'd try on Spenser's lethal stare and found that it fit too well. "This isn't my field," she scowled, hoping to dissuade the woman.

"I don't care," Katherine countered. "As I said, I'll pay whatever you ask."

Sam's scowl eased. In fact, one eyebrow lifted.

Well, she reasoned, *Katherine is Charlie's relative. Sort of. I think. And a Caribbean cruise with Nick is very tempting. Maybe we'll run into that orthodontist…*

Finally she sighed. Mostly for effect. Then she said, "Alright, I'll do my best. You understand that questions will have to be asked."

Katherine smiled and folded back into the chair. The cigarette resumed tapping. "I understand."

"The questions may be uncomfortable."

Katherine stopped tapping, transferred the cigarette to the hand with the case, recrossed her legs, and smoothed the hem of her skirt over the top of her knee.

"I'm willing to do whatever it takes," Katherine said. "I'm a suspect in my husband's murder. This thing needs to be resolved."

Sam took a hard look at Katherine Vandalay. "Even if you are paying me for this investigation, if you had anything to do with your husband's death, I have to report it."

Katherine's face grew red. A tiny vein pulsed on her forehead, above the eye that quivered. "I didn't kill my husband!"

"I sincerely hope not," Sam said. "Are we agreed?"

Katherine nodded, the edges of her anger barely restrained. She rolled the Newport between her thumb and forefinger.

Sam focused on the melon lip print around the mouth end of the cigarette in Katherine's hand while that little voice in her head told her to avoid this woman as if she had the plague. The problem was, no one could tell Sam what to do—not even her Inner Self. After all, there was the Caribbean.

But if the woman really was innocent…Sam's voice softened as she shifted her gaze toward her client. "Look, Katherine. If I'm going to do this, I need your cooperation. Even if it's uncomfortable."

Katherine nodded, quick up and down movements.

"Alright. Now. Do you have an alibi for the time your husband died?"

Katherine blinked away the wetness in her eyes. "No. You see, he was found early in the morning when the shop opened. The coroner thinks the time of death was around one o'clock in the morning. I was home in bed, asleep."

"Alone?"

The cigarette froze in mid-air. Katherine glared at Sam over those high cheekbones. "Of course!"

Sam noticed but went on. "Was your husband often out late at night?"

Spears of light flashed from Katherine's ring finger as she finally put the cigarette back in the gold case and slipped the case into the black leather bag on the floor. She gave her diamond ring a few twists, then drummed her melon nails on the arms of the rocker.

"We have separate bedrooms. He was often out late on business," she hesitated as if thinking about other types of mergers he might have been into, "and didn't want to disturb me when he came in. I had no way of knowing when he came home or *if* he came home. He always left for work early in the morning before I got up."

Sam found herself gazing at the stone on Katherine's finger, wondering how many millions of years it took for the earth's pressure to turn that piece of carbon into a diamond, and how many Africans were needed to dig it out of the mines. Still mesmerized by a piece of the rock, she said, "Were you alone in the house that night?"

"Yes. Except for my sister-in-law, Ula."

"How old is she?

"Ula is forty-six, I think."

"And she lives with you and your husband?"

"Is that relevant?"

This was going to be like pulling those fine orthodontic teeth. "Please," Sam said.

"Yes, she does. It seems strange, I know, but she is Henry's only living relative. She has her own bedroom and living area. In fact, I seldom see her, even though we both live in the same house. Except in the evening. She eats dinner with us." She paused. "Or rather, she ate dinner with us." A tiny wrinkle on her brow suggested she was unsure of her tenses.

"Was Ula at home that night?"

"Ula was devastated by her brother's death. I've never seen such a public display. In the church, she threw herself over the casket and had to be led out before the ceremony ended."

Sam marveled at the woman's inability to be direct, but that could be used to advantage down the line. Katherine's buckshot thought process had already provided more information than Sam had expected. "I see. Was Ula at home the night your husband was killed?"

"I assume she was in her quarters. The house is quite large and her space is in another wing. She keeps to herself."

"Who stands to inherit Vandalay Enterprises?"

Tiny wrinkles crept along Katherine's brow. She took in a slow breath and exhaled. "As his wife, I stand to inherit everything."

"What about his sister?"

Katherine shivered and looked over her left shoulder as if a ghostly hand had touched her. Then she leaned forward and said, in a voice that might have suspected an eavesdropping device had been planted in the shrubbery on Sam's left, "Between you and me and the bedpost, I think she's one can short of a six-pack." She blinked, seemed to remember something, then sat back and lifted her chin.

Startled at the shift in Katherine's vocabulary from precise English to common vernacular, Sam stifled her surprise and said, "He left nothing for his sister?"

"Henry told me that, upon his death, Ula would receive a generous trust payable in monthly installments. And if she chooses, she can live in our house for the rest of her life. She'll never have to worry."

"Do you know of anyone who'd want to kill your husband? Did he have trouble with anyone recently?"

Katherine didn't hesitate. "That's the problem. Henry was ruthless behind closed doors, but in public, he was a saint." She sat back. "Like the street angel-home devil type. Everyone will tell you how charming and generous he was. He gave to charities, he was on the board of the Children's Hospital and the Cancer Fund drive. It wouldn't have surprised me if he helped little old ladies cross the street. Image was so important to him."

The latter statement was a classic case of projection, Sam thought. "So, no one else saw the ruthless side of him?"

"I don't think so. Probably not. He never let his guard down in public."

"Tell me more about Ula Vandalay."

A flicker of disgust was masked by a winning smile, a facial shift not lost on Sam. "Ula was completely loyal to Henry. Whatever he wanted, she did. Cooked his meals, did his laundry. She even cleaned the house. It was as if she didn't want anyone else coming into my home." She sniffed. "Ula acted more like a servant than his sister. You'd think the woman would have more pride."

"Pride goeth before destruction, and an haughty spirit before a fall," Sam thought, remembering the line from Proverbs 16:18. She never could figure out why she remembered quotes and numbers, and not people's names.

"Where is your home, Katherine?"

"In Rye, on the ocean. One can only imagine what Henry paid for the place since there's only eighteen miles of coastline in New Hampshire. But he never talked about money. He was a very private man." Her nostrils flared like a thoroughbred filly. She shook her golden mane.

"I see. When did your husband buy the property in Rye?"

"About two years ago. That's when he moved his business here from Utah. He liked the growth possibilities in New Hampshire, and he found the property when he was here on one of his frequent business trips."

"And Ula followed."

"Yes. What else would she have done?"

Katherine recrossed her long legs, then tugged at the sleeves of her blouse. The creamy material made a "silken sad uncertain rustling."

Sam expected Edgar Allen Poe to walk through her door next. She blinked, forcing her mind back to Katherine's conversation.

"Ula doesn't have a life outside the house," Katherine was saying. "She's not interested in men. Probably because they're not interested in her. She's so plain. She doesn't wear makeup, she pulls her hair straight back in a bun. Every piece of clothing in her closet is black. She dresses like a mortician." Katherine struggled to contain her scorn.

Sam looked down at her hands to find she was tracing triangles in her palm. Given that Katherine didn't seem close to her sister-in-law, Sam wondered how Katherine knew the color of the clothes in Ula's closet.

A clutch of sparrows around the feeder caught Sam's eye. She turned to see a crow swooping through the back yard. The sun, higher in the sky, had shrunk the shadow beneath the feeder to a squat box-like shape.

Sam glanced at the little gold clock on the table between herself and Katherine. Nick had found it at the Brookstone kiosk in the Fox Run Mall during the Christmas holidays. The clock side faced her; in the slot behind, facing her clients, her business cards concealed the timepiece. It was, Nick had told her, a discreet way of monitoring the time she spent with her clients.

The clock read 11:10; the next client was due at eleven-thirty. Although another hundred questions rumbled in Sam's brain, they would have to wait until later.

To Katherine, she said, "I'd like to meet Ula and some of your husband's friends and business associates and see the property on Route 101."

"Of course. I'll leave instructions with Anthony Vernelli at the business site. He was Henry's right hand man, and he's running things temporarily until I decide what to do.

"Also, my husband left instructions with his attorney that, upon his death, his wife was to arrange a benefit party and invite everyone who is anyone. Plus his employees. In lieu of flowers, he wanted the attendees to make donations to the specific charities he selected. I have made the arrangements for the gathering. Sunday afternoon at two o'clock. Casual chic." Her lids fluttered. "You and your husband will spend the

night at my place, either at the main house, or in the cottage if you prefer. Charles and Brunhilda will be there too, of course. If you like, you
may come Saturday afternoon. That will give you time to look around."

Sam didn't like being told what to do but…visions of palm trees and
tropical breezes swept over her.

"Let me check my calendar for this weekend."

Although she knew the weekend was open, Sam got up and walked to
her desk. As her finger traced over the empty Saturday and Sunday
squares she said, "Yes, we can squeeze you in." She couldn't help herself.

She turned toward Katherine. "I will also need the names and
addresses of the people you mentioned." As she returned to her chair,
she added, "And we should discuss my fee."

Katherine promised to have the list ready by the weekend, then she
scrawled her signature at the bottom of a healthy starter check, and
thanked Sam as they exited to the back hall.

Katherine floated through the doorway, slipped into her gleaming
white Lexus convertible, backed out of the driveway to a screeching halt,
then left a strip of rubber as she tore down the street and around the
corner of the common.

Sam noticed the ones and fives on Katherine's license plate. Over the
years, she had observed how the numbers on license plates indicated the
attitudes of the people driving the vehicles. This attitude indicator
applied to telephone numbers as well as home and business addresses.

With the aggressive ones and the impulsive action of the impatient
fives identifying her car, Katherine Vandalay could leave Mario Andretti
in the dust. She was one woman you wouldn't want behind you on a
two-lane winding mountain road.

Sam stared out the diamond-paned window as the dust settled and
their conversation replayed in her mind.

*A cheating husband, the servant sister-in-law, a business worth mil-
lions. And those Tarot cards. In some sort of a cross.*

If Sam remembered her research correctly, the cross could be the ancient Keltic method. If that were the case, the person who killed Henry Vandalay must have had at least a beginning knowledge of the Tarot. It was a place to start.

What with the incident last year, and now this, she wondered what was happening to her rustic town. Should she call upon the Pied Piper of Hamelin to rid her hamlet of plague-carrying rats?

She glanced at the outside thermometer mounted on this, the north side of the house. Sixty-one degrees in the shade. It had been unseasonably cold the last few nights. The Cowberry Festival was coming up in three weeks, and a stretch of Indian summer would be nice. As another hot flash radiated from her chest and climbed up over her face, she decided that cool weather and no rain was preferable.

As she let out a puff of air, her right ankle twinged. An old sprain had transformed her ankle into a reliable barometer. She peered at the sky. There was a storm coming, and it felt like a big one.

Sam glanced down at the silver-colored check in her hands. Once again, she marveled at the numerous ciphers and how easily Katherine had written out the digits. She reminded herself she had done the right thing. She could handle the Fair, her clients, the columns, and the investigation. There was no job too big for this outfit.

Tonight, she would prop this little beauty in front of Nick's dinner plate—*that should whet his appetite.* She smiled at the pun. Then she'd tell him about the Caribbean cruise. *That should soften my involvement in another homicide.*

The icy coils again. She shimmied, as if the motion would ease the chill. How could she be hot and cold at the same time?

Sam had to admit to mixed emotions. Murder was an unspeakable act. To kill another human being created ripples in the Universe. Someone once wrote that you cannot pick a flower but that you disturb a star. The Cowberry Necklace murders last year had taught her that.

She touched her side once again.

And here she was, walking into another sticky wicket. On the other hand, Sam loved solving puzzles, had since she was a child hiding under the bright red patchwork quilt with a flashlight, pen, and puzzle books, long after the family had gone to bed. For a wistful moment, she thought of her father, how he teased her about doing crosswords with a ballpoint pen. "Shows a confident mind," he would say, and gently rub a knuckle under her chin. How she missed him.

Sighing, she set aside the philosophical conundrum, tucked the check into a cubbyhole in the Larkin desk, and wandered back to the sun porch.

The sky had grown dark; thick clouds crept across a dimming sky. A crow swooped down toward the bird feeder, sending the flock of sparrows frenetically swirling into the treetops. The crow, black as midnight, pounced upon the weathered dowel and shifted from one talon to the other before lowering his head to stab at the seeds bunching at the base of the feeder's glass sides.

As Sam watched seeds and shells falling to the dirt, she thought about Henry Vandalay. Death was so final. Henry Vandalay would never see the sky or clouds again. Or savor the pungent smells of fall. Or hear the birds singing.

She folded her arms across her chest, and as if a wraith had whispered a harsh secret in her ear, shivered once again and said, "Quoth the Raven, Nevermore."

Chapter 4

Katherine Vandalay tightened her grip on the steering wheel of her Lexus convertible. *Men were put on this earth to be used,* she thought, *and then abandoned once they served their purpose.* This philosophy had sustained her since she was fourteen years old. Allowing herself a moment of smugness, she had to compliment herself on this particular conquest. Coercing Henry into putting her in his will that night was the smartest thing she had ever done. She acted the role of the distracted blonde bimbo, but the truth was, Katherine was nobody's fool. Her mind was razor sharp.

She drove east on Route 101, over Interstate 95, and swung a right onto the exit to Route 27. That took her through the center of Hampton to North Beach and Route 1A, the road that followed the tiniest coastline in the United States. On any given day during the summer season, Hampton's population rose to a hundred thousand. But now, in early October, the tourists were gone and the two-lane road was all but deserted. Cottages and turn-of-the-century beach houses soon gave way to regal homes with sprawling manicured lawns.

Katherine felt her spirits rise along with the price of the real estate.

On her right, thick, dark clouds crept toward the shore, stalking the sun as it rolled over the stately mansions facing the Atlantic Ocean.

Suddenly, the warm breeze had taken on an underlying chill—a subtle warning of things to come.

Stormy weather, thought Katherine, and she smiled.

Katherine liked storms; they made her feel alive. She had survived more storms than most, and now, after this latest tempest, she almost had it made. One more obstacle—prove herself innocent of the murder. She was counting on Sam to further that end. Then she would be home free.

And what a home! She laughed, her grip on the steering wheel now tenuous. Two wings, fourteen rooms, six large bedrooms with full baths—her own with a step-up black marble Jacuzzi tub and a granite stone shower with a jelly roll entrance and double showerheads. Plus a cottage and a forty-foot swimming pool in the back. Henry had done a lot of renovating since he bought the place. And once the will was read, it would be legally hers.

Katherine rested her elbow on the window frame and glanced down at the speedometer: thirty-five miles an hour. She was tempted to test her prowess on these curves, but that would be foolhardy. She couldn't risk getting in trouble with the law. Not now. Too many things depended on her staying cool until this thing was over.

Instead, she relaxed and let her mind drift. The dimming sun and brisk wind felt delicious on her skin as the car move cautiously over the serpentine coastline road.

Pulling a wisp of hair out of the crease in her sunglasses, Katherine decided approaching the Blackwell woman had been a good idea. Samantha looked low key—no jewelry, dark blond hair tied straight back in an elastic band, the only makeup a touch of lipstick. She could stand to lose a few pounds and she should definitely toss the sweat-pants, but she was still quite attractive in a straightforward and intelligent way. And according to Brun, who'd heard it from Charles, Samantha had a mind like a steel trap. Katherine reminded herself to always play the bereaved widow around the woman.

But she was satisfied with her research on Samantha Blackwell. She ticked off the facts in her mind: Neat white Cape Cod house belonging to one Nicholas Bennett and Samantha Blackwell; Nicholas Bennett owns and operates a flourishing print shop. Samantha's mother, Elizabeth Blackwell, runs A Loosn'd Spirit, the bed and breakfast next door to her daughter's home; Elizabeth's husband died eighteen years ago of emphysema. There are two daughters—Caroline, 24, and Sadie, 22—who have an apartment in Portsmouth, ten miles from Georgetown. Samantha is a syndicated numerologist with three published books, who gained national notoriety when she solved the so-called Cowberry Necklace Murders.

She will have to be handled very *carefully.*

Pleased with her recitation, Katherine's mind, as it did so often these days, shifted into reverse, back to the trailer park. Her eyes narrowed, a stark contrast to the smile of satisfaction that spread over her perfect features.

Suddenly she grabbed the wheel and hit the brakes hard. Around a sharp bend, riding the white line only inches from a low stone wall, two bikers appeared from out of nowhere. Swerving into the other lane, Katherine skinned by them.

"Jesus!" she yelled. Her mouth went dry as her heart climbed a few inches higher in her chest. Luckily she was traveling within the speed limit and no one was coming the other way.

Oh, God. Too close! I can't afford an accident.

Letting out a deep sigh, she relaxed her grip on the wheel and settled back against the buff-colored leather seat.

The wind picked up. A sudden gust whipped Katherine's long hair into furious lashing tails around her sunglasses and wailed harsh cold secrets in her ear.

Let 'er rip, she thought.

Katherine knew she was beautiful, had known it since puberty. She used her God-given weapon as deftly as any highly-trained military strategist did. She had had three secret weapons; two remained—her beauty and intelligence.

She had learned from Vogue and similar genre magazines how to wear makeup and the right clothes. She had spent years observing speech and body language on films and television. But her polished facade was only a carefully crafted veneer that still did not come naturally. She wondered if it ever would. It was such a pain to stay dammed up all the time, and she was really getting tired of the pretense. Still, the stakes were high enough that Katherine would do whatever she had to do.

In spite of her practiced self-containment, however, every once in a while, "Katy" bubbled up to the surface. She loved Katy best of all.

Like now. Katherine had performed well in front of the numerologist, the right impression had been made, and here she was, driving her expensive white Lexus with the smell and sound of the ocean as communion, seemingly a lifetime away from her roots. But roots had a life of their own—those rough, penetrating, searching tentacles that never let loose, never gave up, clinging to the depths for dear life, for *actual* life.

Like the Phoenix rising from the ashes of its own immolation, "Katy" exulted, letting out a whoop and raising both arms straight up over her head. For one adrenaline-driven moment, she reveled in riding on the edge, buffeted by the wild wind. At that moment, Katherine Vandalay didn't exist.

As the car rolled toward the stone wall, Katy grabbed the wheel, pulled back into her lane, and glanced toward her right at the horizon and the approaching storm. Exhilaration rushed through her body, right down to her perfectly painted melon toenails. A defiant smile now lit up her beautiful face.

I can get through this! I always have and I always will.

She sat straighter in the bucket seat and thrust out her chin.

Suddenly sobered, her thoughts shifted to the bloodhound detective in charge of the investigation. Grant something-or-other, Charlie's brother-in-law. In the narrows of her mind, she could see the detective's inflated chest and square jaw, and the hard, cold eyes. She'd seen that look before in her own eyes—hungry, determined, unforgiving. Grant something-or-other would be like a dog with a rotting bone. He would snap and snarl, and not let go until he found the truth—and the truth was something Katherine couldn't afford to have revealed.

A short time later, it was Katy who parked the Lexus on the gravel drive in front of her rambling two-story white mansion and sat looking up at the wing where her sister-in-law lived. Ula was a nothing. A nonentity. Katy would find a way to get her out of the house that now belonged to Katherine Vandalay.

CHAPTER 5

❀

Samantha Blackwell had always led an idyllic life, with the exception of the Cowberry Necklace Murders a year ago, when the demented killer had challenged her by pinning coded messages to his victims' chests. The horror of those events would never leave her. She fumbled under her sweatshirt to find the fleshy scar.

After Katherine Vandalay left, Sam's 11:30 appointment had arrived right on time: a dynamic fifty-eight-year-old woman torn between keeping her husband (he wanted her to retire and travel with him) or keeping her real estate business (which she had built up over thirty years). The woman had just left, still undecided, she told Sam, but with valuable insight into her motivations.

Sam lay on the sofa and looked out the bank of windows facing south into the back yard. She thought about how different Mondays used to be when she'd had two little girls to get ready for school. The crow had flown away, just as her two daughters had flown the coop. But the sparrows had once again taken up residence on and around the feeder. Sam smiled at their raucous chirping.

Although she missed her girls, she savored moments like this. She felt her body relaxing, her mind drifting…

A dead man, Tarot cards laid out in the form of a cross, Katherine Vandalay and all that money, a disenfranchised sister. Perhaps there was a disgruntled employee or business associate.

Sam wiggled her toes as she wondered about the perfume Katherine smelled on her husband. Was Henry Vandalay a two-timing corpse? Somewhat bemused, Sam thought that would be a good title for a mystery.

She stretched her arms over her head, gave her body a good twist, then settled down into the cushions, pulling the green fleece blanket over her. With a deep sigh, she pondered the possibilities: Katherine killed her husband because he played around…or she did him in because she wanted his substantial fortune. Had Sam been hired by a killer? No, that wouldn't make any sense. If Katherine had killed her husband, she would be smart enough to leave well enough alone. Wouldn't she? And what about Ula?

And those Tarot cards. Wouldn't I love to see that layout.

A tap on the breezeway door and a high cheerful voice interrupted further musings.

"I'm out here, mom," Sam called.

Barely five feet tall, if you didn't count the inches of her white bee-hive hairdo, Elizabeth Blackwell hurried into the sun porch, brushed a delicate kiss on her daughter's forehead, and perched on the edge of the rocker opposite Sam.

"You saw, didn't you?" Sam asked. She didn't know why she should be surprised.

"Saw what, dear?" Elizabeth said, patting her immaculate hair. In one sweep, her washed blue eyes took in the room before settling on Sam.

"Mom…"

Elizabeth sat back and folded her small hands in her lap. Her rose-colored linen suit matched the blush in her cheeks. "Well, yes. I saw an expensive car leave your driveway. Wasn't that Mrs. Vandalay at the wheel?" Concern registered on her face.

Sam knew what her mother was thinking. Her eyes softened. "Mom, don't you have an Inn full of guests?"

"Yes, dear, I do." Elizabeth smiled. "And thank goodness for Caroline and Sadie. I don't know what I'd do without them."

Sam forgave that unconscious manipulation—she knew her mother was thinking about the murders last year—and Sam felt her resolve slipping away.

Elizabeth focussed her eyes on her only child, and with the hint of a smile, said, "How about a nice cup of tea?"

That damned cup of tea! Where was Sam's garlic and cross when she needed them? But it was no use. In Elizabeth's masterful hands, that ubiquitous cup of tea elicited confession.

Sam shuffled her feet. She loved her mother, and she understood the toll that had been taken by the loss of Elizabeth's beloved husband eighteen years ago. The Cowberry Necklace murders last year had only compounded her mother's anxiety. Elizabeth didn't want Sam to get embroiled in another murder investigation.

So Sam told her the reason for Katherine Vandalay's visit.

Satisfied that her daughter was involved on the periphery of the matter, and with begrudging assurances from Sam that she would stay close to Nick and Charlie over the upcoming weekend, Elizabeth sat a bit straighter in her chair and said, "So, dear. Speaking of the Vandalay services on Sunday, what are you going to wear?"

*   *   *   *   *

Several hours later, Sam reached for the desk phone to call Charlie Burrows.

"Yeah?"

"Is that any way to answer the phone, Charlie?"

"Oh. Hi, Sam. What's up?"

"I understand we are. For the weekend. At Katherine Vandalay's home."

Sam sank into the flowered sofa cushions and folded her legs over the low pine trestle table. The long cord from her black phone—which she had dragged over from her desk because the portable was recharging—lay in loops in her lap.

"Oh yeah. That." He cleared his throat. "Hope you don't mind Brun gave her your name. They're related…some kind of cousins, I think. Anyway, Katherine sort of just showed up on our doorstep a few years ago, from out of nowhere. And then, when her husband was killed, she came blubbering to Brun about the cops following her around."

"So they do suspect her?"

"Most likely."

"What did Grant, your brother-in-law, have to say?"

"Nada. Talking about an ongoing investigation is a serious infraction of the rules."

"What do you know about Katherine, Charlie?"

"Just a minute, Sam." Muffled sounds came over the wire as Charlie called to his wife that he'd be there in a minute. He came back on the phone. "Brun's getting anxious. She's afraid I'll get called out on police business and she won't get to cross anything off her 'Charlie-do' list for today."

"Katherine Vandalay, Charlie?"

"Oh, yeah. From what I hear, she's some piece of work. Don't let Brun know I said that."

"Is Brun close to Katherine?"

"No. But you know how she is about relatives."

"But what do you really know about her?" Sam asked.

"Wait a minute."

Sam heard the phone drop, then a loud ah-choo! followed by a string of invectives, topped off by a honk that would put a nor'easter to shame as Charlie blew his nose.

"Damn head cold," Charlie sniffled a moment later. "I always seem to get one when I'm on vacation. What were you saying?"

"Katherine Vandalay." By now Sam had the phone cord twisted into a Gordian knot around her fingers.

"Oh, yeah. The Vandalay woman worked at some fancy store in Portsmouth where the rich go to buy things they don't need and they'll never use. Seems Henry Vandalay walked in one day with an open wallet and walked out with her."

"Their marriage happened quickly?"

"Quicker than the blink of an eye. Far as I can recall, it was, like, two months. Surprised everyone, I guess."

Sam's fingers were really stuck now. "What was her name before she married Henry Vandalay?"

On the other end, Sam heard one of the Burrows daughters pleading, "Dad! I need to use the phone. Please!"

"Me, too!" a higher voice added.

"Hold on, girls. I'm almost done. You know, we need five phones in this house. What were you saying, Sam?"

"I was asking if you knew Katherine's maiden name?"

"I don't know. I'll have to ask Brun."

"Charlie, Katherine told me about the Tarot cards that were left beside her husband's body."

"Yeah." He snuffed. "That was really weird."

"She said they were laid out in some sort of a cross."

"Looked that way in the papers." He snuffled again, then coughed. "Hold on." Sam could hear gale winds blowing. "Okay. Let's see. Far as I could tell, there were a few cards in the center surrounded by four more, and then on the right, there was a vertical line of four more."

The Keltic Method, Sam thought. "There should be eleven of them in all."

"Yeah. I think there was. Does that mean something?"

"I don't know. It might." She stared at her imprisoned fingers. Maybe she'd use Alexander the Great's method and cut the damn cord.

"Well, listen, Sam. I gotta go. The girls are lined up for the phone, and Brun is waving her list in my face. You know how she is. Wants everything done yesterday."

Sam smiled at the thought of Charlie juggling the emotional needs of the five women in his home. "We're supposed to arrive on Saturday. Would you talk to Brun and get back to me with the details? And Charlie, see if you can find out specifically what cards were left by Vandalay's body and in what order—that is, if you can talk about it. I don't want you to get in trouble over it. Katherine said she wrote down the exact layout and she's going to drop it by. Whatever you can find out is corroboration."

"Okay." He hung up abruptly.

After a few frustrating minutes, Sam managed to extricate herself from the sinuous black cord without calling for the jaws of life. She put the telephone back on the desk.

Dropping onto the sofa, she leaned into the cushions in a feline stretch like Selket used to do. The twenty-pound orange tabby Sam picked up from the SPCA last year had decided to live next door with her mother and pop in on Sam when the need arose. She was sure the cat had taken Katherine Hepburn's advice. The actress was purported to have said that men and women should never marry. They should live next door to each other and visit occasionally.

But Sam didn't mind. Selket was good company for her mother, who had grown to love the cat, and the cat delighted in all the attention she got from the guests at the inn.

Sam scratched her head, then smoothed the disturbed hair back down. She glanced over at the Brookstone clock on the table between the two stuffed rockers. 5:05.

Without warning, the storm broke with a fury. Rain pounded the ground and the roof of the sun porch.

Sam sighed. *Guess I'd better prepare something warm and toasty for supper.*

But she didn't move. Her body felt leaden. The four o'clock slump. Which, in Sam's case, extended from about three o'clock to five-thirty.

Distracted from the supper menu by sudden ruminations on Katherine Vandalay's name, Sam picked up her six-by-nine clipboard and jotted down the vowels in her client's name, along with their corresponding numbers:

Katherine: A (1)—E (5)—I (9)- E (5), and Vandalay: A (1)—A (1)— A (1).*

Sam easily added numbers in her head. In fact, some time ago she had taken a Rosicrucian course where she'd been taught to multiply numbers without benefit of pen and paper. In bed, after switching off her lamp, she would exercise her mind by mentally multiplying double numbers by a single number, and eventually moved on to multiplying double numbers by double numbers. Her brain cells were as slim and taut as any twenty-year-old's. Even so, she felt more in control with a ballpoint pen in her hand.

The vowel sum of 'Katherine' was a two, and 'Katherine Vandalay' added up to a five. Sam felt the woman was motivated by the secret two, shielding her private life. But she had also developed the five's gift of tongues, the ability to communicate with every level of society, and she was certainly capable of manipulation. So why did she come across so distracted? Was it a ploy?

It was Sam's nature to emphasize the positive side of the numbers, but she had the gut feeling she had been seduced by all those ciphers on that silver check.

Her stomach growled.

I was good today, she told herself. *I just had soup for lunch. Maybe I'll have a little snack before supper.*

* See Appendix for the Number-Letter Code.

Reluctantly, she rose and padded toward the kitchen in her heavy, gray ragg socks. Holding the refrigerator door open and waiting for the Food Muse to strike, she battled the urge to scoop up the last package of Ring Dings. They now sat eye level on the refrigerator shelf of her Amana. She had given up hiding them in the vegetable drawer behind the organic butternut squash.

CHAPTER 6

❀

Carl Gleason knew he'd found the right woman, but he wasn't sure he had the right client! The man had never shown his face, had just contacted Gleason's office through a series of phone calls. Even the guy's voice sounded muffled, as if he were trying to disguise it.

Gleason knew that he should have questioned his client further—like, why was the guy looking for this woman? What was his relationship to her? What was he going to do when he found her? But any semblance of ethics had flown out the window a decade ago during his midlife crises. His penchant for expensive women, fine wine, and designer clothes had finally won out. Now he just wanted to keep ahead of the bills.

Yesterday, per the client's instructions, Gleason had paid for a week at the Port Grande Hotel in Portsmouth, settled into his room, then informed the desk clerk that both his secretary and a client would be calling and to be sure their messages got through.

The city lights by the Piscataqua River looked blurred through the rain-pelted hotel window. Gleason could hear the moaning wind slamming against the plate glass, as if trying to find entrance for a momentary respite. He hoped the weather would clear by morning. He wanted to take the Portsmouth Harbor Cruise, then maybe a ride up to the White Mountains. New England was famous for its riotous fall color.

By a stroke of luck, Gleason had found his quarry in Portsmouth this afternoon. He had immediately called Glenda, and told her to have the client call him at the hotel as soon as the guy checked in with her.

Almost as if the client had sensed something, he called Glenda an hour later. He then rang Gleason in his hotel room and instructed him to stay put and wait for further instructions.

Sure. Why not? The seacoast was scenic. He'd relax, see the sights, sample the restaurants. What the hell—the client was paying for it.

He slipped off his jacket, hung it over the back of a chair by the window, and placed his holster on the seat. Under the chair, he meticulously aligned his mahogany wingtips.

He rubbed his aching right knee, the result of an old football injury, then limped across the carpeted floor in his stocking feet. A quick glance in the mirror prompted him to pull in his gut. Setting his hefty frame on the edge of the bed, he massaged his knee again. His days as a high school quarterback flashed into his mind—the glory days of his lost youth. He shook his head to erase the memory, and reached for the phone to call Glenda.

As expected, his office line was busy. For the next half hour, all he heard was the irritating sound of a busy signal.

Jesus! Didn't she ever stop talking? Who was it this time? Probably Lisa or Cherry or her mother, or, for all he knew, the King of Siam! He had asked her dozens of times to limit her personal calls. Obviously, to no avail.

When Gleason finally got through, he told Glenda he would check in every evening. If he didn't call, and if she couldn't reach him at the hotel or on his cell phone, she was to call the police. He cradled the phone. Why had he said that? Just had a gut feeling that something was wrong, he decided.

Maybe it was the phone call he'd just gotten from the client. There was an edginess in the guy's voice, something almost menacing.

Gleason hoped he was wrong. He wasn't about to take someone out, not for any amount of money. He hadn't sunk that low.

He lay back on the blue floral coverlet and stretched his arms over his head, arching his back to work out some of the kinks. He finally allowed his body to go limp, placing his hands at his sides, fingers separated.

Taking a deep breath and letting it out slowly, he stared at the pebbled white ceiling and let his mind drift aimlessly.

The seacoast of New Hampshire was certainly a refreshing change from Trenton, New Jersey. Not that he didn't love his home town, but he liked variety in everything, including locale. His work not only gave him the freedom to call his own hours, but also took him to new places. And best of all, he never knew what was going to happen next.

Just like now. He'd been after this babe for the past six weeks, and after only one day in Portsmouth, he had spotted her in Market Square! He was sure she was the right one.

That's when he contacted "Mr. Smith."

He snorted. Come on, now. Who was going to believe that one? Anyway, he'd told "Mr. Smith" that in addition to the promised bonus, he'd need another five thousand. The client was hungry and had agreed easily.

Gleason's uneasiness was finally put to rest by the image of those Italian shoes he'd been ogling at Michael's, the shop for the "discerning man."

The discerning man.

Yup. That's me. A discerning man.

For sure.

CHAPTER 7

❁

Sam had laid her trap.

"What's this?" Nick brushed a dark curl back off his forehead as he cocked an eyebrow at his wife across the pine drop-leaf table. "Since when do you make four figures from a client session? What are you up to?"

With a fork, Sam made a circle of garden peas around her slice of lentil loaf. She then positioned six of the green orbs to form a triangle on top of the dollop of sour cream that adorned her baked potato. Six— the number of love. "What makes you think I'm up to something?"

Nick stared again at the check in his hand then said, "Because Clarence Tuttle caught me at McCutty's Market when I was picking up your Ring Dings—which, by the way, I seem to do with increasing regularity." He eyed his wife, then went on. "Clarence saw a white Lexus pull out of our driveway and take off like a bat out of hell. Well, he didn't say it quite that way, but you know what I mean."

Once again, Nick's eyes fell on the silver-colored check. He gingerly held it between his thumbs and forefingers. It seemed as if he were afraid the sweat on his hand would dissolve the paper like the bucket of water Dorothy had used to melt away the Wicked Witch of the West. Life with Samantha Blackwell could certainly be as exciting as any adventure in Oz.

Sam frowned. She dabbed at her forehead with a napkin, wondering if the prickly dampness was from nerves or…No. It couldn't be hot flashes. She was only forty-nine. Dismissing the ridiculous thought, she shifted her attention to Clarence Tuttle. He never missed anything from his perch over Clean As A Hound's Tooth Cleaners across the town green. He had bought the establishment after his wife had run off with Harold, the previous owner, and left Clarence with just a note and one over-starched white shirt. Since then, Clarence has been the eyes and ears of the town.

Sam thought of Clarence Tuttle as *The Scribe* because the vowels in his name added up to Nineteen.

As she had written in one of her columns, 'S,' the nineteenth letter in the alphabet, is the only letter that requires adding twice to arrive at a digit. (19=1+9=10; 10=1+0=1) This process set the letter 'S' apart from the other twenty-five.

She had gone on to tell her readers that the original alphabets were pictorial, their drawings subsequently streamlined into the strokes we know today. In a time when few individuals knew how to read or write, the curves in the letter 'S' suggested a person bent over the writing table, quill pen in hand, recording history.

Clarence's vowels, his Soul Number, the accumulation of all his past lives, were embodied in the number nineteen. Clarence was the official scribe of Georgetown.

But Sam wasn't thinking about alphabets and quill pens this night; she was intent upon her husband's reaction to Katherine Vandalay's scrawled figures.

"Clarence doesn't miss much," Sam said.

Still mesmerized by all the ciphers on the check, Nick laid it down on the table next to his plate, anchored a corner with his left forefinger, then smoothed the surface with the edge of his palm until it lay flat. "No, he doesn't." His gaze shifted to his wife. "So. What are you up to?"

"My, Nick." She cast him a dazzling smile. "You have a suspicious mind. What makes you think I'm up to something?"

Nick leaned in, rested his chin in his hand, and looked straight at her. "Well, let's see. Clues. A sixty-thousand-dollar Lexus was in our drive-way this morning, you've made my favorite *dinner*, there are lighted candles on the table, Roberta Flack is singing in the background, there's an apple pie steaming to my left and a four figure check to my right. And the granddaddy of all clues, you're wearing a dress. And your favorite perfume—Wind Song. Something reserved for weddings and funerals. So you see, I'm assuming you've been employed as a hit woman by the Lexus owner, and your mission is to take out some unsuspecting victim. The only question I have is, am I going to be an accomplice?"

"This *little* black dress?" *How she wished.*

"I happen to know what that little black dress cost. Remember? I bought it for you."

He waited.

"It's not that bad," Sam said with a half grin.

Nick groaned along with the captain's chair as he sat back, a look of resignation on his face.

"Wouldn't you like a vacation in the warm sunny Caribbean?" Sam said, blinking her mascara-covered eyelashes at him. She'd found a tube of the dark, sticky stuff in Caroline's old bedroom.

Nick lowered his head and waited for an explanation.

Chased by a violent wind, the rain beat against the bow window, which showcased a small crescent of green lawn. The buffeted pines and maples hunkered down against the onslaught. For a moment, Sam watched nature's fireworks as deep scarlet, brilliant orange, and pale green leaves swirled in furious maelstroms.

Then she heaved a sigh. "We're under a Hunter's Moon. Well, almost," she offered. "It's coming this Friday. Storms are rather romantic, don't you think? We're tucked in here all warm and cozy, protected from the elements. And if you think this is romantic, just imagine how much fun the Caribbean will be."

Nick looked up at her and shook his head more in disbelief than denial. "Not as fugitives."

"Don't be silly. It's nothing like that."

"Well, what is it like?"

Light from the candles flickered in his dark eyes. Sam gave him her best smile while she thought about how much she loved this man. Even after twenty-six years of marriage, she still got all misty-eyed thinking about that day on the beach.

"What?" Nick said.

"What what?" Sam answered.

He tried not to smile, but the deep dimple in his right cheek gave him away. "Why are you looking at me like that?"

"I was remembering how we met."

"Really. You know what I'm remembering? That old quote you're so fond of when the occasion demands. Something about the English doing idiotic things."

Sam's grandparents had originally come from England, so she felt entitled to recite the line from a long-forgotten author: *Whatever one feels about the English, one must admire the silent dignity with which they do idiotic things.*

Like parading through the New England forests during the Revolutionary War in their bright red jackets, horns blaring, as if they were still on the battlefields of Europe—while the colonists, who had learned from the Indians to camouflage themselves in the woods, hid behind tree trunks and picked them off one by one.

Yes, the English were capable of doing mighty strange things with great dignity. Only tonight, the line wasn't so funny. Still…she'd never been on a Caribbean cruise. Knowing that you catch more flies with honey than vinegar, Sam tried her most charming smile. Something had to work; her repertoire was dwindling.

"You've got to be the world's greatest actress," Nick sighed. "Okay. Cut the soft-soap act, cut me a piece of apple pie, and tell me what's going on. What do you want me to do? You're going to do what you want anyway, so I might as well go along for the ride."

Sam reached for the pie knife and cut her husband a big slab of the warm homemade pie. She placed it on a Rose Chintz plate, and asked if he wanted to top it off with Cracker Barrel cheese or Breyer's vanilla ice cream.

Nick rolled his eyes heavenward. "Save me," he pleaded.

CHAPTER 8

❀

As Samantha Blackwell sliced her apple pie, Ula Vandalay was kneeling in silent prayer before her altar.

On a purple velvet cloth draped over the narrow wooden table against the back wall of her walk-in closet, two white candles flickered, providing the only light in her hidden alcove. On the table to her left lay the Rider-Waite Tarot deck, wrapped in black silk, and missing one card—Key 7, The Chariot—which Ula had propped up against one of the silver candlesticks. A simple gold ring lay close by. Laid out in perfect symmetry before her were the four implements of the sacred litany: Wand, Cup, Sword, and Pentacle.

Ula felt safe in here—her sanctuary—almost as if she were wrapped, protected, and gestating in the Great Mother's womb. She knew that no one would open her closet door and poke around. The clothes rack she'd purchased at Wal-Mart for the purpose of rolling in front of her improvised chapel was all the cover she needed.

Nevertheless, her bedroom door was locked.

It was late. The rain thrashed at Ula's windows with a fury that could not be muffled by the closet walls. Ula thought about Katherine, asleep in the king-sized four-poster cherry bed between white silk sheets, probably dreaming about how she was going to spend Hank's fortune.

But no matter what, Katherine would never would get her hands on the money.

She took a deep breath as a vision of Katherine formed in her mind. A humorless smile spread across her face.

The poor thing's had a hard day. Visiting that numerologist, then having her body massage. She must be exhausted.

Ula's soft laugh was not pleasant. She would enjoy telling Katherine that dinner would not be ready in the future, nor would breakfast or lunch—not that Katherine was ever home for lunch. And furthermore, Ula was through scrubbing floors, polishing silver, and cleaning toilets.

Yes, she would soon be through with it all. But not before she got through Sunday's services. She would play her accustomed role—chief cook and bottle washer. How perfectly she would pretend bereavement, and then she'd have quite a surprise for Katherine.

Hank had been dead for six days now.

And on the Seventh Day, God rested.

Ula thought it befitting that Hank's service was to be held on Sunday, a day of rest, the *seventh* day of the week. The day of the service would be her *Seventh Day*, and it was going to be a doozy.

Key 7, The Chariot.

Ula admired the conquering figure who was master on all levels, particularly the plane of the mind. Key 7 meant rest and victory. Although the black and white sphinxes were not leashed to the Chariot, they were under the mental control of the charioteer.

Yes, Ula thought. *I have triumphed over my enemies.*

She had taken care of Hank for over twenty-five years—given him her youth. The next twenty-five years were hers alone—she almost cackled—and the devil take Katherine and all her whimpering and complaining!

She stood and rubbed her knees to relieve the ache from too many years in the prone position of servitude. She felt on intimate terms with the archaic phrase "housemaid's knee".

I am through with it all. I am not a "housewife!" I am not married to a house! She clenched her jaws so hard her teeth hurt as the words whipped and lashed inside her brain with a silent fury grown stronger over the years.

Making the decision this morning to free herself from her self-imposed slavery felt so good, so liberating. Ula was surprised at how easy it had been—not frightening at all, as she had dreaded. With Hank gone, all her fears were dissolving like a chalk sidewalk drawing in a rainstorm.

Her head tilted as she listened to the pounding rain.

Cleansing her, pounding away her past, washing the slate clean. Only a storm of this proportion was worthy of obliterating the woman she had been until now, of eradicating the parameters she'd carefully drawn around herself for so long. She was free—free!—to draw her own lines on the cement. Hopscotch. Jelly roll. She laughed softly. Maybe even the Cretan labyrinth.

She remembered the story from high school mythology class: Ambassadors from Crete arrived annually in Athens to collect their tribute of seven virgins and seven young men.

Seven. How serendipitous.

These unfortunates were then taken back to Crete and fed to a monster called the Minotaur, who had the body of a man and the head of a bull. Ariadne, daughter of the King of Crete, fell in love with the Greek hero, Theseus, who had come to kill the Minotaur. Ariadne furnished Theseus with a ball of string by which he could guide himself though the labyrinth, kill the Minotaur, and return. Theseus later abandoned her.

Hank had been Ula's Theseus. But over the years, he had metamorphosed into the Minotaur, devouring her life's energy. Then, changeling that he was, like Theseus, Hank had abandoned her when he brought Katherine into their house.

But no more. Ula was finally free! Her inner child rejoiced.

Freedom may come at a price, she thought, *but I'll gladly pay Charon whatever he demands to guide dear Hank across the River Styx.*

Ula caught herself. She had to stop thinking these kinds of thoughts. Her Tarot group's teachings focused on elevating the consciousness, reaching for the higher good, finding a positive channel for negative energies. And she had tried. Lord knows, how she had tried.

At first, Ula was insanely jealous and resentful when Hank brought Katherine into their house. Ula had tried to set aside her feelings, but little by little, she ceased caring about Hank, as if the eternal flame that lit their relationship had been blown out by a ravaging hurricane. The caring was gone and had been gone for the past two years. Although, if she did say so herself, she *had* put on an Academy-Award-winning performance at the funeral. She chuckled, then grew somber once again.

Through all the years of daily rituals tending to Hank and the house, it had been as if Ula was nothing but an automaton—even worse, a zombie—drained of her life's spirit, controlled by the forces around her, doing the will of others. The only time true Spirit filled her was at the Tarot study group.

And when she cast her spells and incantations.

The group did not know about the spells.

Ula did want to rid herself of the last vestiges of hate and resentment for her father…or rather, Hank and that woman. She had worked so hard to do that. Then, as if by magic, Hank's death had miracuously wiped away a maze of tangled webs.

She suddenly realized with some surprise that the last spell she had cast on the pair was over a year ago. Except, of course, on the day before Hank's death, when she had offered up intense and focused prayers.

Surprising how one's thoughts can become manifest if enough energy is put behind them.

Ula had always known, even as a child, that she was different, that she could make things happen if she focused her mind long enough. Her talent had manifested one day, long ago, because of a baseball game.

It was on her twelfth birthday that her father had taken her to Fenway Park to see the Red Sox play the Yankees. In the taxi cab on the way to the ball park, she had told him that, if you thought about things long enough, you could make them happen. He had laughed at the idea, but when Ula insisted, he made a bargain with her. If she could get the batter to hit a foul ball into his hands, he would buy her the pony she'd been begging for. After going to Red Sox games since childhood, her father had never once gotten a ball. Ula could tell by the look on his face that he was sure it was a bet he couldn't lose.

The park was a feast of sights and sounds and smells: Vendors hawking Fenway Franks and crying, "Get your hot roasted peanuts here"; the tantalizing smell of warm nuts filling her nostrils; people milling up and down the cement stairs, in and out of the rows of wooden seats, in endless rills; the cloudless sky of cerulean blue; the manicured field of emerald green; the infamous Green Monster hugging the edge of left field.

This ball park stood as one cathedral among many in major cities around the country. Faithful fans worshiped the players her father spoke of with reverence: Babe Ruth, Denton "Cy" Young, Ty Cobb, Mickey Mantle, Ted Williams, and Hank Aaron, who had single-handedly hit 398 home runs by the end of 1965. She would recall in later years that Aaron retired with a batting record of 755 home runs.

Ula waited with climbing excitement for Boston's "boys of summer" to emerge from the catacombs.

After the National Anthem and amidst the cacophony of settling-down sounds, she had positioned herself in the wooden seat. She drew a breath from deep in her stomach and prepared. She wanted that dappled pony in the worst way.

Every time a batter came to the plate, Ula closed her eyes and visualized the ball arcing high into the air toward the left of home plate, and toward her father, who jumped up to catch it. The vision was so clear, so true to reality, that she knew, just knew! it had to happen. At every crack of the bat, her heart leapt with excitement.

Ula never saw the first six-and-a-half innings. In the bottom of the seventh, she was visualizing once again and was interrupted when the crowd around her rustled, then roared. She opened her eyes to see several hundred people, her father amongst them, on their feet, straining arms and stretching out hands to catch the baseball. It seemed to hang in midair, as if a spirit hand had intervened, then it dropped.

For one brief moment, her father's fingers had hold of the elusive prize, the treasure he had sought since childhood.

In a flash, however, it was over. He bobbled the ball and it fell into the hands of a young boy beside him.

Ula would always remember the hurt, surprised eyes her father had turned on her. And she never forgot the words she said to him. "I got you the ball. It's not my fault if you can't hold onto it."

How could Ula's young mind know that those words bit deep into her father's childhood fantasy, demolishing his ego?

They drove to the hotel silently as her father stared straight ahead, his hands white-knuckled in his lap. When the taxi came to a stop, he turned toward his daughter and said, "What you did today was evil. You are never to speak of this again, to anyone. *Do you understand?*"

His face was the color of beet juice, twisted into a parody of the features she knew, and yes, streaked with fright. She would always remember sensing the angry curls of flame that seemed to emanate from his body.

Ula never got her pony.

Her father's reaction had terrified her so badly that afterwards she had nightmares for months.

Ula wondered if what she had done was truly the work of the devil, as her father had said. Or maybe the power was good, but no one understood it. But somehow, in her child's mind, she knew the power was not of her—it had worked through her.

Out of a deep-rooted fear of her father, she had kept her ability, along with his failed promise, locked in a bitter closet in the recesses of her mind. The lesson was hard: Men were powerful creatures who could turn on you in a moment if you said the wrong thing. Ula learned that security came from keeping your mouth shut and following the rules. From that critical day forward, Ula was the model child—seen and not heard. After her father's death, Hank stepped into his shoes.

Ula had kept that closet door tightly shut and bolted for thirty-three years, until two years ago. With the help of her Tarot study group, she had cast out her demon father and his successor. Now, the closet door opened easily, and she was inside, casting spells.

Well, she thought, not *really* casting spells; she was through with all that. No more hobgoblin rituals. From now on, her attention would be directed to channeling the Light for the good of humanity. Although she had to admit she liked the phrase "casting spells" much better than "channeling energy".

Hmmm. Now that she thought about it, the two phrases meant pretty much the same thing. Semantics had a way of starting wars, both religious and secular.

Ula took a full ten seconds to roll her head clockwise—heard that familiar pop—then reversed the process.

She would relent on this one point, however, because channeling was a more acceptable word in public. Now that Hank was gone, she had a new image to perfect.

Her eyes crinkled at the corners, creating feathery lines that deepened with each passing year.

Maybe the group is working its magic on me after all.

Ula looked down at her makeshift altar. Just in case the police got a warrant to search the house, she had thought about packing up her cards, candlesticks, and sacred implements, and hiding them away in a safe place. Maybe a rental box, just until this business with Hank was over. But a consultation with the cards had told her that the altar in her closet was not an issue. She may have lost faith in humanity, but she trusted her Tarot cards.

Ula Vandalay eye's shone as she lifted the double-pointed wand off the table. Assuming the pose of The Magician, she raised her right hand toward heaven while her free hand pointed at the floor. In a soft rolling chant, she repeated the mantra nine times: "Make me a conduit for Universal Light."

In her mind's eye, energy from the Universe streamed into her raised arm, pulsed through her chest and the fingers of her other hand, and sent showers of sparks toward the floor. The electrical, life-affirming fire of Spirit. She was the conduit between Heaven and Earth.

Carefully, she placed the wand on the table, thinking about the instrument as the symbol of transformation in metaphysical literature: Moses parting the Red Sea with his staff of power, Cinderella's fairy godmother changing her poor rags into a beautiful ball gown by merely waving her magic wand. The group had taught her that the hidden truths in religions, myths, and even fairy tales had the power to change the supplicant if she were worthy.

Well, six days ago, Ula's life had changed drastically. And with each passing hour, she felt the power within her grow.

Her eyes caressed the implements before her on the purple velvet: the wand, the silver cup, the embossed coin, and the newly-polished knife. Three more rituals, and her evening's work would be done.

Shifting her body weight and rolling her shoulders, she swallowed dryly, then became very still. For a long moment, she stared at the knife blade, watching as it reflected the candlelight dancing like a fairy in a misty glen.

She picked up the symbolic sword and tried to focus on the required litany, but her mind, ignoring the call for discipline, wandered off in its own direction. She couldn't help thinking that when the time was right, Katherine Vandalay was in for a big surprise.

CHAPTER 9

Sam wiggled her bare toes in the grass soaked from last night's Biblical down pour. There was something spiritual about standing in cool, wet grass in the early morning, hanging laundry, and watching the sun yawn itself up from its midnight bed to poke through the tree covers.

To greet the day, the sapling maple in the center of the back yard shook tiny droplets from its leaves into the golden locks of the sun. At the edge of the lawn, the recently planted asparagus bed—compliments of the man she had saved last year from a horrible death—was now tucked under its winter blanket. Sam hoped to have a succulent crop next year.

She wiggled her toes again as her taste buds rejoiced at the thought. As if in response, a chorus of birds sang joyful hallelujahs.

Sam breathed in deeply.

Mozart's piano concerto rippled through the open porch windows. She had just bought a double CD of the great master's work. She loved Number 9. Maybe because Nine was her Life Lesson Number, her reason for being here.

To the stirring rhythm of piano keys, she mused on her lifetime assignment: Be an example, speak the truth, be the teacher, extend the open hand.

Lofty goals for one tiny speck of solidified light.

Sam thought it ironic that her childhood fantasy of a teacher was a bearded sage in a book-lined library, pouring over ancient manuscripts. And here she was, standing barefoot in her ragged gray sweatpants, a green foam roller in her bangs, hanging laundry in the back yard. She couldn't imagine herself as the Teacher, the Speaker of Truths—certainly not as a wise old Crone. But in her heart of hearts, that's exactly what she hoped to be one day. Her greatest fear was that she didn't know enough, couldn't possibly learn enough, that she'd never be that wise person of her childhood fantasy. She dreaded the possibility that someday she would say the wrong thing to a client and send them on the path to destruction.

That's a bit egotistical, Sam. As if your words have that kind of impact on people.

Sometimes she was so unsure of herself. Where did that feeling come from? Certainly not from her parents, who had supported her in every way when she was growing up. But, nevertheless, there it was. Those "flutterbys," as Caroline used to call the Monarchs in their back yard. The winged creatures invaded Sam's stomach each time she faced a client. What would her clients think if they knew about the flutterbys?

Some example I am, she thought, as she plucked two plastic clothespins—one purple, the other lime green—from the cloth bag hanging on the line. She stuck one between her teeth and pinned the other to the corner of a sheet. As she inhaled the newly-washed morning air, she looked forward to the smell of sun-kissed linens on her bed.

Considering it a luxury to hang clothes outside to dry made Sam giggle. There was a time when everything got thrown into the dryer. *Even Sadie's rubber dress. What a mess that was!*

As she reached for a pillowcase from the dark green plastic basket at her feet, she heard her daughter's voice.

"Hey, mom. What are you doing?"

Sam looked up at the windows of the sun porch to see Sadie's face pressed up against a screen. "Why are you hanging the clothes? Is your dryer broken or something?"

Sam didn't even attempt to explain. "Oh hi, honey. I'll be right in." She could hang the rest of the clothes later.

In the sun porch, she said, "Would you like some breakfast?"

Sadie was dressed in jeans and a lime green tank top. Pompeii Purple toenails peeked out from the tips of her hot pink Victoria's Secret sandals. She glanced at her watch and said, "Yeah. I don't have to be at Gramma's for another forty-five minutes."

Sadie and Caroline helped Elizabeth Blackwell run the inn next door. Sadie also had a side business, Pets and Pails, which offered home cleaning services and pet sitting. Sam, an amateur cartoonist, had proudly designed the business cards.

"Are you going to wear those wedge heels while you're cleaning?" Sam motioned toward Sadie's feet. "You could trip."

"I brought my sneakers. They're in the car."

Sam nodded her approval. "Bacon, scrambled eggs, fried potatoes?"

"I suppose it's soy bacon, range-free chicken eggs and organic potatoes?"

"You got it."

As Sadie leaned over the divider between the kitchen and the dining area, Sam took two plates from the cupboard, set them on the oven rack, and turned the temperature to warm. She pulled the black iron skillet from the bottom drawer of the stove and placed it on one of the large burners.

"Do you remember those columns I wrote on the Tarot a few years back?" Sam asked, as she gave the skillet a quick once-over with Pam olive oil spray.

"Yeah, why?" Sadie looped a hank of short blonde hair behind one ear.

"Well, you heard about Kenny Ash finding Henry Vandalay in the shop over on Route 101?"

Sadie grimaced. "Yeah. The guy they found knifed to death. God." Her shoulders stiffened, her eyes saucered. "Mom! You're not! Tell me you're not."

Sam turned away and opened the refrigerator door. She pulled out a carton of eggs, a package of Morningstar Farms soy bacon and the left-over potatoes from last night. "I'll tell you I'm not if that's what you want to hear."

"Mom!"

Sam turned to face her. "Look, Sadie. It's not like last time. I'm not the object of some killer's demented fantasy. This homicide has nothing to do with me."

"Then what are you talking about?"

Sam stooped to get a bowl from under the counter. "What I'm going to tell you is private."

Sadie rested on both elbows and watched her mother crack the eggs and drop the shells into the sink.

"Okay. It's 'in the safe.'" Sadie knew her mother's fondness for Seinfeld reruns.

So, as Sam laid the soy bacon strips in the skillet and cut the potatoes, she told Sadie about Katherine Vandalay's visit and the revelation about the Keltic spread.

Sadie cocked her head to one side. "You think the Tarot cards have something to do with finding the person who did this?" She enunciated the word Tarot, dropping the final "t", the way her mother taught her.

"Could be. I just want to talk about it for a while, use you as a sound-ing board, okay? And you can also tell Caroline about the cards, as long as she puts the information in the safe, too." She grinned as she flipped the bacon, then she turned serious. "I know how tuned-in you and your sister are."

Acting nonchalant but secretly pleased that her mother was about to confide in her, Sadie said, "Sound away."

Sam forked the bacon onto a paper towel and dropped the potatoes into the pan.

"I researched the number and pattern implications of the Tarot for my columns. It was an eye-opener. The origins of the Tarot are shrouded in mystery. No one really knows how or where it originated, although some scholars feel the word Tarot comes from the Egyptian *Tar* meaning Path and *Ro* or Royal."

"The Royal Path," Sadie said.

"Exactly. Sometimes called the Royal Road."

Sam sprinkled a bit of parsley, garlic, and onion powder over the potatoes. Sadie handed her the Avon salt and pepper shakers, that were "at least a hundred years old."

"The Tarot is said to be an ancient pictorial book of universal knowledge," Sam said. "The French scholar Court de Gebelin discussed it in a 1781 work—I think it was called *Le Monde Primiti.* Pardon my French."

Sadie let out a groan.

"Anyway, Court de Gebelin was convinced that the Tarot was the one Egyptian book that escaped the flames when the library at Alexandria was burned. He wrote that the book contained 'the purest knowledge of profound matters put forth by the sages of Egypt.'"

Sam had always longed to know more about the priceless manuscripts which had burned in that conflagration.

"Anyway, the legend goes that during a period of illiteracy, the adepts concealed the ageless wisdom in a picture book. That way, they believed it would escape the eyes of the inquisition and live on as a reminder of the universal truths of life and the essential character of the human being."

"Mom! The potatoes."

The skillet was smoking. Sam grabbed a pot holder and a spatula and flipped the potatoes just in time. Luckily, the pieces were just edged in carbon. Perfect.

Sam glanced up at the smoke detector by the Ridgeway grandfather clock. It frequently went off at the slightest hint of smoke.

"You want to drop eight tablespoons of water into those eggs, Sadie, and stir them with the whip." Sam motioned with her head toward the utensil jar.

As Sadie whipped the eggs, Sam went on.

"The Tarot was given to the Romany people—you know, the Gypsies—in the form of a deck of cards. That way, it was protected from destruction by the tyranny of the medieval church. And by the fourteenth century, the deck had been transported to Spain, Italy, and France."

Very clever, these adepts, Sam thought.

"That's cool, Mom. Hiding something in plain sight. You know, most people think the Tarot is just for fortune telling. Medra and I were at Salisbury Beach last summer and this stand had a sign out front that said 'Your Fortune Told', and it listed astrology, palmistry and the Tarot."

Sam shook her head. "I know. It's unfortunate. But every profession has its charlatans—business, politics, medicine, even religion. But there are professional people who practice these ancient arts today, and in some parts of the world, they're openly accepted and very much respected."

But not here in Georgetown.

What would the town think if they knew the pastor's wife, the lovely, gentle Emmaline Loveless, secretly ran classified ads for palm readings through the mail? Sam often wondered how those clients explained why they were pressing their palms on the windows of copy machines. However, Emmaline did a smashing good job at reading palms. Sam knew—Emmaline had done hers. Sam was certain that Emmaline had helped more people through palmistry than her well-intentioned husband did from the pulpit at the Second Puritan Church on the north side of the town green.

"The potatoes are done. Are the eggs ready?"

Sadie handed her mother the bowl, and while she got two place mats out of the dining room closet, Sam scooped the potatoes out of the skillet onto the plates warming in the oven, and dropped the egg mixture into the pan.

"There's orange juice in the 'fridge."

"Has it got pulp in it?" Sadie asked.

"No pulp for you!" Sam said, grinning.

"Caroline and I saw that Seinfeld episode with the soup Nazi," Sadie said as she poured two glasses of juice. "We practically fell off the sofa laughing."

Sam filled the plates and set them on the table. Sadie sat in her usual place with her back to the bow window. As they ate, Sam continued her explanation of the Keltic spread. Eleven cards: two cards in the center, crossed by a third; these cards are surrounded by four more, one at each compass point; while the last four tower up along the right side.

"Is it significant that there are eleven cards in the layout?" Sadie wanted to know.

"I would think so. Just a minute, honey."

Sam dashed to the sun porch and returned with her Saga pen and some scrap paper. She stuffed a few spoonfuls of egg into her mouth, then picked up her pen and mumbled, "There are eleven cards in the Keltic spread, but only ten significant ones. That's because the first card is the querent, or the person who is the center of the question. The querent card has no meaning other than that."

She began sketching the numbers one through ten in a circle.

"The number ten relates directly to recycling in the material world. You see, the zero in the ten is a place holder. It represents the transition point from one series of nine numbers to the next series of nine numbers."

"Like our counting system," Sadie offered. "Maybe we count that way because we have ten fingers."

Sam beamed at her. "How did you get so smart?"

Sadie laughed. "I take after dad." She then examined the bacon between her fingers as if it were made of alien flesh. "What's soy, anyway?"

"Soy is a vegetable. Full of protein. What I don't understand is how you can eat the flesh of animals, yet be suspect of a product made from the simple soy bean."

Sadie nibbled at the corner. "You know, this bacon isn't half bad."

Maybe. Someday, just maybe. To Sadie, she said, "Translation: You really like it but don't want to admit it."

"I wouldn't go that far." Sadie squinted at the bacon as if she expected eye-balled tentacles to periscope up from its variegated surface. "Mom. What's the ten card in the Tarot?"

"It's the Wheel of Fortune."

"So, is Mrs. Vandalay going to inherit a fortune?"

*   *   *   *   *

Sam grabbed the last pillowcase and clipped one corner to the sheet on the clothesline. She wondered which of the seventy-eight Tarot cards the killer had chosen to leave at the scene of the crime, curious whether the Wheel of Fortune had been included. She also wondered whether the killer had subconsciously picked cards that would lead to his (or her) capture. She was anxious to get the exact layout from Katherine Vandalay. Or Charlie.

She plucked another clothespin from the bag—this time, florescent orange. *Where do they get these colors? Well, at the very least, I can find my laundry in the middle of the night.*

What a field day Clarence Tuttle would have if he saw Sam some night, whipping sheets off the clothesline under a full moon. Then her reputation would really be fixed. As it was now, she was considered only a tad eccentric.

As Sam went to squeeze the clothespin open, it twisted between her fingers and fell into the wet grass at her feet. As she bent down to retrieve it, she noticed a spider spinning a web under the porch. The fragile filaments spanned the space between a supporting post and the deck floor. As a gentle breeze played with the silken mandala, tiny diamond drops flashed dots and dashes—Nature's Morse code.

Sam respected spiders, even if she didn't want them crawling over her—like that night she had been awakened by a crawly feeling over her face. She had flicked on the bedside lamp only to freak out at a black hairy spider scurrying across her pillow. Nick was yanked from his deep Delta sleep by decibels matching those of the heftiest operatic soprano.

Sam had to admit, though, that arachnids were magical creatures, spinning homes from within their bodies, over and over, against all odds. This tiny little creature under the porch had lost her hearth during last night's beating rain. But here she was again, undaunted, regenerating like the number ten.

Would Ula Vandalay lose her hearth? Was Katherine the type to oust her sister-in-law from the mansion in Rye? If so, would Ula rise again, spinning and weaving?

We can learn from the spinners and the weavers, Sam thought, smiling at the double entendre.

Another breeze stirred the web, and the spider scurried to the center and hung there motionless, waiting for her breakfast.

Female spiders have a nasty habit of devouring their mates after sex, Sam thought. She wondered if Henry Vandalay had been devoured by his mate—or by someone else's mate—as a result of his sexual appetite. Looking directly at the eight-legged arachnid, she said aloud, "'Oh what tangled webs we weave, when first we practice to deceive.'"

Someone was being deceived here. Sam just hoped it wasn't her.

As she clipped the corner of the last pillowcase to the clothesline and stood back to inspect her neat line of laundry, a strange sense of satisfaction filled her. Within the ordinary tasks of life lie the secrets of happiness.

Just then, Selket waddled around the corner of the garage and rubbed against Sam's leg. She scooched down and rubbed the cat's ears with both hands. "Hello, old girl. How are you this morning? Would you like a treat? How about some Pounce?"

Selket knew the word. The sound of her purring increased in proportion to her desire. As the cat turned and headed for the back steps, Sam picked up the plastic basket and followed her.

As if it were an omen of things to come, a passing cloud blotted out the sun. Sam shuddered and a chill settled into her bones as her mind conjured up a vision of Henry Vandalay's body cocooned like a spider's dinner, eleven Tarot cards laid out beside his lifeless form.

She pulled the sun porch door open, waited for her feline majesty to sweep into her former abode, then stepped in behind the cat. She hoped a lot of questions would be answered this weekend. God! That was four days away! She and Nick and Charlie and Brun were leaving on Saturday at 3:00 P.M. for Rye and the Vandalay estate.

Sam also hoped she could conjure up more than that little black dress from the depths of her closet.

Chapter 10

Carl Gleason's day had gone so well up until now. The air, fresher after the torrential rain the night before, had energized him. He almost felt like that high school quarterback once again, ready to lick the world. So, how the hell did he get into this pickle?

Pickle? It was more like sinking to the bottom of the brine barrel with a sadistic cooper standing by, ready to clamp on the wooden lid. Somewhere deep inside, Gleason sensed this predicament was his own fault, but he couldn't quite admit that to his brain. He was too terrified to hold a rational thought.

"You don't have to do this!"

Carl Gleason backed away, his meaty palms raised in an attempt to ward off the advancing figure, as if flesh could shield him from the hand of death. "Please. I'll give you money. Lots of money!"

In the pale moonlight, Gleason could see his attacker's twisted mouth as his words spit out like poisoned darts. "I don't take what isn't mine."

"But you won't be taking it. I'll be giving it to you." Gleason's words rasped in his arid throat. His heart pounded against his rib cage until he was afraid he wouldn't get the next breath.

The next breath! he thought. *I won't be getting any next breaths if I don't get out of this.*

"Please." He was begging now. "I've got money. Anything you want."

Gleason backed away toward an ancient white pine, catching himself as he tripped over an exposed hump of root. His eyes darted towards his feet as he wondered if he'd scraped his new wingtips. He couldn't tell. He blinked and looked back at the faint silhouette, now so close that Gleason picked up a faint whiff of cologne.

Do killers wear cologne?

Somewhere in a tiny harbor in the back of his brain, an observer looked on, wondering if killers also brushed their teeth and neatly combed their hair before fading into the night to execute their hapless victims.

Gleason's face prickled. He wanted to scratch his cheeks, forehead, chin, with both hands, but he didn't dare move.

The killer's jaw muscles tightened, his scowl deepened. "You money grubbers are all the same," he growled, malevolence dripping from every syllable.

Just for a moment, Gleason thought about running, but he knew he wouldn't get two steps before bullets ripped into his back. And where would he go?

"What do you mean, 'money grubbers'?" His voice sounded tinny in his head.

"You think you can buy your way out of anything with money. You're the kind who will do anything for a buck."

In the last sane corner of his mind, Gleason had an inkling of what the man was talking about. He decided to pursue it. "But, but…I wouldn't do anything for money. I work hard for everything I have."

It was a cold night for early October in New England, and even though the keening wind off the Squamscott River stabbed through his London Fog raincoat, beads of sweat were collecting on Gleason's upper lip. He could feel rivulets running down his back. His hands were clammy, his breath labored. He stared helplessly at his mahogany wingtips, now desecrated with ooze from the river's edge *and* the wetness flowing from his bladder.

Gleason had the strange impulse to reach inside his coat, pull the fine Italian silk handkerchief from his breast pocket, and wipe the filth from his shoes. But he knew such a movement would be misinterpreted. His looked pleadingly at the person who held his destiny.

Gleason's five senses, raw as open wounds, were more alert than they had ever been in his life. Suddenly, a Hindu parable about a monk and a tiger came to mind, only Gleason was the monk being chased by a tiger, grabbing onto a root as he fell over a cliff. But the root was giving way! He was going to fall. Then, he…it was the monk…or were they one? They saw a beautiful strawberry growing out of the side of the cliff wall. A moment before falling to their deaths, he and the monk reached for and ate the most delicious strawberry they had ever tasted.

Gleason came back to his senses, grinding his teeth as his taste buds began to drip.

Hold on!

Don't lose it now.

He rubbed the rough bark, still wet from the beating rain of the night before, as he felt the cold silence vibrating in his ears. He smelled the pungent odor of dead leaves decaying in the mud along the river's edge. He even found a perverse pleasure in the clinging wet gabardine of his Armani slacks. He had never felt more alive. And it terrified him. Almost more than the killer standing before him.

As the muffled sound of a lone car drifted across the river, Gleason thought about screaming for help. But even as he clung to the tiniest ray of hope, he knew it was useless. The town of Exeter, New Hampshire, lay fast asleep under a blanket of night, rumpled only by a few scattered squares of night-owl light from the distant buildings. Windows fastened, doors locked tight, homes soundproofed against the vagaries of the night. Who would hear?

There was no hope on this side of the river, either. Twenty feet from the water's edge where they stood, a thick stand of old growth pines, oaks and maples buffered a wide meadow. Beyond that, a lone road wandered off toward the east, and fifteen miles later ended at the Atlantic Ocean. There were no homes or stores within sight or earshot.

No, he thought, *screaming won't help. Might only enrage this madman.*

The waning moon struggled for dominance against thickening clouds. One greedy cluster momentarily blotted out the light from the fourth quarter sliver. Blue-black shadows were everywhere—springing up from the ground and pressing down from the tree tops. Stirred by a sudden gust of wind, a ghostly orchestra of heavy pine boughs soughed mournfully. Bony maple branches clicked and tapped like Poe's raven with its demon eyes.

Nevermore!

A voice inside Gleason's head screamed, '*There's got to be more!*'

He wanted more.

He was desperate for more.

If only he could reach his weapon. Gleason flexed his left bicep against his side. He could feel the snub nose .38 in its holster under his suit jacket. Useless to him now. He never liked carrying a gun. Only did it to impress the ladies.

Yeah, right! he thought, *that's me—a fifty-five year old Mike Hammer, with forty extra pounds of good eating on my front porch, two ex-wives, and a bum knee from an old football injury. However, I would like to see fifty-six.*

He wanted to laugh, laugh until his stomach hurt, until there were stitches in his side, until he fell to the ground exhausted from laughing.

Then, as the realization of his predicament once again sunk in, a shudder shook his entire body.

He rubbed his left forefinger over the hangnail on his thumb and winced. A terrible habit. Chewing on that thumb. Left over from childhood. Thumb sucking! At his age.

As the slivered moon broke free of the clouds, a rustle in the woods startled them both.

Gleason's heart skipped a beat. Perhaps…He turned to see a pair of black-ringed eyes peering from the underbrush. The creature waddled out, stared at them through curious yellow ovals, assessed the situation, then scurried back into the bush.

With the killer distracted, Gleason started for his gun, but he wasn't fast enough.

"Don't even think about it," the killer snarled, steadying his weapon with both hands.

Any remaining hope was crushed inside a cold deadly cylinder of steel.

Gleason's heart felt as gray and lifeless as the pale moonlit rooftops and ghostly landscape. For a moment, he wondered why he had agreed to come to this blip on the map. But he knew why. He had a taste for fine clothes, fine wines, and fine women. The advance he'd received was more money than he'd seen in a long time—with more to come if he could complete his assignment. By sheer luck, he had.

Gleason thought about the chain of events. He had reported in four days ago. His anonymous client had agreed to lay out another five thousand dollars—for unexpected expenses—before Gleason would reveal the woman's current name and address. The client had assured him that the remaining fee for his services would be in his hands when the job was finished. Gleason didn't know what else the guy wanted but he was willing to wait.

He had enjoyed the past few days of sightseeing and relaxation. The unease he had initially felt had dissipated, and last night he had slept a contented man. His wake-up call had come at ten o'clock this morning.

Was that just this morning?

He showered, shaved, dressed, and guided by the brochures he had picked up at the front desk after breakfast, he went into Portsmouth and toured the historic John Paul Jones House, walked the grounds of the restored Strawbery Banke Outdoor Museum, and viewed the tugboats on the Piscataqua River from quaint Ceres Street.

Then he treated himself to a fine dinner at the Cosmo. He dined on Chateaubriand, baked potato garnished with a dollop of sour cream and chives, baby carrots sautéed in onions and Marsala wine. He had sipped Opus One, Vintage 91, mentally spending the money that would soon be his. The evening had been superb, marred only by the persistent eerie feeling that he was being followed.

Gleason should have listened to his instincts. This Cretin had snatched him from his car, and waving a deadly Smith & Wesson .357 in his face, driven him to this isolated spot and was about to end his life. Was this person his anonymous client? Had Gleason gone too far in asking for more money?

As if he had drunk from Socrates' cup of hemlock, Gleason's limbs began to freeze, a creeping paralysis that numbed his feet, clawed up at his knees, and sent tremors through his groin.

This isn't happening.

That tiny harbor of his mind still had the capacity to disbelieve that he would meet his maker in a place like this. He was meant for better things. He had places to go, women to conquer.

Whorls of blinking lights, like a Ferris wheel gone mad, erupted before his eyes. The dizzying swirls threatened his balance. Was he passing out? He felt himself sinking toward the dirt.

No! He wasn't going to die. And certainly not on his knees.

Breaking the paralytic fear with an almost superhuman surge of adrenaline, he pushed his unwilling body upright, gulped at the cold air.

He tried to speak. Dry, strangled sounds accosted his ears. Was someone else there? He glanced right, then left, searching the silvery gray landscape for a savior, someone, anyone, who could rescue him from this killer. Then he realized the pathetic noise came from his own parched throat.

Swaying, he fought the dizziness, the heart-clutching fear. He had to live.

He fell back against the tree trunk, arms extended, groping for something to steady himself. The rough bark tore at the flesh on his palms. The pain was excruciating.

"What do you want?" His voice cracked. He coughed, struggling to speak. The guy had to be "Mr. Smith". In a last-ditch attempt, Gleason pleaded, "How can I make things right? Please! I don't need any more money. You can keep the five thousand."

As the moon finally succumbed to the dense curdled clouds, Gleason's world plunged into a darkness he had never known.

The killer chuckled, an eerie almost feral sound. "We don't want any loose ends now, do we?"

Gleason felt a thump in his chest, then another.

He turned toward the tree, clutched at the root with his damaged hands. He hadn't noticed it before, the strawberry growing out of the gnarled and striated trunk of the white pine. The taste buds on each side of his jaw line began to tingle, salivate. As he felt the root pulling away, his body beginning its downward spiral, he grabbed for the plump, juicy red strawberry and plopped it into his mouth.

Carl Gleason's body was dumped into the cold Squamscott River where it sank like a rock.

CHAPTER 11

It was Friday the thirteenth, Freya's Day, Queen of the Norse Gods, the Great Woman who brought the souls of slain warriors to Valhalla. Sam had to wonder if synchronicity had placed her here on the road to Vandalay Enterprises on this rare and feared day. Would she be able to extract a clue from one of the employees that would lead to the arrest of the killer and lay to rest the soul of Henry Vandalay?

Her thoughts thus occupied, she headed for the site where Henry Vandalay was murdered. She needed to talk with Kenny Ash, the man who found Henry's body, and Tony Vernelli, the company foreman.

A few minutes before four o'clock Friday afternoon, under a cloudless blue sky, Sam approached the turnoff to Vandalay Enterprises. She slowed down, then darted in between two dump trucks, taking a left onto a short stretch of macadam. She wended her way over a road thickly lined with trees and emerged onto a large dirt ellipse carved out of the woods. Sprawling metal buildings gleamed in the sun.

As convoys of red dump trucks rumbled past, stirring up dirt twisters around her Honda, Sam could feel the earth beneath her tires vibrating as if Thor, the Thunder God, were driving his goat-drawn chariot across this ravaged land. She closed her windows against the choking dust.

Like so many mindless mechanical warriors, the trucks lined up against a small hill behind the corrugated steel buildings. Sam counted twelve dump trucks, and they were still thundering in. In addition to the battalion of trucks, off to the side in front of a huge pile of dirt were three yellow Caterpillar excavators, two yellow Caterpillar bulldozers, and a skidster loader.

Sam parked her car next to the office door at the peak end of the main building and lowered her head to look out the windshield. Shading her eyes from the sun glinting off the metal buildings, she estimated the seamless galvanized roof of the main building was about thirty feet above her.

One door was up, opening into a cavernous interior with a cement floor and I beam frame construction. In the shadows at the far end of the builidng sat an old army vehicle with a crane mounted on the back that had been used to retrieve tanks.

Sam hesitated, her fingers tapping the steering wheel. Grimy men in work boots, jeans, frayed plaid shirts, and hole-ridden tee shirts streamed around her car as if she were a stationary rock in a fast-moving river. Some of the workers carried yellow hard hats. They looked tired, anxious to punch out and get home for the weekend.

Sam stepped out of her Honda, waving a hand in front of her face to dispel the dust.

Above the roar of metallic chariots, a voice behind her growled, "You the Blackwell woman?"

Sam spun around to find a man built like a wedge. He had short muscular legs and a broad chest that threatened to burst through a grimy gray tank top. Above the tangle of black curly hair sprouting from the open neckline of his shirt rose a twenty-inch neck. A solid line of black eyebrow seemed to slice his swarthy face in half. The man's head shone like Thor's mighty hammer.

"Yes. Yes, I am." Sam almost stuttered. "And you must be Anthony Vernelli." She stuck her hand out.

He ignored it.

"Tony," he said, fixing her with a murderous stare. He then turned and headed for the office door.

"I hope this is a good time," Sam said to the back of his head, running to keep up. "Mrs. Vandalay suggested I stop by at four o'clock today."

"She told me," he said without turning around. He grabbed the closing door and yanked it open. The stream of bodies around him temporarily came to a halt.

Sam followed Tony Vernelli past the human statuary into the office and waited silently while he pulled a red-checkered neckerchief from his back pocket. He wiped the sweat running down his face, and bellowed something about scheduling to the gray-haired secretary behind the gray metal desk. Seemingly, the only one able to do so, the woman ignored 'Tony the Tiger' and continued handing out white envelopes to the men lined up at the counter.

The entire room was gray, Sam noted. Functional.

"Down here." Tony jerked his head toward the short hallway that led to his office.

Tony Vernelli's office was a ten-foot-square cubicle that reeked of cigarette smoke not dispelled in any manner by the one tiny window set high in the wall. A gray metal desk dominated the room. There were two chairs, one behind the desk—gray with padded arms, and one by the door, also gray, of the folding metal variety. Except for a plain-faced, large round clock centered on the wall behind Tony's desk and a large white board to his left, the walls were void of any sign of a human presence.

Tony pointed Sam toward the metal chair. She expected the next command to be 'Sit!'

"I appreciate your seeing me," Sam said, offering the olive branch. She wondered if all his tee shirts were gray to match the decor of his office.

Tony dropped into his chair.

"We do what we're told around here," he said, without looking up. Seemingly absorbed by the few papers laid edge to edge before him, he suddenly scooped them up, tapped the edges into alignment, and lay them neatly in the bottom of a two-tiered metal tray to his right. With a thick hairy hand, he pulled a red marker from a Dolly Parton coffee mug on the desk, took two steps to the white board, and made a notation under the column marked 'Monday'.

A red marker?

Crazily, the red block printing on the board reminded Sam of the one splash of color in the black and white film, *Schindler's List*. Turning her attention back to the desk, she noticed a large glass ashtray next to Dolly. Filled with butts, it seemed an anomaly in this otherwise sterile room. Sam counted thirteen crushed cigarettes.

Key 13, the Death card in the Tarot, she thought, *the card representing major change—death, transformation, and rebirth.*

Switching to the happier side of the card, Sam recalled how the birth of Caroline had changed her life and Nick's. *The birth of the first child is the death of the marriage as it was, transforming the couple into the trinity of mother, father, and child.*

Although in the case of Henry Vandalay, the killer wasn't thinking about the esoteric meaning of trinities and transformations. Death had been very literal. She wondered if the Death card was one of the cards in the Keltic layout left beside Henry Vandalay's body.

That's when she noticed that some of the crushed butts had lipstick smears.

Tony was still at the white board, so Sam leaned forward and squinted. Were those melon or pink lip prints on the butts? Were they Newports? She couldn't make out the brand name. Not that it would have been unusual for Katherine Vandalay to check in with the foreman of her dead husband's company, but Katherine claimed she didn't smoke. Yet, the vision of Katherine tapping an unlit Newport against her shiny gold cigarette case caused Sam to question the woman's protestations.

Sam hovered.

Dare she reach out and slip one of the butts into the pocket of her sweats? She glanced once again at the broad back in front of the white board, then tentatively reached toward the ashtray.

Tony whipped around, and growled, "Whaddya doing?"

"Doing? Oh…" Sam feigned looking under the desk. "I thought I saw a piece of paper on the floor. My mistake." She straightened up and cleared her throat.

Since Tony Vernelli was a man of few words, Sam got right to the point. "Who found Mr. Vandalay's body?"

Tony lowered himself into the gray chair and stared into his hairy hands. "Kenny Ash."

"One of the workers here?"

"Yeah."

"So I take it Mr. Ash was the first one at work that morning?"

Tony scowled at her, his long black eyebrow knotted like a hangman's noose. "That's right."

Why is he so angry? Sam wondered. She wished there were a clue to his personality somewhere in this office, but other than Dolly and her obvious attributes, there was nothing that gave Sam any insight into the man. Not even his handwriting. Block letters. No arcs or telltale squiggles. It was almost as if Anthony Vernelli intended to blend into his gray landscape, a bland and colorless chameleon protected from predators. She had to wonder what he was hiding.

"What time did you arrive at work that morning?"

A vein throbbed in Tony's thick neck, and a twitch appeared at the man's stubbly jaw so slight it made Sam wonder if she had imagined it. She didn't, however, imagine Thor's tiny hammers in Tony's black eyes waiting to pound the life out of her.

"'Bout two minutes later."

Sam steeled herself into interrogation mode. "Where was Mr. Ash when you arrived?"

"Standing over the body."

"And you saw this how?"

"The bay was open."

"How do you know when Mr. Ash arrived?"

"Time cards."

Tony Vernelli sat back and folded burly arms across his chest. He studied Sam as if she were an alloy he could beat into any form he desired.

Nevertheless, she persisted. "Is it possible that he arrived earlier than his time card stated and forgot to punch in right away?"

Tony leaned menacingly across the gray desk and growled, "Look lady. You'll have to ask *him* that."

Two whole sentences! She was impressed, if a bit shaky.

CHAPTER 12

Foreman Anthony Vernelli left his office to go and find Kenny Ash. Next on the list of suspects, he jawed to himself. Where was the skinny little grunt anyway?

Tony stomped his way through the front office, where men were still picking up their checks, out into the yard, bellowing, "Ash! Where the hell are you?"

The last truck had finally parked, its motor now burping into silence. Tony scowled at the line of apple-red vehicles, making sure they were lined up neatly. Then he spied Kenny climbing down from the last truck in the row.

"Ash!" he bellowed again. "In the office. *Now.*"

A few workers, pay envelopes in hand, were climbing into pickup trucks when a '98 powder blue Monte Carlo slued to a stop before the bay door at the far end of the building. In the rising dust, a slim woman with spiked blonde hair hopped out of the car and tugged at her white short shorts. Surgically enhanced breasts strained at the red polka-dot halter tied around her chest.

With a fleeting glance at Vernelli, she called, "Kenny! Kenny, honey! Over here." She waved a bedangled arm in his direction while casting eyes at the quivering inhabitants of the pickup trucks. Sets of leering eyes surveyed her terrain as she bent over to check her lipstick in the side view mirror. She dabbed at the corners of her mouth, apparently finding everything satisfactory.

Candy ass, Tony glowered, and thumbed Kenny toward the office door.

Kenny nodded slightly in his wife's direction, then skittered across the threshold into the empty office. Everyone was gone, including the secretary. Tony was glad she wasn't there. The bitch showed him no respect.

If there was one thing Tony needed—no, demanded—it was respect. He'd done bad things to people who failed to pay him his due. He thought about the night he got the "BORN TO BE BAD" tattoo on his right buttocks. He had been *real* bad that night.

"Get your ass in there and talk to that Blackwell woman," Tony barked at Kenny. "Orders from the top." He then plunked himself down in the secretary's gray chair to wait.

He scowled at her name plate, the long eyebrow a black slash across his face. The secretary had been at Vandalay Enterprises as long as he had. Hired the same day, as a matter of fact. He rubbed his finger back and forth under his nose. She didn't even have a resume.

Berma Battles. He laughed. He liked to think of her as Berma Battles the Bitch. She wasn't easily intimidated, as Tony had discovered in very short order. He envisioned her as an ex-prison guard. Probably in a men's prison! Even Hank Vandalay had stayed out of her way. She had the eyes of an eagle and the behavior of a buzzard; she saw too much, and could pick a man's bones clean without a whole lot of effort. This past week, Tony fumed, Berma Battles had seen way too much.

*   *   *   *   *

Kenneth Robert Ash had married Candace Mary Ploski right out of high school. They had 'done it' for the first time three months before graduation. Although it wasn't Candy's first time, he didn't care.

In the beginning, they were like a couple of rabbits, and two months later, Candy was pregnant. He thought poking holes in the tips of his condoms had been pretty smart. She never knew, and he would never tell her.

Now, eight years and three kids later, Kenny loved her more than when they first met. Just last year, he sold the heirloom watch and the Winchester 44-40 his father had left him. That gave him enough for a down payment on the Monte Carlo Candy now drove. Candace Ash was the center of Kenny's universe. He would do anything to keep her happy.

Anything.

He gritted his teeth as he stepped into Tony Vernelli's office.

*   *   *   *   *

Samantha rose and smiled. "Mr. Ash?" She hesitated to put out her hand, but decided not to let Tony the Tiger dictate her etiquette.

"Uh huh." Kenny's hand shake was limp, his hands rough and dusty. A thatched roof of straight sandy hair hung over his forehead. He swallowed hard, twice, his prominent Adam's apple bobbing up and down as if it were in a tub of water during a child's Halloween party.

Kenny looked around the stark room, seeming to notice Tony's seat for the first time. He made a move for the chair, appeared to think better of the decision, then jammed his hands into his jeans pockets. Two of Kenny could have fit inside the green plaid shirt hanging over his thin, bony frame. Even motionless, he appeared to be quivering.

Sam smiled to put him at ease. "I really appreciate your talking with me. I won't keep you long."

"That's okay." He fidgeted, then pulled a pack of Marlboros and a book of matches from his shirt pocket. He pointed the pack at Sam. "Smoke?"

"Uh, no thanks."

Sam's eyes cut to Tony's dirty ashtray on the desk. She had decided not to pick up one of the crushed cigarette butts after all.

"Mind if I do?" He was already taking one from the pack and lighting it.

Sam minded it very much, but she would tolerate anything to get through this interview. Kenny needed to feel relaxed if he was going to open up to her. "It must have been terrible for you to find Mr. Vandalay like that."

"Yeah." He nodded his head jerkily, leaned a shoulder against the wall, and lit the Marlboro. He drew in a deep, lung-filling fix. Savoring the nicotine high, his body relaxed as he watched the stream of smoke issue from his mouth and lift toward the ceiling.

Sam felt a familiar flush in her chest, her initiation into the crone stage of life.

Not now, she commanded, but no one was listening. A fine sheen of sweat broke out on her forehead. She felt like Neuman sweating under the hot lights while grilling Jerry Seinfeld, who sat comfortably in the shadows.

She glanced up at the clock. A quarter to five. She thought about the Ring Dings in the refrigerator at home and her stomach rumbled. Kenny had his Marlboros, she had her Ring Dings.

Pulling herself back into the now smoke-filled room, Sam stifled a cough. "Would you show me the spot where you found Mr. Vandalay's body?" *Anything to get out of this room.*

"Sure."

Kenny also seemed glad for the chance to leave. Maybe he was claustrophobic, or maybe he just couldn't remain still very long. He appeared to be a stereotypical nervous chain smoker; even the whites of his eyes had that yellow tinge often found among heavy smokers.

Sam followed Kenny down the hallway into the front office, past a sullen Tony Vernelli, through a side door into the huge main building. As they made their way, their footsteps echoed in the dead air space.

Sam wasn't sure if she was ready to view this spot and sure as hell hoped there would be no telltale evidence of the violent crime. She wondered if any of the workers were spooked when they walked past the scene of the bloodshed.

As Kenny pushed ahead of her, Sam watched the cigarette smoke swirl around his head. She felt just as sorry about his addiction as she did about her own.

Like the enchantress Circe who turned men into swine by means of a magic drink, Ring Dings and Marlboros had the power to transform the undisciplined: Kenny into an almost anorexic caricature of himself, and her into—yes, a swine. Or swinette. Well, maybe a chubby piglet. Anyway, pigs made wonderful pets. And they were intelligent. They just needed a better press agent.

Kenny stopped by a metal rack and pointed at the floor. "It was right here I found him."

Sam's eyes followed Kenny's finger to a dark stain on the cement floor. She felt her mouth go dry. Fighting to regain her composure, she forced a steady gaze. "How was he lying when you found him?"

"On his back."

Sam couldn't control the shudder that ran through her body. Kenny didn't notice. He was also staring at the dark stain on the cement. He took another drag while the forefinger of his left hand tapped repeatedly at his thigh.

"I opened up that morning 'cuz Tony thought he might be late. His wife wasn't feeling good, so he called me to come get the key."

"What time did Mr. Vernelli call you to pick up the key?"

"Um, I think it was about five-thirty."

"And you found Mr. Vandalay that same morning, when you got to work?"

"Yeah."

"So Tony usually opens in the morning?"

"Yeah." He bit at his lips, then drew in another lungful of tobacco, coughed, cleared his throat, then said, "He's got the only key so he opens up. He's always the first one here."

"How did Mr. Vandalay die?" Sam already knew, but asking questions often led to unexpected answers.

"Knifed in the back. More than once, I heard."

Sam rubbed her forehead, then held a closed fist against her lips. She tried to swallow, and couldn't. She thought she was going to choke, but managed to get enough saliva in her mouth to come up with a tiny swallow. She felt her heart thump erratically. "Did the police find the weapon?"

He looked down at his feet. "Don't think so. Anyway, I didn't see one."

Sam looked at Kenny's bent head, taking a moment to allow her bodily functions to normalize. Had there been trouble between Kenny and Henry Vandalay?"

She looked out through the open bay door and saw a young blonde woman in shorts leaning against a car.

Kenny noticed. "That's my wife," he beamed.

Sam smiled at him. "She's very pretty."

Then she wondered. Did some of those lipstick stains belong to Kenny's wife? If so, was Kenny really naive enough to agree to open the shop the morning after he'd killed his boss, leaving the body there for the world to find? He could have made any kind of excuse to get out of it. Unless it was a clever ruse to deflect suspicion from himself.

"Was Mr. Vandalay a good employer?"

Kenny stood stark still. After a moment he said, "He was okay." His jaw muscles suddenly twitched.

"So you and Mr. Vandalay were on good terms?"

"Yeah, I guess."

Sam wondered if Henry Vandalay's late night 'business meetings' included the voluptuous Mrs. Ash, but she was afraid Kenny would clam up if she pursued that line of inquiry. Perhaps Sunday, when all the players arrived for their command performance at the Vandalay estate, more of the script would unfold.

"Anything else unusual about that morning?"

Kenny's Adam's apple bobbed. "Yeah. Those cards."

"The Tarot cards."

"Right." A furrow planted itself on Kenny's forehead as he fixed pale eyes on Sam. "Do you think he was killed by some fortune teller?"

"That's for the police to find out, Mr. Ash. What about the cards?"

"I don't know. There was a bunch of 'em. Looked like someone laid 'em out careful-like 'cuz they was nice and even. I gotta go. My wife's waitin' for me outside."

"Alright. Thank you for your time, Mr. Ash. I take it I'll see you at the Vandalay estate on Sunday?"

"Yup. Candy's looking forward to it."

Candy? Sam thought. *Candy Ash? What's in a name, indeed.*

She followed Kenny into the front office, where Tony was waiting. Tony grumbled about being kept late and practically pushed them out as he slammed the door behind them.

Kenny headed toward the powder blue Monte Carlo on which Candy, her back resting against the windshield, lay stretched to the waning sun.

Sam noticed that the last few pickup trucks rumbled out of the yard slower than one would have expected from a group of tired, hungry construction workers late on a Friday afternoon.

"Hi, honey." Candy waved at her husband, then took a wad of gum out of her mouth and tossed it on the ground. She slid off the car and tugged at her shorts. It didn't help.

Kenny beamed, then paused and turned back to Sam. "It's really weird," he said, his yellowed eyes curiously animated. "Now that I think of it, one of those cards—it had an eight on it—had these knives all over it."

The Eight of Swords? Sam couldn't remember what that card looked like.

Kenny scooped his wife into his arms and kissed her lips, then scurried around to the passenger side of the Monte Carlo. As the pair took off in a dusty cloud-of-happiness, Sam wondered if that glint in Kenny's eye was from the vision of his wife or some perverse pleasure in finding the brutalized body of his boss. Or could the pleasure lie in the performance of the act itself?

She was also curious about Kenny's sudden burst of clarity in recalling one specific Tarot card from the crime scene.

Finally, she had to wonder if Henry Vandalay had found Candy Ash as appealing as Kenny did.

CHAPTER 13

Katy Thayer was terrified.

Cowering under a sheet on her single bed in her tiny fake-wood-paneled bedroom, she listened to her stepfather ranting at her mother through an alcohol-induced rage. Katy could only imagine what would happen next. He would burst through her bedroom door and do what he had been whispering in her ear for the past six months.

Six days ago, Katy had turned fourteen. Over the past year, she had developed high firm breasts and a slim waist which accentuated long shapely legs. She spent many hours staring at her face in the bathroom mirror—the planes that carved high cheek bones, the seductive violet eyes, and the creamy skin that begged to be touched. She didn't revel in her beauty. It came at a price: leering looks and groping hands. Gene would laugh and pretend he was joking. Her mother didn't notice—or maybe she didn't want to.

Although Katy tried to hide her body, Gene's bloodshot eyes couldn't miss the swelling womanhood beneath the baggy clothes. Her stepfather snapped her photograph every time she turned around. Once, he even caught her stepping out of the shower and got his friend at the camera shop to develop the film. He had taken photos of her sleeping at night with her mouth open and her nightgown hitched up around her hips. He would wave the glossies in her face and tell her he was passing copies around to his friends. She never knew if he really did. But his friend at the camera shop sure got a good look.

Katy knew it was just a matter of time before Gene tried to rape her. But she was determined not to be a victim like her mother and the women in the magazine articles Katy devoured. She knew what to do. She had her weapons. All she needed now was enough money and a little more time. If Gene didn't come through her door that night, he would soon. She knew it.

Lady Luck smiled on Katy that muggy night when her stepfather came home from the races and *did* come through her door. He had fifteen one hundred dollar bills crumpled in his drunken fist. Her mother was working the late shift at K-mart.

"Look what I've got for you, Katy, my Katy," he slurred, waving his fist in the air.

Katy rubbed sleep-filled eyes and tried to focus on the swaying hulk in the doorway. Gene staggered to her bedside and let the hundreds drift down over her sweat-covered body. Katy skittered up her pillow and pulled the sheets protectively to her chest screaming, "Stay away from me!"

Emboldened by the alcohol and the flush of big money, Gene Meeker threw himself on his stepdaughter, kissing her neck, running his rough hands over her breasts.

"It's about time, don't you think, baby? You know you want it." His sour breath turned her stomach.

As she kicked and pushed at the unkempt hulk pressing down on her, she could hear the crinkle of bills between their bodies.

Money. All that money.

Even in his drunken state, Gene Meeker was too powerful for the slender fourteen-year-old. She stopped resisting as her mind screamed. *Think! Think!*

She cleared her throat and took a heart-thumping breath. "Gene. I *do* want you. But…" Gene pushed himself up on two elbows and stared unbelievingly at his step-daughter through foggy eyes. "But first, I have to pee. And I want to put on my perfume. Make it nice for you. Okay?"

Crevices formed around Gene's sunken eyes as he squinted at the supple girl beneath him. "You promise?"

"Yes. I promise," Katy whispered.

"Alright, baby!" He rolled onto his side, forcing his eyes into focus as she slithered out from under him. Still suspicious, he said, "We have a contract, Katy. You get the money, I get you."

Terrified, Katy nodded mutely, and started for the door as Gene fell back on the bed to await his fifteen hundred dollars worth.

A minute later, it happened—and Katy screamed.

She screamed and screamed, fighting up through a red river of blood, struggling in vain against the thick sticky fluid. It filled her mouth and nose and ears. She gurgled and bubbled, and finally felt herself giving in to it. She was drifting. It wasn't so bad. Not half as bad as she imagined.

She was drowning...

Drowning...

Katy bolted upright in her four-poster cherry bed. Drenched in sweat, she clutched the silk sheets against her to ward off her attacker. But he was gone. The tiny bedroom and sweltering trailer were gone. She was alone in the king-sized bed in her rambling mansion by the sea.

As this realization sunk in, Katherine Vandalay fell back into the down pillows, her golden hair twisted into damp strands, her body drained.

The nightmare had followed her through the years. She never knew what happened to Gene Meeker. She had left him sprawled on her bed, his legs trailing in the narrow space between the bed and the trailer wall. One foot had been twisted against her navy blue school bag. Squiggly claret-colored lines had trickled down his blank expression.

He had been stone still.

Clutched in Katy's right hand was the beach stone she used for a paperweight, splattered with claret-red drops matching the streaks trickling down Gene's face; fisted in her left hand were fifteen one hundred dollar bills. Katy left home twenty minutes later, never to return.

Left behind that sticky summer night was the broken-down trailer park, her drunken step-father, her weak martyred mother—and Katy's childhood. She left with a small bag of her belongings and fifteen one-hundred dollar bills stuffed into her bra.

And three powerful weapons. Henry Vandalay had succumbed to one. Katherine had saved her virginity for just such a man. It only took two months after he first laid eyes on her in that gift shop. The night when she brought him to the edge of ecstasy, but wouldn't give it to him, Henry begged her to marry him. After Henry made a few phone calls, they flew to Las Vegas where marriage is easy: no blood tests, no waiting periods. The Marriage License Bureau is open seven days a week: Monday through Thursday, 8:00 A.M. to midnight, and twenty-four hours on weekends and holidays. Thirty-five dollars (in cash) for the license.

Henry and Katherine were married in a hokey little wedding chapel, and two days later, Mr. and Mrs. Henry Vandalay flew back home.

So Katherine had gotten exactly what she wanted, and now that her husband was dead, life was going to be so sweet.

The white and gold Louis XIV style clock on the bureau read 2:15 A.M. Katherine let her gaze drift around the redecorated bedroom, dimly lit by the frosty light of a full moon. Except for the cherry bed which Henry had refused to part with, the room was a symphony in white—a thick white carpet and creamy silk wallpaper, off-white end tables, and matching antique bureaus set off by bouquets of white silk freesia. Clean, fresh, untainted. White lent clarity.

Katherine sighed, and stretched into the luxury of the silk sheets. She turned on her side and burrowed her head deep into the pillow. Her nightgown lay draped over the end of the bed. She never wore nightgowns anymore. Too restricting. Like Marilyn Monroe who wore only *Chanel No. 5* to bed, Katherine Vandalay wore only *Hypnotic Poison* when she slipped between her silky sheets.

She tried to still her mind. Sleep was essential. She would need her strength and all her wiles to get through the weekend. Paramount in her mind was the need to keep her language refined around Charles and the Blackwell woman. She'd also have to monitor the caterers, the food, the musicians, and especially Ula. God, she hoped the woman wouldn't come draped in a mourning shroud. The guests had to be the focus of tomorrow's celebration. It was going to be interesting to see which philanthropist would make the biggest contribution so his name (or her name, Katherine thought, as Agatha Coldbath came to mind) could be splashed across the newspapers. Well-fed, happy guests made big contributions, and Henry Vandalay was going out in style.

From the folds of her pillow, her drooping eyes lit upon the nightstand next to her bed. A curious smile touched her lips. The highly-polished black-and-gray speckled beach stone, now cleansed of its claret spots, stood as silent testimony to her success.

CHAPTER 14

"What am I going to wear, Nick?" Sam cried, her head in the closet. "I have nothing to wear!" It was Saturday morning and she was desperate.

"That's because you never go clothes shopping," Nick answered. He stood in the bathroom doorway, toothbrush in hand, with that I-told-you-so look on his face. "You could outfit an expedition to the summit of Mt. Everest with what you spend on books. Think how nicely you could dress if you took some of your book funds and went on a shopping spree. The girls would go with you. Your mother would go with you. Hell, I'd even go with you."

"That isn't helping, Nick!"

He glanced at the digital clock on the bureau. "It's only eight-thirty; we don't leave until three. Why don't you run over to the Fox Run Mall and find yourself an outfit?"

"I'm not buying a thing until I lose thirty pounds."

Nick sighed and rubbed the nub of his nose with his free hand. "Isn't that circular logic? You have nothing to wear, but you won't buy anything until you lose thirty pounds."

"Everything in life isn't logical," Sam said, a bit of irritation in her voice. She knew she shouldn't be upset with Nick when she was really disgusted with herself. How did that package of Ring Dings find its way onto her bedside table last night while she was reading, long after Nick had fallen asleep?

"Hey," Nick said, raising his hands in the universal sign of surrender, "Don't shoot the messenger."

Sam took a deep breath, then said, "I'm sorry, honey. I'm not mad at you."

He winked at her. "I know."

"I'll take my black dress. Good. That's settled."

Nick started into the bathroom, then turned and said, "Don't forget to pack your green hair roller." Grinning, he executed a quick retreat.

Sam stood, arms akimbo, trying to decide if she should laugh or toss a throw pillow at him. She could hear him brushing his teeth vigorously and humming *The First Time Ever I Saw Your Face.*

That's when her heart went mushy.

She sank onto the bed, on the red patchwork quilt from her childhood. She flopped back, her arms spread like wings, listening to Nick's deep muffled voice. He had told her when he heard Roberta Flack sing that phrase that it took him back to the special moment when he first laid eyes on the woman who was to become his wife. It was his favorite song.

Sam stared at the ceiling as tears collected at the corners of her eyes. She loved this man. Too intensely, she sometimes felt. How was it possible for a woman to love a man so much that it physically hurt? That was only for the heroines in Barbara Cartland romance novels.

She got up, slipped into the bathroom and wrapped her arms around Nick's naked waist.

"What?" He half turned, toothpaste trimming his top lip.

Sam laughed. "Got milk?"

"What are you talking about?"

"I'm talking *to* the most gorgeous man in the world."

*   *   *   *   *

Thirty minutes later, as Sam leaned over the bathroom sink wiping toothpaste off her cheek, the phone rang. She ran to grab the portable off the bureau.

"It's me." Charlie Burrows' usual greeting.

"Hi, Charlie. What's up?"

"Brun can't make it. She was up all night. Probably got the flu or something. I hope I didn't give her my cold on top of it."

"Oh, Charlie. That's too bad. You're still going, aren't you?"

"Yup. Me and my box of Kleenex."

Sam said, "Nick's not excited about going. He grumbled a little about giving up breakfast at The Bog tomorrow."

The Bog Cafe was the watering hole and gossip center for the Georgetown locals. It was also the site of last year's fight between Jimi Duncan and Bobbie Hammand. Bobbie's father had been found sliced open in the frozen fish section of McCutty's Market.

"Hmph. That's where I'd rather be than all gussied up for some lawn party."

"It's not a lawn party, Charlie. It's a fund raiser in honor of Henry Vandalay. Where's your community spirit?"

Charlie grumbled something unintelligible, then said, "Do you suppose Agatha will be there?"

"Absolutely. Katherine said she was inviting 'everyone who is anyone,' and Agatha is definitely *anyone*. Lest you forget, Coldbath Cowberry Chutney is the third largest business in New England."

"Agatha is the berries." Charlie tittered at his own joke.

"Have you had any luck with the Tarot cards?" Sam asked.

"Yeah. I managed to get the exact layout. Hold on." He sneezed, performed some other rituals that Sam could only imagine then continued. "But, Jesus, don't tell anyone I'm giving this to you. Although the whole affair, including these cards, will be in the papers soon enough. You know how those things go."

She certainly did. It hadn't take longer than a wink for the coded messages during the Cowberry Necklace affair last year to make the front page of Publick Occurrences. *And* the national tabloids—above the fold.

"It's in the vault, Charlie. But it's not a problem. Katherine said half a dozen of the employees at Vandalay Enterprises saw the cards. Besides, she called last night to tell me she'll have the Tarot layout for me this weekend. I would have found out sooner or later. So, why not sooner?"

"Right. Be right back, Sam."

Sam cradled the portable phone between her ear and shoulder, smoothing that last wrinkle on the bed quilt. The cover was starting to show its age—some of the floral rectangles were wearing thin, some had pulled out of the seams. The replacement material Sam bought last year still sat on top of the sewing basket in her closet. Another project she would get to some day.

This winter, she told herself, *when the nor'easters blow, and the fireplace is blazing, I'll drape this quilt over my lap and hand sew these pieces while I watch TV.* She needed her fantasies.

On the sun porch, Sam set the portable phone down on her desk and switched to the speaker phone. She took a piece of paper from the blue stationery box where she kept the used sheets from her work, and twiddled her favorite gray Saga pen while she waited.

Suddenly remembering, she made herself a note to order refills for the pen. They had to be ordered a box at a time—twelve packets of two each. You couldn't buy *one* of anything anymore. She still regretted the closing of Woolworth's in Exeter three years ago, where you could buy one of just about anything.

"You ready?"

"Yes," she said, feeling the flutterbys in her stomach that accompanied challenges. "Go ahead, Charlie."

*   *   *   *   *

The Rider deck Sam had bought while doing research for the Tarot columns a few years back was found in the bookcase under the sun porch windows, behind a stack of books: Paul Foster Case's *The Tarot,* Barbara Walker's *The Secrets of the Tarot* and *The Woman's Encyclopedia of Myths and Secrets,* Eden Gray's *A Complete Guide to the Tarot,* and Stephan A. Hoeller's *The Royal Road.*

She blew the dust from the top flap, opened the box and drew out the seventy-eight cards. Clearing a spot on her desk, she fanned the cards in an arc, leaving room in front of her for the Keltic layout.

Legend had it that the multicolored symbols on the cards contained priceless wisdom. Would they also reveal who killed Henry Vandalay?

Sam recalled that the word Tarot itself contained a secret message. She pulled in a deep breath, and closed her eyes for several moments while she fumbled through her brain cells for the ancient acrostic. Some researchers felt the final 't' in the word Tarot was used to confuse the uninitiated. Using the letters t-a-r-o as the key, she mouthed, *Rota Taro orat tora Ator: The wheel of Tarot speaks the law of Hathor.*

Hathor, variously named Ator, Nut, and Isis, was the Egyptian Queen of Heaven. Hathor had never been created; she always *was*, before the beginning of time, present and omniscient. She was the milk-giving Goddess whose holy river of blood, the Nile, nourished her land and its people.

The Mother of all gods and goddesses, Hathor took many forms, one of which was the Nile goose, from which Mother Goose and her fairy tales emerged.

Sam smiled as she thought, *Fairy tales, just like old wives' tales, contain ageless truths.*

In ancient Egypt, the star-shaped Easter lily was Hathor's flower and is still a present-day symbol of birth and resurrection. Sam knew from history that victorious nations overlaid their own religions on the holidays and symbols of the conquered peoples to make the transition palatable. According to some authorities, even though Jesus was born in

March, his birth is celebrated on December 25th, which is the period of pagan ceremonies honoring the birth of the Sun, the winter solstice.

Folding her hands across her belly, Sam thought, *Old truths never die or fade away. They just take on different forms. The Tarot deck is more than a stack of picture cards.*

For many minutes, she sat and listened to the silence, waiting for her inner voice to speak. All she heard was "Idle hands are the Devil's workshop."

Time to get down to it.

She fingered the silky surfaces of the cards, straightening and rounding the arc. The symbology embedded in the figures, buildings, backgrounds, colors, and numbers was mind-boggling, but she had more mundane matters to attend to. Someone had used this honored set of cards during an horrendous act, desecrating the Sacred Wisdom.

To her left lay the sheet of paper with the list Charlie had given her of the specific Tarot cards found at the crime scene. The Death card and the Wheel of Fortune (the card Sadie had asked about) were among them.

Sam searched for the card the killer had chosen to represent Henry Vandalay and slipped it out from the others: the King of Pentacles, a man of wealth.

In the Keltic method, the first card was designated to represent the querent, and was not part of the interpretation of the spread. She placed Henry's card on the desk in front of her.

Following the instructions in the Tarot book lying open on the notepaper, she drew out the first official card in the reading, Key 6: The Lovers, and aligned it exactly over the King of Pentacles. The Tarot book said this card represented the general circumstances and influences surrounding Henry Vandalay.

The circumstances surrounding Henry prior to his death were symbolized by The Lovers.

What do we have here? A lover's triangle?

Katherine mentioned that she had smelled other women's perfume on her husband, and that he was often out late. Maybe all night. What would a contractor be doing roaming the countryside during the wee small hours? *He probably wasn't polishing his excavator.*

Sam grabbed another sheet of scrap paper, made a note, and tossed the pen aside.

The book said the second card indicated opposing forces. According to Charlie's list, this was the Three of Swords. Against a gray background of storm clouds, three pale blue swords pierced a blood red heart. Interpretation: confusion, sorrow, loss. She placed this card horizontally across The Lovers.

Someone didn't like what Henry was doing.

She crossed her legs and leaned her chin into a cupped hand to stare at the broken heart.

If Henry Vandalay was tomcatting around, he could have stirred up animosities. Perhaps there was more than one woman, and the more possessive of the two paramours decided to carve him up. Hell hath no fury like a woman scorned. It was an old story.

Sam drew up from memory one of the most talked-about cases of the twentieth century. A woman named Jean Harris claimed that, while attempting suicide, she accidentally killed her lover of fourteen years, Dr. Herman Tarnower, author of The Scarsdale Diet. The respected headmistress of the exclusive Madeira School for Girls in Virginia was subsequently found guilty of murder. The 1980 trial provided salacious material for the tabloids for months. Jean Harris was a woman scorned. Of course, Sam reasoned, an enraged boyfriend, or a husband like Kenny Ash, was not out of the question either.

Then there was Tony the Tiger. What reason would he have to kill his employer? As foreman, he probably made pretty good money; you don't bite the hand that feeds you. She wondered if there were a Mrs. Tiger and if she liked to meow.

She paused. Was she reading more into the cards than was really there?

Sam had a family reputation for asking too many questions. It was a trait that had gotten her into more than one thorny thicket, to the great exasperation of her husband, who often pondered God's oversight in not branding his wife's forehead with a question mark as a warning to others.

She was asking questions right now. Did the killer thumb through a Tarot book, see the Keltic layout and select the cards at random, with no other intention?

Even if that were true, the perpetrator would still have been revealed. For the past twenty years, Sam had observed how clients subconsciously revealed their true selves through their choices and actions: by the colors and types of clothing they wore, their makeup and jewelry, their body language, the verbs and adjectives they used to describe their situations and feelings.

Each of us is an open book for those who can read.

Like Katherine, the nonsmoking, cigarette-tapping widow.

Once again, she wondered about the lipstick-ringed butts in Tony Vernelli's ashtray. She made another note and sat back.

Tony Vernelli.

His office was a study in mathematical correctness. Perhaps the man was obsessive-compulsive about his surroundings. Both Charlie Burrows and Kenny Ash mentioned that the Tarot cards left at the scene of the crime were neatly arranged.

Sam recalled Thor's twin hammers, and knew that Tony Vernelli, after stabbing a man to death, would not be able to leave the bloody scene until each Tarot card was ruler straight. Was this obsession a fatal mistake?

She rubbed her forehead.

The third card was Key 15: The Devil.

Tucking a loose strand of hair into the elastic at the nape of her neck, Sam stretched her arms high above her head. Her neck was getting stiff. She rubbed it, then settled into *The Thinker* mode once again.

The Devil card is the querent's foundation, something that is already part of his past…

Her thoughts were shattered by the shrill jangle of the phone at her elbow. She jumped, then grabbed the receiver, reminding herself for the thousandth time to turn the volume down.

"Hi, Mom."

"Oh, hi, honey. What's up?" Sam leaned back in her swivel chair and looked up at the paddle fan above her head where dust strands hung like Tarzan's jungle vines. Another thing she would get to one of these days.

"What are you wearing this weekend to the Vandalay service?" Caroline asked.

"Why?"

"Mom, you know you need help. I don't want to hurt your feelings, but you usually look like you got dressed in the dark."

Sam stifled a giggle. "I don't know what I'm wearing. I was thinking of taking that black dress dad bought me."

"You wear that everywhere."

"Well, I've never worn it to the Vandalays'."

"What am I going to do with you? Don't go anywhere. I'm almost through helping Gramma and I'll be right over. You and I are going to the mall. I'm not having you go out in public looking like an accident victim." Caroline hung up before Sam had time to respond.

Sam just knew that her mother had put a bee in Caroline's bonnet. Still, feeling all warm inside, Sam slowly replaced the receiver in its cradle. She savored the moment. Even the horned, goat-faced Devil whose white eyes stared up at her from the desk couldn't dispel the mood.

She lifted one eyebrow. *The card does look ominous*, she thought.

The Devil sat atop a half cube to which a naked man and woman were loosely chained. They are in self-imposed bondage to their carnal desires because they can see only half truths—represented by the half cube. The inverted pentagram on the Devil's forehead indicated the five senses gone astray.

Sam picked up her pen and began twisting it between her fingers. Was the killer saying that Henry was in bondage to his sexual desires?

Sex is a powerful motivator. She had read somewhere that men think about sex every six minutes. Sex and six—as in Key 6: The Lovers— sounded suspiciously alike.

As these thoughts rolled around in her head, she unconsciously drew a six-pointed star on the scrap paper. Then, shifting gears, she started to make a note about adjusting the telephone volume and dusting the paddle fan, when she actually noticed the six-pointed star she had drawn.

Ah, yes. The Great Yantra.

Although the Jews had adopted this star as their symbol, its origins lay with Tantric Hinduism where it represented the 'union of the sexes'. The downward-pointing triangle, the female Yoni Yantra, existed before time. Eventually, the Goddess created a spark of life within her triangle, which developed into a male, her future mate.

Bindumati, a personification of the Great Yantra, was known as the 'divine harlot'. Ruling nature, she could "command storms by the power of her magic and halt rivers in their tracks," a miracle subsequently copied by Moses.

Those guys stole our thunder! she thought, *then they blamed us for the sins of the world!*

Behind Sam's closed lids, the Garden of Eden rose in all its lush glory. She could see Adam cowering behind a bush while Eve busted her buns to pick him an apple. He ate it, then let God put the blame on Eve. Adam even had the nerve to name the fruit after himself.

Adam's apple, indeed!

As usual, she was getting off track.

Opening her eyes to erase the image, Sam forced her attention back to the doodle. The Great Yantra was an apt symbol for the six, the number of love, home, and hearth, and for The Lovers in the Tarot deck. Yes, she reasoned, if there was a deliberate selection behind this spread, there had to be a woman involved.

Sam glanced back at the list of cards. The Nine of Cups was next. A well-fed man sat before nine elevated cups. He looked content, implying material success and satisfaction. She placed this card to the left of the querent, in the westerly position; the influence that is passing away.

Self-explanatory, she thought. Henry Vandalay's influence and wealth no longer mattered to him.

The next card, in the north position, indicated what might happen in the future. She slipped the Eight of Swords out of the rainbow of colors.

That's when her breath caught in her throat.

CHAPTER 15

In their bright yellow lacy kitchen, Tony Vernelli groused at his wife about the coffee, the runny yokes of his fried eggs, the black pellets she called fried potatoes, and the carbon-dated Wonder Bread toast. You'd think after eighteen years of cooking two meals a day plus packing lunches, that practice would have made perfect—but it hadn't helped Maria Vernelli one damned bit. Tony thought he was probably the only man in the world with an Italian wife who couldn't boil water.

He snorted. No wonder she couldn't cook a decent meal. She spent all her time going to that damned Tarot class. Why were women so superstitious? According to Maria, even Hank Vandalay's sister went to the same classes, as if that lent any credence to her own involvement with that group of muddled-headed women. Tony would have bet that Ula Vandalay wished she'd stayed the hell away from those stupid Tarot cards, now that they'd been found beside her dead brother's body. His mouth twisted into an evil smile. *The bum had it coming.*

He wiped his face with a paper napkin decorated with watering cans and tossed it into his plate. A corner of the napkin curled as it absorbed the runny yokes.

His thoughts drifted to his wife once again. They were more benevolent this time. Maybe Maria's superstitious pastime was innocent enough. As long as his home was clean, meals were on the table (such as they were), and she was available in his bed, he would allow her this one pleasure.

He shoved the half-eaten breakfast aside, tracing a line of thought back to yesterday afternoon. That Blackwell woman could spoil any man's appetite, snooping around like she was some god-damned detective. He saw her looking at the ashtray on his desk, at the lipstick. It was stupid of him not to get rid of those butts. He was usually careful about such details, but Hank's death had thrown a monkey wrench into his routine. Not that the guy didn't deserve it.

And why the hell did Vandalay request that he and Maria return after the services tomorrow to hear the will? What did the bastard have up his sleeve? Tony hoped it had nothing to do with the time he strong-armed Vandalay into giving hefty raises to the crew. Tony didn't care about the rest of the men, but he wanted more money for his hard work and long days. He was worth it.

And when Vandalay won the big state contract a year ago, Tony struck. He organized the men and threatened a walkout. He had Vandalay over a barrel that time, and the guy caved. There had been no love lost between them since then, but they coexisted.

His presence at the reading of the will certainly wasn't because Vandalay wanted to fire him. He snorted at that thought.

Tony pushed himself up from the table, scowled at his wife, then headed for his workshop. He had two obsessions in life: model trains and women. His trains he kept in the basement; he would have kept his women there, too, if the law (and his wife) allowed such indulgences. Those Hindus had the right idea—burn 'em up if they don't satisfy you. Sometimes he thought about dousing Maria with a can of lighter fluid and tossing a match at her. Then she'd be carbon-dated like most of her meals.

It irked him that he couldn't control his wife in the kitchen. Tony Vernelli loved to eat, but more than anything in life, he needed to be the man in control, top dog, king of the hill. Being in complete charge of the men at work filled him with unspeakable satisfaction. If it weren't for Berma the Bitch, his hours on the job would be so sweet. Maybe Berma would be next.

He thought about that for a while, then turned his attention back to the model trains. Operating the complex lines of tracks that carried the metal engines, passenger cars, and box cars he had religiously amassed over the years gave him endless hours of pleasure.

At least his trains had some value—unlike all the Madonna figurines his wife had stationed in every nook and cranny throughout the house. One doe-eyed Virgin even watched them screw in their bedroom. Perhaps the presence of the Virgin lessened his wife's guilt about the pleasure she received from her husband's body.

Women. He smiled. He loved women. He especially loved what they were created for, and once he had them, his domination was total. The church taught him that pride was sinful; nevertheless, Tony held his prowess in the bedroom (or wherever else an opportunity was provided) as a badge of manliness. He never hurried, and he knew how to linger over the erogenous zones like a hummingbird sucking nectar from a morning glory. Once the bitches had a taste of this hummingbird's bill, they became insatiable. Let the golden boys flex their steroid-inflated biceps. They were all show. Tony Vernelli was a man of substance, and the babes knew it.

He leaned over the miniature manicured landscape, and picked up the 260 Roger's steam engine he had just bought at auction on eBay. With satisfaction, he surveyed the station house, church, stores, and houses, the little wagon pulled by a plow horse, the forests stretching over hills in the background.

Squatting down to eye level with the board, he examined the symmetry. It was only from this perspective that he could tell if everything looked just right. He reached up and placed the steam engine on a track. Then he turned a horse an eighth of an inch to face the road.

As he grasped the edge of the landscape table to stand up, he remembered the scene some nights ago in his office—a pair of shapely legs, a flat belly, and spectacular twin peaks waiting for him across his gray metal desk.

He felt himself stiffen as he stood.

He laughed. She had tasted his nectar; she was his territory now.

"Yeah," he said, fondling the steam engine, "Tony Vernelli is a stud."

But Tony had one big problem. In spite of everything, he still loved his wife.

CHAPTER 16

At the sight of the Eight of Swords, Sam felt her blood turn icy.

Against a gray background and clad in a red robe, the despondent figure stood on a marshy landscape amidst a field of swords. The figure was blindfolded—"hoodwinked"—and bound with strips of material. Almost indiscernible in the distance sat a castle atop a rocky cliff.

Henry Vandalay was blindfolded and bound with rope. And killed with a knife—which is a sword of sorts. Now she was convinced that the killer had deliberately chosen specific Tarot cards to send a message.

Sam placed the card in the north position, above the King of Pentacles, The Lovers, and the Three of Swords.

Quickly, she ran a finger down the instruction page of the Tarot book. This fifth position indicates what might happen.

Well, Sam thought, *obviously it did happen so let's look at the key words.* The Eight of Swords meant indecision, fear and betrayal.

Indecision. Was Henry indecisive concerning something that brought about his death? Henry Vandalay was a successful business-man. Making decisions was what he did best.

Then there's fear. From what Katherine said and what Sam had heard about the man from numerous newspaper articles and on the six o'clock news, fear also seemed incongruous with his nature.

Given the fact that Key VI, The Lovers, and Key XV, The Devil, were in the Keltic spread, surely the third interpretation, betrayal, was the intended message. Henry Vandalay's lust finally got the best of him.

As old as human history, there was nothing more lethal or more titillating for the public than a lover's triangle. Right here in New Hampshire—how could she forget?—a Winnacunnet High School teacher named Pamela Smart and her young lover were convicted of murdering her husband. Media from around the world mobbed the outside of the old County Court house in Exeter for months, irritating citizens and creating traffic jams.

A lover's triangle. Sam folded her hands between her knees and leaned over her desk. *Triangles are aggressive sexual symbols, and, as they say, three's a crowd.*

Given Henry Vandalay's reputation, it would seem he had cast his triangles all over the countryside, and by extension, pricked the egos of a number of men by bedding their women. Yes, right up there with the scorned lover was the possibility of an enraged husband or boyfriend.

Or was this card speaking for the killer rather than about Henry Vandalay? Did the indecision of the Eight of Swords indicate that the killer had been indecisive about murdering Vandalay for a long time?

As if to stimulate the seat of intuition, Sam rubbed the spot between her eyebrows.

Indecision and betrayal. *Hmmm…*

She would hold on to those thoughts.

*　　*　　*　　*　　*

"What do you think of this, mom?"

Caroline held a black crocheted sweater and a long dark floral skirt against her body. "It's subtle but not somber, with just a touch of mauve and mint green in the skirt to give it some life."

Sam cocked her head. "I don't know."

They stood in the women's department of Filene's at the Fox Run Mall among tubular racks of sweaters. Sam took the items from Caroline and held them under her chin in front of a full-length mirror. "I think I look like the sofa in my sun porch.

Caroline chuckled. "The skirt does have the same colors."

Sam turned sideways. "Do you think this outfit makes me look fat?"

"It's a good line for you. And you'll be comfortable. I know how important comfort is for you. You should have been born a Hobbit."

Sam tilted her head toward her shoulder, pulled in her stomach, and gave the sweater and skirt another once-over. "Well, if you think so."

"I do." Before Sam had a chance to change her mind, Caroline grabbed the hangers from her mother's hands and headed for the sales clerk.

Sam followed her to the counter and rummaged in her oversized needlepoint bag for her PETA wallet. She handed the clerk a Humane Society credit card.

"Promise me, mom," Caroline pleaded, "that you'll leave that black dress at home."

Sam nodded.

"Okay," Caroline said, "shoes are next. I saw the perfect pair at Macy's."

As Sam signed the credit card slip and took the plastic bag from the clerk, she was thinking about the Saga pen refills she needed to order from Staples. Turning, she noticed a gray-haired woman rummaging through a sale rack. Sam frowned as she ruffled through her mental filing cabinet. Where had she seen that woman before? She and Caroline were almost out the door that emptied back into the mall when it hit her.

She hesitated.

Caroline turned toward her mother. "What's the matter?"

"Um. Nothing. I just thought of something. You go on ahead and I'll meet you at Macy's."

One of Caroline's exquisitely shaped brows lifted with that knowing expression. "Mom. I know that look. What are you up to?" The tiny scar on Caroline's forehead, along her hairline, was barely visible now. It would always serve as a painful reminder to Sam of the Cowberry Necklace Murders.

"It's nothing. Trust me."

Caroline sniffed. "You know what they say about people who say 'trust me.' Okay. Just don't get into any trouble. I saw you staring at that woman in the sweater department. She has something to do with Mr. Vandalay's death, doesn't she?"

"Not really. She works in the office." *Yes, and she's the only person there who seems impervious to the growling of Tony the Tiger.*

Caroline sighed. "Okay. But don't be too long. You need shoes to go with that outfit. Your black Reeboks just won't cut it." She turned and headed into the mall.

Sam watched her oldest daughter float away, as if she were being carried on the shoulders of a gentle breeze. Caroline's dark hair was pulled back in a silver barrette. Her slender body seemed regal even in baggy tan chinos and a short-waisted white sweater.

Where did she come from? Sam wondered, as pride played with her heartstrings. Sighing, she headed back to the sweater department.

The gray-haired woman was gone. Sam looked up and down the aisles until she spied the back of the woman's head. The secretary from Vandalay Enterprises was angled toward the outer doors, her mission apparently completed, because she was carrying a plastic Filene's bag. Had the woman also bought something new to wear to the Vandalay services?

Sam threaded through milling shoppers, past the perfume counter, and through the men's department, just in time to see the secretary push through the outer doors. She wanted to ask the woman a few questions, but held back for some reason she didn't understand. She waited a few seconds, then slipped through the large glass doors leading into a glassed-in foyer with doors opening obliquely on two sides. Flattening her body against the pebbly cement wall, she watched the woman march toward the parking lot.

Sam shaded her eyes from the sun's glare glinting off the windshields. What was her name? Something odd. Melba? Berba? Berma! That was it. Berma Battles. That's what was printed in white block letters on the brown name plate on the woman's desk at Vandalay Enterprises. What an unusual name. It reminded her of the staggered Burma Shave signs along the roads she'd traveled as a child.

Sam smiled at the thought of her dad's hearty laugh, his bronzed arm out the window, his eyes checking the rearview mirror every few minutes to make sure his daughter was alright. She blinked away the wetness and focussed.

Berma was at her car, a brand new bronze Taurus. *A sturdy car for a sturdy woman.* The thought evoked an image in Sam's mind of Taurus the Bull.

Sam sidled through the door and skittled behind the trunk of one of the tall pines that lined the outside wall. The plastic bag containing her new outfit caught on a broken branch, but she didn't try to extricate it. Let it hang there. No sense in drawing attention to a woman lurking in the shrubbery. She had to ask herself why she was following the woman. What was she going to do? Leap into action like Mercury and race after the Taurus in her winged sneakers?

Berma stuck a hand into the pocket of her slacks—apparently fumbling for her car keys. Suddenly, from between a white panel truck and a dark green Plymouth Voyager, a figure jumped out behind her.

Berma spun around to confront her attacker. She tossed her bag onto the trunk of her car, planted her feet a good half yard apart, fisted her hands on her sturdy hips, and fixed her eyes upon Tony Vernelli. She never flinched. In fact, it seemed to Sam, Berma leaned into the fray with joy.

Tony got within inches of Berma's face. He thrashed his burly arms at the air. He stomped his foot. He pounded a thick fist on the trunk of the Taurus. The plastic Filene's bag bounced, then slid a few inches toward the back of the car. Words erupted from Tony's mouth which Sam couldn't distinguish—and wasn't sure she wanted to.

With the calm assurance of an animal trainer who has a wild creature under the control of a whip, Berma remained fixed, silent, and prepared.

It suddenly became clear to Sam. *The woman knows something. Something that Anthony Vernelli is very afraid of.*

Tony Vernelli sensed defeat at the hands of the gray-haired secretary. It seemed the Tiger was no match for the Bull today. With a final crude gesture, Tony Vernelli turned and stomped away.

A big smile crossed Berma's lips as she gathered her bags. She got into her shiny new car and drove away.

CHAPTER 17

Kenny Ash worried about his wife. She'd seemed out of sorts the past month; he hoped she wasn't pregnant again. Candy was on birth control pills, but sometimes she forgot to take them. He could barely afford to support the five of them now. With another mouth to feed…well, he just didn't know what he would do.

The kids were playing outside on their rusty swing set. Inside the forty-foot trailer, Candy was cleaning the kitchen. They had been invited to the Vandalay estate for the services tomorrow and for the reading of the will in the evening. Kenny didn't know why they had been invited for the reading of the will. He was afraid he'd done something very wrong; Candy had no idea what to think. She was, however, in a state of animation and indecision about what to wear.

Kenny sipped the coffee in his chipped Vandalay Enterprises mug as he looked over their tiny kitchen. The tan linoleum was curling up in the corner behind the chair leg. The frayed cord of the toaster oven needed to be fixed; he'd better get to that before someone got electrocuted. The roof had a leak that dripped into their bathtub, and the back door handle was loose from the kids yanking on it. The yard needed to be mowed, and someday he'd get rid of the old tires behind the trailer. They collected water and bred mosquitoes every spring. Sometimes, like today, he felt like his trailer. Falling apart.

Then he looked at Candy. Two smooth slivers of round buttocks showed beneath her jean cutoffs. Kenny admired her long, curvy legs—the envy of any Las Vegas show girl.

At the sound of a ruckus outside, Candy leaned over the sink and pulled the Cape Cod curtain aside. Her breasts threatened to spill out over her halter top. "Hey, you kids! Stop that fighting right now or your father will be out there to stop it for you!"

Kenny wanted to bury his face in those mounds. Forever. When Kenny Ash looked at his wife, he was filled, total, complete.

Candy picked up the glass coffee pot and waved it at him. "More coffee before I dump this out?"

"No, thanks, honey. I'm done." He slurped the remains in his cup to punctuate his statement. His eyes dropped to her waist, at the little bulge of her stomach. That had come after Robbie, their third child. For the past few weeks he had been wondering if another baby was growing in his wife's womb. And he wondered if it were his.

His insides felt like broken glass. He dragged at his Marlboro as his mind drifted back to the morning he stood over the dead body of Henry Vandalay. Who would have thought that Kenny Ash would be victorious over that scum-sucking, womanizing bastard? He laughed to himself. And all it took was a knife.

Kenny drew in the last lungful of nicotine, then stubbed out the butt in the glass dime-store ashtray. That had been his fourth cigarette this morning, and it wasn't even nine o'clock yet. Sobered by what he saw, he scowled at the evidence of his addiction. Coffee and cigarettes. The breakfast of champions. He knew he had to give them up. They were killing him.

Picking up his mug, he dumped the dregs into the sink, rinsed the cup, kissed his wife on the cheek, and disappeared into their bedroom with cup in hand.

In their back yard moments later, inside the eight-foot square work shed built from scrap lumber, Kenny vented his rage. He smashed the

Vandalay mug on the floor and stomped the porcelain shards until his legs got weak. Then he grabbed a knife from the workbench and viciously ripped his three apple-red Vandalay tee shirts into shreds.

Spent, his breath coming in short painful gasps, he slumped against the wall. He stared at the slivers of white porcelain and the tattered red shirts on the floor, and finally, at the knife in his clenched fist.

Tears rolled down his hollow cheeks as he slid down the splintered boards and collapsed on the wooden floor.

He was convinced his wife was pregnant.

"It's *my* baby," he whispered. "It's *my* baby."

But somewhere deep inside, he wondered if it was.

CHAPTER 18

The trip to the mall with Caroline proved successful, and the beautiful weekend weather materialized as promised—cloudless, in the mid-seventies. Sam was thankful. Maybe she'd get through the service without dripping like a tropical rain forest in monsoon season. And maybe this positive start was a harbinger of even better things to come, like clues to the Tarot riddle.

She glanced at the Ridgeway grandfather clock. Charlie would be along in about ten minutes to pick them up. She had programmed the VCR to tape the nightly news and Seinfeld, all the windows were shut and locked, and she had left the Vandalay telephone number with her mother.

The stuffed black bag at Samantha's feet held her new skirt and sweater, underwear, a plaid nightshirt, her toothbrush, and shampoo. Everything else in the bag was Nick's. He had packed something for every occasion, from confronting an enraged grizzly to paddling the St. John River.

Sam rummaged in her needle point handbag plopped on the dining room table for one last check: lipstick and a comb, one green foam hair roller, her wallet, and a small silver jackknife (a gift from Nick last Christmas—for protection. Besides, you never knew when she might need that to ward off the grizzly). She also had her deck of Tarot cards with the list tucked inside, a copy of Eden Gray's *The Tarot*, and Dan Brown's novel, *Angels and Demons*. Somehow a package of Ring Dings had found its way into the bag as well. What else could a girl want?

Nick hurried into the dining room. "I think I've got everything." He eyed the overnight bag, the furrow between his brows revealing his uncertainty. Sam could almost hears the cogs clicking in his brain, checking off items.

"What about the kitchen sink?" Sam said.

"Don't get smart," he countered. Nick squatted down, unzipped the bag for the tenth time, stuck a hand in and lifted layers of clothing. The wheels were turning. "Hey," he looked up at Sam, "I don't see your black dress. Aren't you taking it?"

"Not if you want Caroline to ever speak to me again."

"But you've only got one skirt and a sweater." He looked distressed.

"It's an overnighter, Nick. How many outfits do you think I need?"

He shook his head. "Well, what about shoes?"

"I have these low black heels Caroline picked out." She nodded at her feet. "They'll go with my new outfit."

Nick zipped the bag shut, stood up and looked his wife over. Sam was wearing a long-sleeved soft green Eddie Bauer dress and small gold hoop earrings, and she had her hair pulled back in a flowered green scrunchie.

"You're not going to be hot, are you? Fanning magazines in your face every thirty minutes?" Sam evil-eyed him but it didn't work. Concern crossed his face. "When are you going to see the doctor about your hot flashes?"

"I am NOT having hot flashes!"

"Okay, okay. You're not having hot flashes."

Sam's mouth set in a straight line, then she proclaimed, "Really!"

"Alright."

"And I've packed everything I need."

"I believe you."

She knew he didn't.

*　　　　*　　　　*　　　　*　　　　*

Sam wished she had brought a cotton blouse to go with her new skirt in case it got hot, but she wasn't going to mention that to Nick. And where was a magazine when you needed one?

They were motoring along Route 1A in Charlie Burrows' old, but pampered, mist green Oldsmobile 98. Because of his worsening cold, Charlie had the windows battened down tighter than the Andrea Gale's hatches in *The Perfect Storm*. The car's interior temperature had to be approaching ninety degrees, closing in on *The Perfect Temperature* for the cloven-footed one and his hellish minions.

Outside, the Atlantic Ocean sparkled millions of tiny points of light. Sam yearned to taste the cool breezes that skipped over the ruffled waves. If only this heat didn't kill her first!

"Heat kills infections," Charlie said over his shoulder to Sam. Her arms and legs were spread wide in the back seat as if she were staked out on the Devil's ant hill. "Brun read about a test with viral-infected mice."

Through sweat-clouded eyes, Sam examined the necks of the two men she loved most in the world. Not one drop of perspiration! Not the slightest sheen of dampness. Did they have ice water in their veins? She dropped her head back on the seat and attempted to cool her plumbing, to visualize ice water running through her veins. It didn't work. Through the searing heat, she could hear Charlie's voice droning on.

"Six mice were given aspirin and kept in the shade. Six had no aspirin and were left in the sun where their body temperatures rose. And the six in the sun got better 'cuz their higher temps killed the infection. The six cold mice died."

Sam felt sorry for the cold dead mice, but didn't want the higher temps in Charlie's car to send *her* to rodent heaven. As her gaze once again shifted out the side window, she wished herself onto the grainy gray sand where the frigid waters of the Atlantic could wash over her burning body.

A lump of lifeless fur by the road's edge interrupted her fantasy. She sighed, let her lids fall shut and silently recited her mantra for road kill: *Your soul has risen in joy and peace.* Even though she had been known to bless rag heaps and crumpled paper bags, unidentified roadside lumps were always sent to creature heaven with a prayer, just in case. Someone had to care.

Finally, Charlie swung onto the pebbled drive that cut through an opening in the three-foot stone wall fronting the Vandalay estate. As the car rumbled down the drive, pebbles crunching and spurting from beneath its tires, Sam mentally recited, *One for the money, two for the show, three to get ready and...* The Olds slowed to a stop. *Four to go!* her mind screamed. She leapt out of the back seat as if tossed by a searing tsunami.

A salty breeze teased a damp strand of hair by her ear. She stretched her arms out and gulped the cool air into her lungs. She would have fallen to the ground in prayerful jubilation, but the cooler air was at a higher elevation.

Nick climbed out of the car, a knowing look dawning on his face. "What's the matter, babe?"

A quick reply. "Nothing." Too quick, her voice an octave higher.

Nick turned to Charlie and said over the roof of the car, "That's doublespeak for 'there is something wrong but I'm not going to tell you.'"

Charlie broke into his high-pitched giggle. "Yeah. With five women in the house, I've had to learn the language."

In unison, they all turned toward the Vandalay mansion. A two-story winged beast, it stood on manicured grounds amidst a profusion of beach roses hugging the wide verandah. Mountains of rhododendrons stood sentinel at the corners and disappeared along the white clapboard sides. Two giant cement urns bursting with white chrysanthemums flanked the broad porch steps.

To the right of the drive on the massive green lawn, a huge white tent had been erected for Sunday's services. It seemed stark and lonely somehow, Sam thought, sitting out there, waiting for music, food, and the mingling of voices. Then the ceremony would be over, and the tent would come down. Henry Vandalay would be just a memory.

Sam bit at her bottom lip. It was likely that one of the guests at tomorrow's festivities would be a murderer. She felt a sense of déjà vu. It had only been last year, at the services for Doug Hammand, that she had rubbed elbows with a killer. That time, she wasn't aware of it. This time, she would be more alert.

She pulled a tissue from her dress pocket and dabbed at her forehead. Which wing was Ula's? she wondered. The large one-over-one glass windows, typical of the mammoth beach homes along Route 1A, gave no clue. Their curtains were so similar as to be identical.

A three-car garage, obviously added later, was attached to the left wing. Its doors were closed. Eight-foot high arbor vitae hedges, extending from both sides of the house across the lawn and then toward the rear of the property, ensured the privacy of the back yard. Sam surmised that's where the swimming pool and cottage must be.

As the trio crunched their way over the pebbled walk toward the house, Sam noticed the gold numbers above the double Christian doors. She blinked twice.

8778. *Secrets and power struggles lay in this house.*

Sam recalled an article about Hong Kong license plate auctions where bidders were known to spend tens of thousands of dollars for possession of the number eight.

Absolute power corrupts absolutely, she thought. *And the number eight has the power to do just that.* Sam always told her eight-empowered clients that the avaricious eight succumbs to the seductive trio of power, sex, and money, whereas the altruistic eight uses these material gifts to advance not only itself, but society as well. With eights ruling this house, Sam wondered if Katherine Vandalay would be as generous as her husband was purported to have been.

8778. Secret sevens closed in by two power eights. Things could get very interesting.

Perhaps when she got behind closed doors, as Kenny Rogers sings, Katherine Vandalay would let her "hair hang down" and with the loosened tresses, reveal a slew of secrets. And the sister-in-law, Ula. What could she tell? Sam was encouraged, knowing that people were more relaxed in their own environment.

Once again, Sam examined the palatial home, marveling at the size of the building. Her entire house would probably fit in the foyer. Given that the New York City building code required eighty square feet of living space per person, and well-behaved inmates at Attica State Prison were afforded ninety square feet, Sam felt fortunate to have 2500 square feet of her own on the town green in Georgetown. She wondered how much territory the Vandalay mansion covered, and how many New Yorkers would fit inside. It was easy to believe that Katherine and Ula seldom saw each other.

The sparkling white double doors of the mansion were flung open, causing Sam to reel her thoughts back in. Like an angel descending from above, Katherine Vandalay emerged in a diaphanous white dress. The breezes played with the yards of material, lifting the hem to reveal long tanned legs. Katherine floated to the edge of the wide verandah to greet them.

"Welcome to my home. Come in." She half turned and motioned toward the doorway. "Your rooms are ready. Ula will show you the way."

"Thank you," Sam replied. "Your home is beautiful." Followed by Nick and Charlie, she stepped past Katherine and into the cool foyer.

In sharp contrast to the bouquets of white flowers on side tables, thick oriental rug on the shining parquet floor, and glistening chandelier high above their heads, Ula Vandalay stood like a miniature Charon the Ferryman, waiting to guide them across the River Styx.

No smile greeted them.

About five feet tall, Ula was dressed in a black wool skirt, boxy black cardigan sweater, black stockings, and low-heeled black shoes. She could have been a child pretending to mourn for the loss of her doll. Ula's dark brown hair was pulled back in a tidy bun that framed the sallow planes of her face. The only signs of Ula Vandalay's tension were the white knuckles of her fisted hands held stiffly by her sides, and the barely-concealed fire in her large brown eyes. These were telltale signs that could easily be overlooked because Ula Vandalay was easy to overlook.

"This is my sister-in-law, Ula," Katherine said in her throaty voice, the fingers of her right hand rubbing against her thigh. Sam wondered where the Newports were. "She's prepared your rooms." Katherine never glanced at the somber woman. It was as if she weren't there.

Sam reached out her hand as the pungent smell of lilacs drifted over her. "Hello, Ula. It's nice to meet you."

Ula took the hand reluctantly. Either Sam's hand was burning hot or Ula's was deadly cold.

Katherine said, "I will retire for a few hours." Her voice was tight, implying that she didn't hobnob with the servants. "I didn't get much sleep last night, and I have some last minute details to attend to. So please make yourselves at home. There's a television and magazines in the living room." She motioned toward a large square room to her left. "And books in the library. Ula will get anything you need. Refreshments, drinks. Dinner is at eight. I planned a vegetarian dish for you, Samantha. Now, if you will please excuse me."

With that, she started toward the staircase. She stopped abruptly, turned, and said, "Oh, Ula. There's a list of names on my desk in the library. Would you give it to Ms. Blackwell?"

Katherine swept up the wide staircase like Scarlett O'Hara, turned right at the landing, and disappeared down a hallway.

She never said please or thank you to Ula, Sam observed. How much humiliation could one person take before she let loose with an axe and gave someone forty whacks? As a shiver wiggled down her body, she told herself to put a lid on it.

The trio waited silently in the foyer while Ula fetched the list. Sam's mouth twisted as she pondered the answer to how Katherine knew she was a vegetarian. Had the woman been checking up on her?

Ula returned, handed the list to Sam without a word, and proceeded up the staircase. Charlie and Nick, with bags in hand, hurried after her.

Sam lingered behind, taking in the smells, colors, architecture, furnishings. A cut glass vase—Baccarat?—of white iris and baby's breath caught her eye. She sidled over and dropped her face into the bouquet. Inhaling the cool scent, she thought about Iris, Goddess of the Rainbow and messenger between heaven and earth. She had to chuckle at the mythological appellations—Ula as Charon and Katherine as Iris, black and white, night and day. The two Vandalay women were opposing forces in the Vandalay universe. Sam had to wonder if a super nova was imminent.

It was when she lifted her head from the flowers that she saw the name.

Sam frowned. Between her two hands, she stretched the pale blue stationery that Ula had given her and scanned down the tight vertical script to the last notation. Printed in a different hand and pen than the others, the block letters at the bottom of the suspect list read: 'KATY.'

Chapter 19

❀

Berma Battles worried about her son.

She had never approved of him hooking up with that woman. But young men were nothing but walking hormones, and Candy had slim hips and the kind of breasts that could smother a man. Although Berma would never forgive Candy for trapping her son into marriage, she had played the noninterfering mother-in-law these past eight years, waiting for her daughter-in-law to get tired of living hand-to-mouth.

Berma had control over the digits in Kenny's pay check (something he didn't know and never would). She saw to it that he earned just enough money to survive. Maybe, if things got tough enough, Candy would leave him. That's what Berma hoped for. When that happened, Kenny would be compensated for the eight years of meager pay checks, and Berma's three grandchildren would get plenty of gifts from their father as well as their grandmother. Although she worried about what would happen to the kids if Kenny and Candy got divorced, Kenny's welfare came first. It always did. In any case, the grandkids would be well taken care of. Candy *was* a good mother, Berma had to give her that.

But "tough love" was Berma Battles motto. Her son had to learn his lessons the hard way. Just like she had.

If nothing else, Berma was the epitome of discretion. She had kept her mouth shut all these years, and as a result, had pretty much feathered her nest: a neat Cape Cod home, a double garage housing a new Saturn and a dark green Mitsubishi Spyder, money in the bank, and a job that kept her busy, where she could keep tabs on certain people. Life should have been oh-so-sweet, but there were still a few remaining twigs stuck in her craw.

Now that Hank Vandalay was dead, the last twig was about to be dislodged. She was planning to do something special at the services tomorrow. As for Hank, the man couldn't keep his zipper shut. He'd deserved what he got.

She did get a nervous twinge every time she thought about the invitation to be present during the reading of the will. Even with Hank dead, she didn't trust him. He was up to something.

Berma felt that same twinge a few hours later as she turned off the 6:30 evening news and watched as newscaster Aaron Brown faded into blackness. Then she pulled an old scrap book from the living room bookcase and settled into the soft, dun-colored sofa by the front windows. She had been meaning to buy a new album; the photos kept slipping out from under the plastic pages. She supposed the sticky backing was gone, dried up by age like her.

It was Saturday evening. The sun retired around six o'clock these mid-October days, and Berma's tree-lined street was quiet. The neighborhood kids had been called in for supper, and by now were most likely protesting their homework, baths, and bedtimes.

Berma reveled in the peaceful autumn evening and in her freedom. She thought briefly about her childhood: her mother in that stupid blue-and-black striped apron tied up around her neck, following her around, shaking a wooden spoon, and railing endlessly about Berma's laziness. The tirades always began with "Idle hands are the devil's workshop." An image of the devil should have been engraved on her tombstone. As for her father, he was useless. His epitaph should have been, "Your mother's right." When Berma left home, she vowed nobody would ever tell her what to do again. Her hands would do exactly what she wanted them to do.

Berma had spent most of Saturday going through seed catalogues, planning her patch of vegetable garden for next spring. She was also going to plant roses along the front of the house—Rosa rugosa maybe, or the apple-scented Rosa rubiginosa—she couldn't decide which. They were both hardy and could withstand the harsh New England winters.

The day had been quiet except for the two hours she'd spent at the Fox Run Mall. She had gone there to search for a new outfit for Hank's services tomorrow and had run across Tony Vernelli in the parking lot.

She laughed out loud.

The man was so obvious, strutting around like some kind of oil sheik, ogling women from under that black slash of eyebrow as if appraising the ones he would select for his harem. Who the hell would want him anyway? And why didn't he pluck that ridiculous eyebrow? Berma couldn't imagine having to look at that long black strip in the mirror every morning. It would drive her crazy. But men didn't seem to have the same concerns as women. They had only one thing on their minds.

Suddenly, her faced closed down. It always did when she got on this line of thought. Her past stupidity and naiveté had cost her dearly, but it would never happen again.

Berma leaned back into the sofa, switched on the table lamp beside her, and stared at the *Fleurs du Jardin* framed print on the wall above the fifty-one-inch Mitsubishi television. Rexford's poppies in a glass vase had the power to pull her in—almost, she thought, like that old Twilight Zone episode, where a criminal, in a desperate attempt to escape the authorities, fled to a museum and melded into the fishing boat scene he had always admired. In the darkness, he never realized the painting had been replaced by one of an agonized Jesus on the cross. That's where he was found in the morning, in eternal pain. But in Berma's case, the poppies drew her back to memories of her summer gardens where the sun had warmed her back and butterflies danced through her flowers.

Slowly, as her mood softened, she rubbed the cracked surface of the red scrapbook on her lap. Irregular shapes of colored light from the stained-glass lamp played across her hands and over the rivulet-like veins connecting her fingers to her wrists. Those veins had become more substantial over the past few years, as had her weight. Longingly, she remembered when she was an athletic 119 pounds. Her hair was sandy then, long and loose. She had loved life and…how long ago was that?

She patted the back of her neck. She kept her hair tightly curled and out of her face now. She had no one to impress anymore. At forty-seven, the sandy locks had turned prematurely gray. A number of times she had hesitated before the L'Oréal boxes at Walgreen's drugstore, but each time, she was visited by a vision of Candy's spiked blonde hair. That was always enough to make Berma ditch the whole idea.

Berma flipped a few of the plastic pages until she came to a photograph of Ollie Battles. His head was so round, she used to call him Mr. Pumpkin Head. He was one of the few good men.

As her hand caressed the slippery page, she recalled the first time he stuck his grinning face in her car window and asked, "Fill 'er up?"

At first, she didn't know what to make of him. He was so sunny and happy and outgoing. Berma's life had been a struggle for so long, happiness was a stranger to her. But a year later they married, moved to Georgetown where no one knew her, and started a new life together.

Kenny was a toddler then. Ollie never asked about Berma's past or displayed any signs of resentment over Kenny. He loved them both without reservation. She'd been lucky to have him for those thirteen years, until he ate himself into his grave. That was nine years ago. Although she had tried to keep his diet clean and had encouraged him to exercise, he ballooned to 350 pounds. When Ollie was at work and on the road, his taste for greasy burgers and fries, donuts and Schlitz always got the best of him. She held his photo against her breast and blinked the wetness from her eyes.

The phone rang, jolting her out of her reverie.

Berma gritted her teeth. She knew who it was.

Setting the scrapbook on the cushion beside her, she struggled up off the sofa and crossed to the wall phone in the kitchen.

"Hi, Berma. What are you doing?"

"I was watching the news," Berma answered. Candy would never know how Berma felt about her. There would be no reason to drive a wedge between Berma and her son.

"Oh." Pause. "What are you wearing tomorrow to the Vandalays'?"

"I haven't thought much about it." Which was a lie. On Friday, Berma had spent hours thinking about it, and on Saturday, she had pawed through sale flyers and then spent two hours rummaging through the racks at Filene's.

"I just don't know what to do," Candy whined. "You think it's dressy? I mean, it *is* in the afternoon. I wouldn't think it would be too dressy. Should I wear a dress, like short or long? What do you think?"

Berma rubbed the side of her face, rolled her eyes and answered pleasantly, "I think you should wear what you want to. Whatever you feel comfortable in."

"But I want to fit in."

Berma wanted to tell her if she wanted to fit in, she should cover her boobs, keep her hem down, and get rid of the blonde spikes and the gum. But instead she said, "I'm sure you'll make the right choice."

In the background, Berma could hear the youngest grandchild pleading, "I want to talk to Gramma."

"Just a minute, Berma. Lucy wants to say hi."

"Hi, Gramma."

"Hi, darling. Are you having a good day? Have you colored that picture for me like you promised?"

"Oops." Lucy dropped the phone and ran off, apparently to fulfill her promise.

Muffled sounds accompanied the transfer. "Sorry about that, Berma," Candy said. "Now, what I was wondering about tomorrow…"

"Oh…," Berma interrupted, "there's the door bell. I've got to go."

"You sure have a lot of company," Candy said, disappointment infusing her voice.

"I know. It never seems to stop. I'll see you tomorrow, Candy. I'm sure you'll look just fine."

The doorbell wasn't ringing and Berma never had company, but Candy hadn't caught on in eight years.

Berma crossed back to the sofa, picked up the scrapbook, and returned it to the bookcase. Outside her window, she noticed one of the neighborhood teenagers doing wheelies on his red bike in the street. Berma winced as he skittered through a pile of leaves and almost lost his balance. The kid looked around, obviously embarrassed, then took off down the street like the hounds of hell were after him.

Berma walked back to the sofa, knelt down, and reached underneath. She extracted the gold-striped box Ollie had given her on their first wedding anniversary, with a black negligee inside. She looked good in it then, and how Ollie had smiled when she wore it for him that night.

After pushing herself upright with one hand, grunting as she stood, she once again settled into the sofa. She squared the box on her lap and brushed her fingertips over its cover.

"Open Sesame," she whispered.

She lifted the gold lid and placed it on the sofa cushion next to her. The box had brought her so much happiness when Ollie had given it to her; it would bring her happiness again. Inside the box lay the secrets that would set the seacoast buzzing and atone for past wrongs done to her.

She knew she would use these photos and documents and cigarette butts to her advantage.

Her hands trembled.
She just knew she would.

CHAPTER 20

A sniffling Charlie was deposited in the bedroom across the wide hallway from Nick and Samantha's, next to Ula Vandalay's suite. Sam was bursting at the seams to tell Charlie about the list in her hand, but he looked so miserable, and after he announced he was going to take a nap, she didn't have the heart to say anything.

"Nick!" she whispered, as soon as their door was shut and Ula's efficient footsteps clicked off into the distance.

Nick was placing their overnight bag on an old wooden chest at the foot of the sleigh bed when he turned to see his wife pressed against the bedroom door. She was saucer-eyed, waving a piece of light blue stationery at him.

"Jesus, Sam!" he said. "You scared me." He shook his head and raked fingers through his thick curly hair. One piece fell deliciously over an eyebrow, but Sam dismissed the thought it inspired. "We just got here. Can't you relax for one minute? Why are you so intense?"

One of Sam's eyebrows lifted. "Do you remember the time we went for massages and the therapist said to you, 'Your wife is intense'?"

His eyes softened. "Yup."

"What did you say?"

He crossed the room and took her in his arms. "I said, 'That's why I love her.'"

She pecked his cheek. "Right. So, look at this." She waved the paper in his face.

His head went back as he looked down his nose. Loosening his grip on Sam's waist, he took a step back as she handed him the stationery. He held it at arm's length and squinted. "What? It's the list you asked Katherine Vandalay to make for you."

"Yeah, but look at the final name."

His squint deepened. "Katy. No last name. That's odd."

"Not only that, but notice the handwriting is different."

"It's printed."

"More than that, Nick. Look how deeply indented the paper is under the letters K-A-T-Y. You think *I'm* intense."

"Hmmm. And the ink is a different color, too." He handed the paper back to Sam.

"Right, my darling. Someone other than Katherine wrote that name. And Katy is a nickname for Katherine. Whoever wrote KATY wants us to pay attention to the lady of the house."

Tony Vernelli printed on the whiteboard in his office at Vandalay Enterprises, but how would Tony know about this list, and how would he get into Katherine's home undetected?

Sam felt a flush coming on, and without thinking, fanned herself with the list in front of Nick.

"Why don't you lie down for a while?" Nick asked, leading her to the double bed. "You look beat."

She dropped onto the mattress, kicked off her shoes and lay spread-eagled on the white tufted bedspread. "I'm not having a hot flash!"

Nick sat on the bed beside her. "Why won't you admit you're having hot flashes? Then you can do something about them."

Sam folded her arms across her chest, crumpling the blue stationery under an armpit, and stared silently at the high ceiling. The room had the sweet smell of lilacs. An image of Ula, purple spray can in hand and purpose in mind, materialized in Sam's thoughts.

Nick persisted. "Are you afraid of getting older?"

She looked toward the foot of the bed as images flickered like a silent movie before her eyes: the girls in the sandbox in the back yard, their roles in the school plays as sunflowers and shepherds, their first proms, their graduations—it had poured during Sadie's outdoor program and everyone ran for the cafeteria.

Blinking her damp eyes, she said, "It's not so much that. I guess I just don't want the girls to grow up too fast. Then they won't need me."

Nick scooped her up in his arms and kissed her forehead. "Of course they'll need you. They'll always need you. Just like I'll always need you." He kissed her lips.

Sam clung to him, finding strength and warmth and comfort in his embrace. Then she disentangled herself and said, "Fifteen minutes is all I allow myself for self pity. Now, back to this list."

Nick sighed, stood up, and raked both hands through his hair. "Okay, woman. Talk."

Plumping the bed pillows behind her, Sam scooched up against them. She attempted to smooth the wrinkles out of the delicate stationery on her lap. "Obviously Katherine wouldn't put her own name on the list."

"You wouldn't think so," Nick replied from the foot of the bed.

"The only other person in the house is Ula. She could have written Katherine's name on the list, but why write Katy? I can't imagine the stoic Ula calling her sister-in-law 'Katy.' Besides, that name doesn't seem to fit Katherine." Her thumbs moved up and down the edges of the paper. "Nick. Would you get a pen from my bag, please?"

Nick tugged her smiley-faced sack from the overnight bag—along with his *Outdoor* magazine. He handed the pocketbook to his wife and settled into a stuffed chair by the window. Sam fished around for her Saga pen, found it, then pulled out a small notepad and began talking as she wrote out Katherine's name.

"I did Katherine's name earlier," she said. "Her vowels add up to a two."

As Sam had written in her books and columns and told countless clients, the vowels in your name, or your Soul Number, represent the inner you, hidden from others, and sometimes even from yourself. It's what unconsciously motivates you. At the age of twenty-seven (when you gain your soul, according to Plato) or twenty-nine (when you officially become an adult, according to astrology), you have more of a handle on your inner motivations. Katherine and Ula were both past that coming-of-age point.

"Why are you working with just her first name?" Nick wanted to know.

"Because your first name is your biggest imprint," Sam answered. "Over a lifetime, think how many times you're called Nick or Nicholas rather than Nicholas Wentworth Bennett. The vowels in your first name sort of jump start your instinctual reactions, which are then carried out through the sum of the vowels in your full name."

Nick's head began to droop. "Mmm."

With her head bent over the note pad, Sam said to no one in particular, "With a two in Katherine, she is the power behind the throne, a lot smarter than she lets on. Toss the dumb blonde routine."

Sam tapped the pen against her lips. Once again, she chastised herself for not seeing through the rambling discourse last Tuesday morning when Katherine sat opposite her on the sun porch.

Then, tracing the two with her pen and making it into a block number, she went on. "Two is the number of magic, where much is happening beneath the surface, although it remains invisible. It always reminds me of the pregnant woman wearing a jersey with an arrow pointing down to the words: Under Construction."

Catching his nodding head and knowing that his services wouldn't be required for some time, Nick opened his magazine. He settled deeper into the chair by the large windows overlooking the back yard, and propped his feet on the matching hassock. He would mumble an occasional "Uh huh," and that would be sufficient.

"If we add the A's in 'Vandalay' to the equation," Sam muttered, "the vowels from her full name add up to a five. She instinctively knows how to say the right thing, how to communicate with any level of society. There's an abundance of nervous energy coiled inside her. And she has an innate curiosity…she stores information like bees store honey in a hive for later use. Hmm…curiosity…"

Sam's eyes skirted the perimeter of the ceiling.

"Uh huh," was Nick's contribution.

"…and she's curious about me, I think. To get me to take this case, first she waves Charlie's name in my face, knowing how much Charlie means to me. Then, when I'm teetering, she offers me a substantial check. A winning combination, I have to admit."

Islands, here we come.

"And then she knows I'm a vegetarian. She's planned a veggie dish for me for dinner." Her eyeballs screeched to a halt, both eyebrows dipped. "I hope I'm not being manipulated." She looked to Nick for denial of that thought but none was forthcoming. She did get another "Uh huh."

Holding the frown, Sam rotated the pen in her fingers for a moment, then returned to her notes. "Anyway. The name 'Katy' is a one. Katy, whoever she is, is a loner. She's either very centered or out for herself. She has to make choices about the direction in her life and channel her energies so they won't go wild."

Sam gazed at the ceiling once more as if Katy's identity lay scrawled on its blank white surface. She did some of her best thinking on that convenient *tabula rasa*. "The one is extremely independent and isn't afraid to go it alone."

Focusing on the notepad once again, Sam said, "Then there's Ula." Even though Sam had already added the numbers in her head, she scribbled them on the pad. Motor responses also helped her think.

"Ula. Her first name adds up to four." She began drawing squares. "Ula has a strong need for security. She'll work hard for what she wants. Practicality and possessions are important to her. So is stability. She doesn't like change.

"Ula Vandalay. Add the three A's in Vandalay to Ula and her Soul Number is a seven. No flies on this lady. In ancient times, if sevens were prominent in the birth pattern, the girl would have been put in a temple to become a priestess. That sheds a whole new light on the taciturn Ula Vandalay."

Nick had read the same sentence six times. He burrowed deeper into the chair and said, "Uh huh."

"So," Sam went on, oblivious to the grunt from across the room, "we have Katherine's two and five, implying a sensuous, curious, more excitable woman with secret stirrings, and Ula Vandalay's four and seven, suggesting a steady, patient, enduring sort with a need to hang on to the status quo. A woman who bides her time, but has a well-thought-out plan. Wait a minute. I just thought of something."

Sam rooted around in her handbag and pulled out a small black-edged invitation.

"Katherine gave this to me last Tuesday. She sent these invitations for Henry's services to a number of people. Yes, I thought so. Her full name is Katherine Anna Vandalay. That means her vowels add up to a seven! Like Ula. How do you like that! They're like opposite sides of the same coin, connected by the hidden motivations of the seven. Yet on the surface, they're very different. Yin and yang, black and white."

Defeated, Nick threw aside his magazine. "How can Katherine be a two and a five and a seven?"

"Different things to different people, Nick. Because we exhibit behavior according to our circumstances, we are called by variations of our name. First names and nicknames are personal—loved ones, relatives, friends use our given names. Your mother called you Nicky until her dying day. Your colleagues at Hampton Rotary wouldn't call you that."

Nick smiled at that thought.

"Our first and last name, and sometimes a middle initial, is our public persona, used in more social settings, or in the newspaper or on our mail. It tells a little more about us, but not the entire story.

"But the full name—first, middle, and last—gives the whole story, warts and all. That's on our birth certificates and other legal documents. Now, in most cases, the general public never knows that full name, so ordinary people like us have sides to us that are not known outside the family. In the case of famous people however, a number of things can happen depending on how they commonly use their names. For instance, if celebrities use their full names, they either have nothing to hide or they feel so powerful, they fear no one."

"Henry David Thoreau and William Randolph Hearst," Nick said.

"Exactly!" Sam clapped her hands. "You are so smart. They're great examples of the two facets I just mentioned. Now contrast those names with H. G. Wells. Would the person on the street know the writer as Herman George Wells? I doubt it. The man had a private side that said 'you can read my books but don't get too close to me.' Hearst, on the other hand, didn't fear anyone. And the existentialists also let it all hang out, albeit for different reasons. Henry David Thoreau and Ralph Waldo Emerson." She chuckled. "Imagine calling them Hank and Ralphy? It's like calling Wolfgang Amadeus Mozart, Wolfy—which his wife did, but she knew him intimately."

"What about Kenny Ash?" Nick said. "His name is on the list and so is that foreman you told me about."

Sam scribbled again. "Kenneth is a ten. Ha! The Wheel of Fortune. That's the last card in the Keltic spread found beside Henry's body. Given Kenny's circumstances..." *and his wife. Candy looked the type to require more upkeep than Kenny could afford.* "...money could be a big motivator for him. I wonder..." She plucked at a white tuft on the bedspread.

"Sometimes we do things unconsciously that give us away. He certainly doesn't seem the type to be interested in the Tarot, but you can't judge a book…"

"You said he described one of the cards quite well," Nick added as support.

"Right. The Eight of Swords. He could be a closet Tarot reader. I've given up trying to anticipate the variety of ways that people satisfy their needs. Let's see. With the addition of his last name, his vowels total eleven."

She looked across the room at Nick. The shadows were deepening. They'd have to freshen up for dinner soon.

"From what I saw of Kenny at Vandalay Enterprises yesterday," Sam said, "he seems unstable. Chain smoking, fidgeting. The eleven is powerful because of the double ones, but it can act precipitously in some cases. And because eleven adds to two, relationships are usually the root cause. I wonder what the problem was between Kenny and Henry Vandalay." Again, Candy Ash came to Sam's mind.

"And the foreman?" Nick asked.

"Anthony Vernelli." More scribbling. "Seven in the first name and eight in the full name. Another thinker with a intense passion for power. There pulses a clever brain beneath that bald pate. Or course, we're talking about a negative use of the number energies here."

"I know," Nick said, a grin spreading across his face accentuating the dimple on his right cheek. "'The numbers just are. It's your choice what you do with them.' You don't have to protect the numbers from me. But you just can't help it, can you? You protect kids and animals, old people, flies and spiders. Even the numbers. As if they can't stand on their own merit and be counted." The last was said in his best Jerry Seinfeld imitation. Nick's grin widened at his own cleverness.

"'I yam what I yam,' as Popeye used to say," Sam said, jiggling her left foot. She recognized one more name on Katherine's list: Berma Battles. Why would Katherine put the secretary's name on the suspect list? Well, why not? Berma saw Henry Vandalay every day, knew his business, perhaps did his books. Maybe Berma had stuck her nose too deeply into Vandalay's affairs—business and otherwise.

There were seven other names, all male. Business associates or perhaps disgruntled clients. Sam would check the connections before the services tomorrow and have Katherine point out the suspects.

Hunched over the notepad, Sam rubbed her mouth with an open hand. The full birth name was the ideal starting point, and the letter 'Y' added more dimensions to the Soul Number patterns. Still, these shortened versions had stories to tell. She began twiddling her pen while her mind drifted up to her *tabula rasa*.

"What are you thinking?" Nick asked, while he re-crossed his ankles. The *Outdoor* magazine rustled in his lap.

"I was thinking about the cover story in last summer's *Time* magazine about the two scientists—Collins and Venter, I think—who mapped the human genome code. The article said that if you take any two individuals on the planet today, their DNA would be 99.9% identical. Isn't that amazing? How much alike we all are?" She thought of Tony Vernelli and blessed that errant one-tenth of one percent. "Plus, the six billion people on this planet can be traced back thousands of generations to a small founding group of sixty thousand people. It does prove that we're all interconnected, just one big happy family. That fact alone should make racial intolerance obsolete. Sometimes I wonder how a cosmic presence could create such an interlocking universe."

"I wonder about things like that all the time," Nick said.

"Yeah. Right," Sam said.

Nick grinned, lowered his head, and looked up at her with a lustful gleam in his eye. "How about interlocking with me?"

With that, he leapt onto the bed. "Okay, you ravishing beauty. That's enough." He tossed her bag and notepad aside. "You're all mine now."

Sam squealed. "Nick! Stop it!"

But she didn't mean it.

CHAPTER 21

Inviting warm and tangy smells filled the spacious, well-appointed dining room. An ornate mantle clock daintily chimed eight times as Ula set a large Wedgewood bowl of steaming pasta primavera before Sam on the polished dining room table. She had already laid out a garden salad and platters of hot breads and breasts of chicken in raspberry vinaigrette sauce, plus delicate white Wedgewood dishes filled with a variety of dressings and small silver spoons. Embossed butter squares floated among slivers of ice in silver bowls with matching silver forks on the plates beneath. Sam looked down at her place setting and admired the subtle raised grape pattern on the solid white plate.

As she straightened her silverware, she took it all in. Through the large plate glass window and beyond the stone wall at the end of the pebbled drive, the ocean lay calm, waiting and blinking under the ambient moon. Moonbeams had crept on "little cat feet," into the dining room, scaring shadows into the corners.

Sam shivered. Early October, the Hunter's Moon. How appropriate. This weekend, she was the hunter and the guests were her prey. Quite a bloodthirsty thought for a vegetarian.

La Luna. Charlie had told tales of the destructive effects that shimmering celestial ball had wrought: more fights than usual, excessive bleeding, a rise in the number of accidents, and a generally crazed population.

Under one such moon, a cop at Hampton Beach actually pulled in a man who was crouched on the sands baying at the silvered Lady.

It was those positive ions, Sam had told Charlie. They're more numerous during full moons, collecting on the skin and unsettling the psyche. People who are emotionally unstable tend to go off the deep end; more stable individuals have restless nights.

This evening, invisible positive ions filled the Vandalay dining room, and Sam knew anything could happen before the weekend was over. The three guests and their two hosts sat in the eye of a moonlit storm.

Katherine raised her wine glass, her emerald-cut diamond ring sending bolts of white light through a sea of ions. "I'd like to make a toast." Four glasses raised in unison. "To my husband, Henry Vandalay. A generous and loving man. May he rest in peace."

Henry Vandalay was an eight, Sam calculated quickly, the power number.

Five pairs of lips sipped the wine. Actually, it was only four pairs, Sam noted, since Ula lifted her glass to her mouth but didn't drink. Sam glanced at Katherine and wondered how Henry, in death, became a 'loving' man? What happened to never forgiving him 'for selling my silver Ferrari?' Was there absolution in the wine? Sam looked down at the golden liquid in her glass. Wine *was* used in the sacraments. Red wine, that is. Like blood.

"Please, help yourselves," Katherine said, waving a delicate hand. "We don't stand on ceremony here."

Sam looked at the faces around the table. *Five for dinner, a full moon. The conversation should be lively.*

On the table, reflecting light from clusters of flickering white candles, crystal glasses flashed fiery tongues. Silver napkin rings, engraved with flourishing V's, bound stark white cloth napkins in their metallic grips, reminding Sam of the Tarot's Eight of Swords. From a low centerpiece of white orchids, leafy green arms snaked across the polished wood surface. She hadn't seen this much elegance and matching china since Jackie Kennedy's White House tours.

Yeah, Sam thought, *Jackie tours the House of Usher.*

But beneath all the elegance—the silver and china and crystal and flowers and warm wonderful smells—this was not Camelot. Something was very wrong. Sam felt almost disconnected, as if the silver thread that bound her soul to her body was wound tighter than a blood pressure cuff and was about to snap.

Suddenly, her vision clouded. Her chest felt tight, as if she were suffocating. Her eyes seemed to roll back into her head.

Sam closed her lids tightly and took a deep breath, fighting off the image of a body—a man's body—floating and twisting in cold swirling currents, his flesh nothing more than food for the myriad marine life tearing at his hands and face. The man called to her through blue lips, bubbles frothing from his mouth as if from a child's plastic bubble maker. His words were muffled and unintelligible, his ravaged hands were raised in supplication.

Sam took a quick gulp of wine and gripped her glass with trembling hands. Her body was shaking. Glancing around the table, she realized no one had noticed. Charlie and Ula were picking at their food, each for different reasons, and Nick and Katherine were exchanging pleasantries. Sam's encounter with the dead man had gone unheeded.

The man in her vision wanted to tell her something. What, she didn't know, but he was somehow connected to...to what? A cold breath brushed her ear, as if icy lips were whispering a horrible secret. Her shoulders hunched as shivers rippled across her shoulders and down her legs. She looked to see if a breeze had stirred the curtains, but they hung motionless. She couldn't cope with this right now. She just wanted to erase the grisly vision from her brain cells.

The amber liquid slid over her parched tongue and down her throat. The wine's chill settled into a pleasant burning sensation in her stomach, helping her release some of the tension twisting her gut. She took another mouthful for good measure, then forced her attention back to reality.

Look around. Notice.

With her back to the marble fireplace, Katherine Vandalay laughed her throaty laugh at something Nick had said. She sat poised at the head of the table, the fingers of her left hand turning the gold cigarette case as ceaselessly as the ocean tides turned outside the mansion.

Katherine had changed from her yards of white, and now wore a pale pink silk blouse tied at the waist over a long black crepe skirt. Her blonde hair was softly twisted, leaving tendrils falling gracefully before each diamond-studded shell-like ear. And then there was that ring, shooting fire into the room.

Sam still wore her green flowered dress, but Nick had changed. Gray slacks, light blue button-down shirt, and red and navy striped tie. His hair was slicked back and his blackberry eyes glistened in the candle-light as he surveyed the feast before him.

Even Charlie looked dapper, if a bit wilted, in a gray suit jacket and starched white dress shirt, unbuttoned at the neck. He'd given up the green work pants and wore dark slacks. A touch of Brun, Sam was sure.

Ula looked like a hired mourner at an Italian funeral.

Charlie wiped at his nose with a tissue, then stuffed it in his jacket pocket. Beside him, Ula sat with her hands folded in her lap like an obedient schoolgirl waiting for the bell to ring. The chair at the foot of the table remained vacant.

Or did it?

Shakily, Sam reached for the salad. Charlie already had a piece of chicken and two slices of warm bread on his plate. He was reaching for the pasta when he hesitated, then offered the dish to Ula.

"I hope your accommodations are comfortable," Katherine said to Nick.

"Thank you," Nick replied, smiling affably. "The room is very nice. We hope we're not putting you out, staying here the night before the service." Ever the diplomat, he added, "You and Ula must have a lot of last minute details to take care of."

Dead man floating... Sam wiped her brain slate clean, *tabula rasa,* and glanced at Ula who was staring at her plate, watching her fork as she toyed with an errant cherry tomato. Tiny muscles bunched and loosened at the base of Ula's unadorned ear lobes as she set her fork down and accepted the dish from Charlie. She spooned pasta onto her plate. They had yet to hear her speak.

Sam put a hand over her mouth to muffle the clearing of her throat. Since Ula seemed to be either catatonic or mute, Sam asked Katherine, "How many guests do you expect tomorrow?"

"Over three hundred. It's quite a tribute to Henry," she responded, cutting a dainty triangle of chicken. She swirled it in the raspberry sauce and placed it in her mouth.

The tiny wrinkles at the corners of Ula's eyes deepened. With a deliberate hand, she punctured the cherry tomato, placed it between her teeth and yanked the seed-oozing orb into her mouth. Candlelight danced over her. The shadows accentuated the cords and faint beginnings of veins on the back of her hands. Ula pressed a white napkin against her lips.

A slight depression around the third finger on Ula's left hand caught Sam's attention. The kind of crease left from years of wearing a ring.

Ula wore a ring? The woman without a trace of makeup or jewelry? The ring must have been taken off recently to leave such an impression. Why would she have worn a ring? Katherine said there were no men in Ula's life, that all her time had been devoted to her brother. Perhaps Katherine doesn't know the entire story behind her sister-in-law. Had Ula been married before? Even engaged for a long time? Was the floating dead man connected to her?

With effort, Sam shook that vision away and kept her eyes averted from the pale chicken flesh floating in red raspberry sauce. There was a story behind Ula's stoic façade, and Sam was determined to find out what it was.

Then Ula's left hand disappeared, properly deposited into her lap.

"The pasta is delicious, Ula," Sam said, wiping a dab of the creamy sauce from the corner of her lips. "May I have your recipe?"

Ula nodded, but her eyes never left her salad. She punctured another tomato.

"Yes," Nick added. "Everything is delicious."

"So, Sam," Katherine interrupted, "did you talk with my foreman?"

Glad to get away from the floater, Sam shifted her attention to the business of another dead man. She wondered how much Katherine knew about her murdered husband's construction business. "Yes. I spoke with Mr. Vernelli yesterday afternoon. He didn't seem to know much. He had asked Kenny Ash to open the shop for him…" She paused as she played with the right words. "…that morning. It seems Mr. Vernelli's wife was ill."

At that moment, Charlie muffled a gargantuan sneeze into a tissue, apologized, then looked longingly at his dinner plate. Charlie Burrows was the master of food shoveling, a habit left over from too many hungry days when he had shared Sam's double-packed lunches in grade school. But he wasn't shoveling tonight.

Illness and death seemed omnipresent, Sam thought, fixing an eye on her old friend for a few lingering moments. The ragged scar running down the left side of his face and onto his cheek seemed to pulse. Sam hoped that someday he would tell her how he got that childhood gash and let loose the flood of anguish that lay buried beneath its shiny surface.

Sam said to Katherine, "I understand Mr. Vernelli opens the shop each morning because he has the only key."

"Yes." Katherine began turning the gold case once again. "Tony is punctual and quite reliable. He is the only employee with a key. Of course, Henry had keys."

"Did anyone other than Tony and your husband have access to the keys?"

"I did, of course. Henry dropped his keys on the hall table each night when he came in. And Ula had access as well." Katherine's attention shifted down the table to the dark bent head as her fingers stilled around the cigarette case. When Ula remained silent, Katherine said, "As I told you, Sam, we were both at home that evening." The little vein wiggled on Katherine's velvety forehead.

Was Katherine baiting her sister-in-law...waiting for Ula to leap onto the table like a Flamenco dancer and proclaim that she had killed her brother? That she couldn't take it anymore...that she wanted to click her castanets and dance on his grave...that even if Katherine were to inherit every last penny of the Vandalay fortune, it was worth it?

No. Staid, stoic, enduring number four would never do such a thing. Ula would hold her tongue as she always did, from what Sam had seen of her. But Sam had to wonder if Ula had bigger castanets to click. She would figure out a way to get the woman to talk to her.

Katherine picked up her glass. "Ula, more wine, please."

Ula placed her napkin beside her plate, got up, and went for the wine bottle sitting in an ice bucket on the side board. "Would anyone else like more wine?" Katherine's exquisite brows lifted.

Charlie shook his head, Sam said no thanks, but Nick smiled. "Yes. I'd like another glass. It's exceptionally good."

Ula poured the golden liquid into Nick's goblet, then filled Katherine's glass before seating herself once again.

"How long has Kenny Ash worked for Vandalay Enterprises?" Sam asked.

"Oh, right from the beginning." Katherine reached for her wine glass and fondled the stem with long fingers, *almost to the point of arousal*, Sam thought. "He and Berma were both hired when Henry first moved his business here. Berma keeps a sharp eye on that son of hers."

"Son?"

"Oh, yes. Didn't I mention that? Kenny is Berma's son from her first marriage. I really can't fathom why Henry kept him on. He used to complain that Kenny wasn't worth a lick of salt, but I guess he felt sorry for Berma. She's a hard worker and he didn't want to lose her."

Son?

What's going on? Something's going on. Kenny is Berma's son? He finds the body, remembers in surprising detail the Eight of Swords. Then, Tony Vernelli has a verbal altercation with Berma outside the Fox Run Mall. Was he grousing about Kenny? No, more likely she's got something on him. Berma's not the least bit intimidated by Tony. And whose lipstick was on the cigarette butts in Tony's office? Katherine's? No, that isn't possible. Katherine doesn't smoke—or so she says.

Sam glanced at the cigarette case lying beside Katherine's plate.

Candy's lipstick, maybe, but what would she be doing in Tony's office? And then there's Berma. Does she smoke?

Sam couldn't remember seeing an ashtray on the secretary's desk.

But if she does smoke, melon lipstick? I don't think so. Then there's silent, brow-beaten Ula with her indented ring finger. And who is the floating dead man?

Sam's mind was so muddled with questions, she couldn't have straightened her thoughts with a ruler. That's when she did it.

"Who's Katy?" she asked.

CHAPTER 22

❀

The words sprung from Sam's lips like a jack-in-the-box and hung there, wobbling.

"What?" Katherine's irises seemed to shrink, even in the dimness of the candlelight.

The room fell deadly silent. Even Charlie froze, sensing through his snuffling fog that they were about to crash on a rocky shore.

Sam put down her fork, folded her hands in her lap, and repeated, "Who's Katy? That list you made for me, the one Ula got from the library. The name Katy is written at the bottom…"

No one moved. Waves of silence pounded in Sam's ears.

"…not written, actually, but printed…in block letters…" Sam aligned her knife with her plate. The sound of silence was deafening.

"…with a pen…but the ink's a different color." Sam's fork seemed a bit askew also.

Finally, Katherine spoke. "You're telling me that someone added the name Katy to the list I had written out?" Katherine's voice sounded shrill as it rose from its soft deep octave. Stress hung on every syllable as she squeezed the words from her throat.

Sam knew she had struck pay dirt! Her intuition told her Katy was Katherine. But her short-lived euphoria was immediately replaced by frustration as more unanswered questions arose to shake their fingers at her mind.

Nick shuffled in his chair, darting one of those look-what-you've-said-now glares at her. He hated confrontations as much as she did, but he knew how to hold his tongue. Sam had had "foot-in-mouth" disease from the moment she opened her little pink mouth to speak her first word. And that word was "Why?"

"Yes," Sam said, "someone added Katy to the list. If you didn't, then who did?"

The only movement in the room, besides the gold cigarette case which now spun in Katherine's hand, was a wayward moth fanning its white wings furiously at the flaming candles. Sam noticed its struggle and was mesmerized by its darting dance with death and its fascination with the light as the moth's approach-avoidance behavior brought it ever closer to its fiery destiny. Was the ecstasy of the flame more potent than the thought of death? Did the moth think it could escape the murderous heat? Did it think at all?

The sound of a voice broke her trance.

"I have no idea." Katherine's words seemed wrung from her throat. "And I have no idea who Katy is."

Bleak shadows carved hollows in her face, making it look as if it were about to crumble. Her eyes darted toward the doorways, then around the table, and finally lit on Ula. As if she needed a depository for her fear, Katherine flung her suspicions against the only other person living in the house.

"Ula! What's the meaning of this? How did the name Katy get on the list I wrote out?"

Ula slowly lifted her head, squared her shoulders and, for the first time, smiled sweetly. "How would I know, Katherine?" Her voice was light, melodious, with the lilting innocence of a young girl.

Everyone's attention was now focused on Ula.

"*You* went to the library to get the list," Katherine pounded at her. "*You* were the last one to handle it!"

In a soft voice, her brown eyes fixed on Katherine, Ula said, "I didn't look at the list. I gave it to Mrs. Blackwell, as you instructed." Although the innocent smile never wavered, a fire burned deep in her sable eyes. There was primal life simmering in those subterranean chambers, stirring a cauldron of passions Sam could only imagine. Ula Vandalay might just leap onto the table, and fling herself into a wild and voluptuous Tarantella, the spider's dance, then turn on her mate for a tasty dinner.

Sam was suddenly reminded of the spider web under her sun porch and of Robert Frost's exquisite verse:

We dance round in a ring and suppose,

But the Secret sits in the middle and knows.

In the case of Henry Vandalay's murder, someone sat in the middle and knew. The big black spider in the middle of the web took on the face of Ula Vandalay in her mourning weeds. Or maybe it was Katherine's face. Or Berma Battles'. Then there was Tony the Tiger and Kenny Ash, the Cigarette Man. It was then that the connection between Ash and cigarettes made its way into Sam's brain.

"But it had to be you!" Katherine insisted, both fists on the table, one still clutching the gold case. She started to rise from her chair, leaning on the table as if for support. Her shoulders hunched as she thrust her head forward. Sam thought she resembled a vulture who spied an easy, if not totally dead, dinner. "Ula! Who else could it have been?"

Who else indeed? Sam could only wonder.

Ula pushed back her chair, stood, and in her little girl voice said, "I will have an announcement to make tomorrow. I'm retiring now, Katherine. You can clean up this mess."

And with that, she left the room.

*   *   *   *   *

Aghast, Katherine's dropped her gold cigarette case onto the table. It made a loud metallic clink. She pressed a delicate hand against her throat, swaying as if she were about to faint. But she caught herself, then said in a voice that spoke of great restraint, "I must apologize for my sister-in-law's behavior. I can't imagine what's gotten into her." She slowly dropped into her chair, brushing at a thick clump of golden hair that had come loose from her twist. She looked puzzled and confused.

After a long silent moment, she reached behind her head, and pulled out a hairpin, fumbling with it before securing the wayward tress.

"Please. Don't concern yourself," Nick said. "Ula must be very upset over her brother's death. The stress of things like this hits people in different ways."

Charlie had a puzzled scowl on his face as he observed Samantha. She knew what he was thinking. He was wondering why she hadn't told him about the note. And then he was probably thinking she had the interviewing skills of an aardvark, which Sam had to admit was probably true. But sometimes, things just popped out like that. And Katherine and Ula's reactions *were* something, weren't they?

Her interior voice kept telling her that 'Katy' was Katherine.

What is the woman hiding? Sam wondered. *And if Ula didn't write that name on the list, who did?*

Sam glanced toward the empty doorway.

And here we have Ula, the steady Eddy, who suddenly picks up and leaves the cleanup mess for Katherine? With all these abrupt personality changes, I feel like I'm in a psychiatric ward.

Somehow, personality disorders notwithstanding, Sam just couldn't conjure up an image of the elegant Katherine Vandalay in a lacy apron, scraping dirty dishes and piling them into the dishwasher. She wondered who would clean up the mess.

"Would you like us to help you clear the table after dinner, Katherine?" Sam asked.

"No, no," Katherine said, waving a hand back and forth in front of her face as if to fan away a pesky insect. She seemed to have regained some of her composure. "I'll call the caterers. They'll send someone right over."

At nine o'clock at night? This lady has some pull.

Charlie resumed picking at his chicken with his fork and wiping his nose with a tissue drawn from the supply in his pants pocket. He had continued stuffing the used ones in his jacket.

"I apologize if I've upset you," Sam said. "But you did hire me to investigate your husband's murder. I have to ask questions. Katy *is* a nickname for Katherine. That can't be a coincidence."

Nick seemed intent on his butter-soaked crusty French bread. He broke off a small piece, took a bite, then laid the piece next to the larger one, adjusted the angle of the larger one, then the smaller one, and finally turned his bread plate one-quarter of a turn to the right. The shell game had to be next, Sam thought.

Katherine drew herself erect. "My name is Katherine. I have never been called Katy." Period. End of discussion.

But Sam persisted. "Not even when you were a child?"

The moth now lit on a trailing leaf from the white orchid center-piece, quivering, as if contemplating its next line of attack.

"No. I've always been called Katherine." Her voice was icy.

"That just seems so odd," Sam said. "No one ever called you Katy? Not your parents or siblings? Friends? A teacher maybe?"

Whether it was an instinct buried in the group mind or the little guy made an independent decision, Sam would never know. She watched as the moth rose above the candles, hovered for just a moment, then did a kamikaze dive into the flames. A brief singe, and it fell to the elegantly appointed table, its passing unnoticed by everyone but Sam.

Suddenly, Katherine stood. "You'll have to excuse me. I'm not feeling well. I need rest. I have so much to do tomorrow. Please take your time finishing dinner. Leave the dishes for the help. I will see you in the morning." She swept from the room without looking back.

Charlie and Nick looked at each other, their brows raised in unison. Sam stared at the still, lifeless body of the moth.

During World War II, kamikaze pilots were fed raw meat before their suicide missions to make them more aggressive. Then they were given just enough fuel in their bomb-ladened Zeros to reach the enemy ships. They had a date with Death. Just like the moth. Just like Henry Vandalay. And like the *floating dead man?*

As Sam blessed the dead moth, Charlie wiped his mouth with the thick white napkin and dropped it on his plate. He stood up, his jacket pocket bulging like a chipmunk with the mumps.

"Seems you struck a nerve, Sam," he chuckled. "You have a way of doing that."

Sam sensed a dollop of admiration in his voice.

CHAPTER 23

❀

"Wow!"

"You can say that again. Whatever possessed you to drop a bomb like that, Sam?"

In the shadowed room, propped against two pillows in the sleigh bed, Sam was drawing circles under the covers with her right foot. She watched Nick strip off his shirt, fold it in half, and lay it over the back of the stuffed chair by the window.

"I couldn't help it. It just came out." She gave him a lopsided grin. "You have to admit, it did produce results. What do you think, Sherlock?"

She watched him slip out of his pants and lay them neatly over his shirt in the rectangle of moonlight that bathed that side of the room. As expected, coins came tumbling out of his pants pockets onto the cushion of the chair and slid down into the side cracks. "For crying out loud!" he exclaimed, as he began fishing for the coins.

Sam refrained from telling him for the millionth time that he should empty his pockets before getting undressed. But, she had learned a long time ago that old habits don't die, they just cause arguments. So, she just sat there, admiring his strong, muscular legs.

When she finally had his attention, she said, "So?"

"Let me wash up and I'll be right with you."

Ten minutes later, the bedside lamp glowed softly (some kind of Victorian affair with an intricate metal base and fringed ivory shade), and Nick was under the covers beside her. He rolled onto his side and threw an arm over her lap. And laughed. "I see you never leave home without them."

She knew exactly what he was going to say.

"The Ring Dings." With his index finger, he pointed at the night table. The plastic-wrapped package sat on top of two books and next to Sam's deck of Tarot cards.

"I've got some reading to do," she countered. "It could be a long night."

He gave a fake groan. "I can see it's going to be a long *long* night."

She knew he was kidding, but she sniffed anyway. It was a game with them. "Nick, since when does my reading keep you up? You're usually asleep before I can count to ten."

"Wouldn't nine be a more appropriate number? Since nine represents endings?"

"Funny man," she said, and kicked his leg gently. "Really though. What do you think of our first, and probably last, evening at the Vandalay estate?"

"I think you hit a nerve. Do you really think Katherine is the Katy on the list?"

"Yes, I do. And I think she's hiding something. But is it something worth killing for? That's the big question." She idly stroked Nick's hair. "And there's another thing." She then told Nick about the floating dead man.

"Jesus, woman." He lifted his head to look at her. "Where do you get these things from?"

"It just came. The man was trying to tell me something. I know it's connected to this case somehow."

Nick rolled over on his back, and in so doing, pulled half the covers with him. Sam often woke uncovered in the morning because Nick was wrapped in the bedding like a caterpillar in a cocoon. She tugged the sheet and blankets back over her legs, the response so automatic that she barely noticed it.

"Sorry, babe." Nick smoothed the covers on his side and folded his hands across his chest. "Another body?" He ruminated a moment. "I don't know. I haven't seen or heard anything about that on the news, have you?"

"No. But that doesn't mean anything." While she frowned, her eyes lit briefly the Ring Dings. "The other body hasn't been found yet or we would have heard something. Along with Henry Vandalay's death, the papers would play that up big time. Of course, if this man's in a river or the ocean, he may never be found."

"How do you know he's around here? Maybe some surfer in Hawaii bought it in a big wave."

"No. Whatever happened, happened here. And he didn't jump into the river of his own accord. I just feel it. You know, I was thinking…" And, as she looked at the ceiling for the *tabula rasa*, she went off on a number of theories.

The next sound Sam heard was the zzz's. Nick was asleep with his mouth open, and the decibels were rising. She smiled and gave him a little nudge so he'd turn over. He mumbled, and with the sheet, blanket, and coverlet tight under one arm, rolled away from her onto his side and fell into an acceptable deep rumble. Sam eased the white tufted coverlet (the only piece of bedding she could extract without waking him) over to her side, just enough to cover her legs and lap.

Then, with one eye on the Ring Dings, she picked up the Tarot cards and slid them out of the box. The five cards she had laid on her desk, just before Caroline called, were on the top. With the Keltic layout list on the nightstand beside her, Sam placed the Three of Swords over The Lovers and the King of Pentacles. The Devil, the Nine of Cups, and the Eight of Swords were set around them in the south, west and north respectively.

According to the book, the next card—position six, in the east—represented what was before Henry Vandalay.

It was the Death Card.

No explanation needed there. She scratched her head, then picked up the Tarot book once again.

What the querent fears is indicated by position seven at the bottom of the vertical line of cards to the right of the spread. Sam pulled out the card.

The Tower.

She spread her legs wider to make room and placed the card on the bed.

An ominous looking scene. A bolt of lightning strikes a gray tower, dislodging the tower's crown. Two figures—one common, one royal—appear to be falling to their deaths on the rocks below.

Sam rubbed the side of her nose. *What the querent fears.*

And then a thought struck her. It was almost as if a shift had happened in the consciousness of the killer—as if the killer was now expressing his or her own feelings, rather than Henry's. Henry was dead after all; he had no feelings after the Death card. With the Death card in position six, nothing was before him. Henry became a non-player. What would he have to fear now?

Sam eased open the Ring Ding package—with one eye on Nick—and took out one of the round chocolate cakes, putting a toothy arc in it. A few crumbs fell on one of the cards. She picked up the card, tapped the crumbs into her hand, popped them in her mouth, and then wiped her hands on a tissue from the nightstand.

Licking at the corners of her lips, she read position eight: the influence of family, friends, and the environment.

The Five of Pentacles. She rummaged through the deck, found the card, and placed it above The Tower.

Through a snow storm, a ragged woman and a crippled man struggle past the window of an opulent home. They seem unaware of the light inside. The images suggest those who live in outer darkness, unaware of their inner light.

Definition: loss of job and/or home, loneliness.

Seems the killer felt pretty isolated and alone. No family support. Loss of a home? Could that be Ula? Then again, maybe Tony the Tiger feared losing his job for some reason. Was he in major debt? But how would killing his boss help him out there?

Sam let out a big sigh. Too many questions.

Tucked in the middle of the definition of the Five of Pentacles was: "Lovers unable to find a meeting place."

Hmm.

Sam took another bite of the Ring Ding. When she tried to pick up a fallen crumb, it smeared on the white tufted spread. "Damn," she muttered under her breath. She slipped out of bed, tiptoed to the bathroom and returned with a wet face cloth. After scrubbing the brown smudge out, she draped the face cloth over the shower rod and crawled back under the covers, avoiding the large damp spot on the bedspread.

She leaned back into the pillows, and for the hundredth time she wondered who killed Henry Vandalay and why. Katherine stood to inherit almost everything. Over millions of reasons right there. But what about Ula? Why would she kill her brother?

She looked down at the layout, which was now a bit askew from her chocolate episode. She bit at a corner of her lip as she realigned the cards.

The ninth placement was the querent's hopes. *Or perhaps the killer's hopes?*

Thumbing through the deck, Sam found the Queen of Pentacles. She placed it over the Five of Pentacles. A Queen sits amidst a scene of fertility—fruit, green fields, red roses overhead—contemplating the pentacle in her lap. In a layout, the card indicates opulence and practical use of earthly talents.

Sam blinked a few times, yawned, and then popped the last wedge of Ring Ding into her mouth. As she munched, she ran her thumb back and forth over the deck of cards in her hands. Pentacles represented wealth. It would seem someone was after money. And that could be just about any one of the people on Katherine's list.

Sam was getting tired. She could barely keep her eyes open as she read the tenth placement: *the final outcome. Yes, the Wheel of Fortune. Success, new conditions.*

She stared at the pattern cast by the moonlight on the rug next to the bed. She had a feeling she had missed something. Something right under her nose. What was it?

Her blinking was almost steady now, as if beach sand were collecting beneath her lids. She was getting loopy. She rolled her shoulders. Nick stirred beside her, then fell back into rhythmic rumbling.

Everything looked blurry. She shook her head, focussed once more on the layout. All but three of the cards came from the Major Arcana, the twenty-one cards in the Tarot deck which follow The Fool.

As sand dunes continued to build behind her eyes, Sam started to add up the numbers at the top of the Major Arcana cards, but she couldn't focus. Besides, this line of thinking was a bit far-fetched, even for her.

She yawned again, rubbed her eyes with the heels of her palms, then gathered up the cards and put them back in the box along with the list. Flexing her feet a few times, she rolled her bangs around the green sponge roller on the nightstand, then plumped her pillows into a comfortable position.

As she reached for the second Ring Ding and Dan Brown's book, *Angels and Demons,* she wondered once more about "Katy," before settling down for a nanosecond of reading.

*   *   *   *   *

It was in the hallway. The sound.

Sam bolted upright! The book lay between her and Nick, and the lamp was still on. On the nightstand, in a tiny pool of light, lay a ripped cellophane wrapper and a rectangular slip of white cardboard.

Nick was into heavy breathing now, deep in delta sleep. Every cell in Sam's body strained to hear...

Yes! There it was again. The unmistakable sound of a floor board creaking. She squinted at the walnut mantle clock on the bureau. A few minutes past three.

She slipped from the bed and scurried across the rug to the bedroom door. With her heart at attack mode, she placed a sweaty hand on the brass knob and prayed the door would not creak open like in the intro to the old radio program, *Inner Sanctum*.

Do it quickly, she told herself, like ripping a Band-Aid off a cut. She hoped this rip wouldn't hurt. She took a deep breath and pulled the door open about a foot. Not one creak, thank the Lady in Heaven.

With her head stuck out into the hall, she looked to the right toward Ula's room. Nothing. Then to the left, just in time to catch movement at the head of the stairway. Someone was out there, and that someone was heading down the staircase.

At three in the morning?

Charlie's door was closed; his room dark.

The sweet smell of lilac drifted into Sam's nostrils, conjuring up a vision of a black-draped Ula wafting down the wide hallway, a candelabra dripping wax in one hand and a can of deadly lilac spray in the other.

Through a window at the head of the stairway, a lacy pattern from the full moon rippled over the deeper shadows in the hall. A moving mandala created by a tree, Sam surmised. Had those undulating forms created the illusion of a skulking figure? If the figure was real, was that figure a man or a woman?

She supposed Ula or Katherine could have gotten an attack of the hungries—Sam often did in the middle of the night. But model-thin

Katherine? She didn't think so. And somehow, Ula didn't seem the type to fry up a grilled cheese sandwich at three in the morning. But what other reason could either of the women have for sneaking down the stairs at this unholy hour? Well, maybe they weren't sneaking, but it sure seemed that way.

Perhaps she hadn't really seen anyone. Was her imagination working overtime again as a result of too many old horror movies? Dr. Jekyll and Mr. Hyde crept to mind. Sam especially liked the 1941 version of the film with Ingrid Bergman and Spencer Tracy. As Leonard Maltin wrote, that version "stressed Hyde's emotions rather than the physical horror."

Were she and Nick and Charlie sleeping in a house with an emotionally unbalanced counterpart of Hyde? The lump in her throat was making it difficult to breathe.

Too many visions accosted Sam's tired mind: dead bodies, secrets from the past, a big drafty house, specters floating down hallways at three o'clock in the morning. And the Hunter's Moon with its positive ions. This weekend, all the ingredients were present to bring out the beast in people. Sam hoped the apparition she had seen was just that— her embodiment of the collective emotions residing in this old house and not some real flesh-and-blood monster.

She shuddered once and closed the bedroom door. She took a ladder-back chair from next to the bureau, wedged it under the doorknob, and went back to bed, where she would lie awake and listen for the rest of the night.

CHAPTER 24

Katherine Vandalay stretched like a cat, long and luxuriously.

From bedroom windows overlooking the ocean, she saw the sun had risen before her and was now moving through a raspberry-colored sky. She was pleased she didn't have to contend with rain and whipping winds that would put a damper on the festivities, maybe cut them short.

Funny that she thought of the services today as festivities. She yawned, her hand over her mouth. It *was* a chance to show what she was capable of: organizing the caterers, flowers, servants, even the parking had been carefully planned. She hadn't overlooked one detail. And now that she had Henry's money, she would finally be accepted by the people she had always envied. Maybe she'd join the country club.

Yes, this was her day. Just a few more hours and the games would begin. Katherine kicked the silk sheets aside and slowly, sensuously, massaged her stomach.

Herman Lawlor, Henry's lawyer, would be arriving from the Serengeti sometime today, cutting his vacation short. Per Henry's instructions, Lawlor was to read the will after the guests had left. Katherine had decided she would ask Charles, Samantha and Nick to stay. She wanted Sam to watch the reactions of the gathering, particularly Ula, and maybe pick up some more ammunition against the bitch. That Henry had requested the presence of Berma, along with Kenneth

Ash and Anthony Vernelli and their wives, disturbed her. But she didn't want to think about that right now.

Katherine's left eye quivered. Images from last night seeped into her sleepy brain.

Katy.

She felt her shoulders stiffen.

How the hell did that name get on the list? She draped her forearm over her eyes. *It had to be Ula...but how would she know my old nickname? She knows nothing about my past. Unless she hired a private detective, which I wouldn't put past her. Is that what she plans to announce today?*

Katherine took a long, deep breath, trying hard to calm herself. She could feel sweat beading on her forehead.

That kind of scandal would be her ruination. All her plans down the drain. She had done everything right, followed her plan religiously. She wouldn't let success be snatched from her now because of that four-letter word, "Katy." The horror of the thought that Katherine could fall from social grace was almost more than she could bear.

She clenched her teeth so hard, her jaw hurt. She'd have a talk with Ula, threaten her with eviction—which she planned on doing anyway, but Ula didn't know it. Katherine was sure she could break Henry's will in that regard if she had to. She'd find a way. Maybe declare her sister-in-law incompetent because of those stupid Tarot cards and that weird altar in her bedroom closet. Who but a loony would hide in her closet with a deck of cards imprinted with knives and devils and pierced hearts? And light candles and wave wands and drink God-knows-what from that cup.

Katherine thought about the Tarot card spread beside the dead body of her husband and wondered how long it would take the police to get a search warrant for the house. Regardless, Ula belonged in an institution. And with Ula safely put away, no one would believe her tales about Katy.

That resolved, she pushed herself up into a sitting position and let her legs dangle over the side of the bed. She liked the high mattress. On most days, it made her feel like the princess in the fairy tale, *The Princess and the Pea*—but not today.

She sat for a moment, staring across the room, waiting to fully awaken before pushing off into her busy day. Her eyes watered as she yawned once again.

For no apparent reason, a vague sense of uneasiness came over her, seeping into the cells of her skin like an insidious fog, and sending a chill through her warm body. Something was wrong in her room. What was it?

She stood, pulled her nightgown on over her head in an unconscious defensive gesture, and listened to it rustle down over her body. Then she canvassed the room.

The air felt heavy, strained, as if her space had been violated. She couldn't seem to shake the cold anxiety that prickled her skin. To dispel the feeling, she paced back and forth from the windows to the bedroom door.

Then, more out of desire than belief, she blamed her sense of violation on nerves. After all, she was a suspect in her husband's murder. Charles and Sam would probably be watching her like a hawk, as would the other guests. The assembled elite and Henry's employees had to be wondering about a murdered wealthy older man leaving behind a very wealthy young wife. She would be like a bug under a microscope. Who wouldn't be uneasy?

Katherine Vandalay finally shrugged off her jitters, slipped out of her nightgown, and wound her way into the granite shower. The hot water from the double shower heads beat at her body, wringing out the last vestiges of tiredness and fear. She stood motionless, eyes closed and face lifted to one stream of water as the other pricked at her back like fine-pointed needles. It felt so good. So relaxing…

Suddenly, her eyes snapped open!

Katherine raced from the shower to her bedside and stared at the night table. While water streamed from her hair and body, soaking into the carpet at her feet, her mouth fell slack, her face registered disbelief.

She dropped to the floor and lifted the bed skirt.

Nothing!

She stuck her hand in between the mattress and the box spring, then jumped up and stripped the bed, throwing sheets and covers on the floor. She yanked the nightstand away from the wall, knocking over the crystal lamp. It clattered to the floor and broke in half.

Nothing behind the stand.

She pulled the drawer out and emptied the contents onto the bare mattress.

Oh, God! It wasn't there!

Katy slid down the side of the mattress and curled into a fetal position on the wet spot on the carpet.

Her rock…her polished, speckled beach rock. It was missing.

*   *   *   *   *

Sam saw Katherine coming down the hallway looking pale and distracted, but Sam had another concern at the moment. She'd knocked on Charlie's door and found him still in bed, running a fever.

"Katherine, could I trouble you for some Advil or Tylenol? Charlie isn't feeling well."

Katherine waved Sam toward Ula's room. "I'm sure Ula has something like that in her medicine chest. The woman always seems to have a headache."

"But…should I go in there?" Sam said. "I mean, wouldn't Ula mind?"

Katherine was distraught. Sam could see it in her eyes and the tight set of her shoulders, but she was more concerned about Charlie at the moment.

"Ula has been up for hours," Katherine said, hurrying past Sam. "She's downstairs with the caterers. I'll tell her that you're getting Charles a pain reliever from her bathroom." She turned and whooshed down the staircase.

Well, if you insist, a delighted Sam thought. She wasn't so sure that Ula wouldn't mind, but...

Mingled with her concern for Charlie, Sam could hardly wait to get some insight into Henry's sister. As she passed a scowling Nick in the doorway of their room, she smiled. "I have permission."

Sam reached for Ula's doorknob. She heard Nick muttering behind her, "You're incorrigible."

Ula's room was large and austere, but well appointed. Two tall windows dressed with simple white sheers and dark burgundy velvet panels looked out over the front lawn. On the floor were hooked wool rugs in subtle browns and creams. The room was sparsely furnished: between the windows was a brass double bed covered by a striped comforter in rich shades of plum, gold, and tan, and a two-drawer oak nightstand on which rested a Victorian lamp similar to the one in Nick and Samantha's room. To Sam's right, between the opening into Ula's sitting room and the closet door, sat a large bureau with oak-leaf pulls and a matching mirror.

At least a dozen New Yorkers could settle in here, Sam clucked.

As she almost tiptoed across the room toward the bathroom door on the left, she did notice the closet door was ajar. Fighting off an evil impulse to peek inside, Sam shifted her gaze and her thoughts to the top of the bureau which was as bare as the moon's landscape. Not one thing sat on its surface. Nada. The walls were bare, too. A furniture store display had more personality.

The one exception was a stack of books on the nightstand. Sam read the titles: C.G. Jung's *Four Archetypes*, Solomon's *How To Really Know Yourself Through Your Handwriting*, and J.C. Cooper's *An Illustrated Encyclopaedia of Traditional Symbols*.

Interesting if eclectic reading material, Sam thought, *especially the book on handwriting.* The printed name "Katy" came to mind.

Sam headed into the small bathroom. She blinked at the gleaming white fixtures, white shower curtain (actually a white liner, not a curtain), and small white rug draped over the tub. On the sink, there was a generic toothbrush (white) and a half-squeezed tube of Crest with its bottom rolled neatly and tucked into a Vandalay Enterprises mug. Sam knew about the toothpaste tube because she looked inside the mug. A plastic packet of dental floss lay next to the cup. There were no water spots on the faucets. The sink was dry.

Sam pulled open the door of the fingerprint-free mirrored medicine chest. Two shelves were empty. The third shelf held a white nylon hair brush and black comb (with no hair strands in either), and one bottle each of aspirin and Tylenol. A bottle of Listerine mouthwash sat on the bottom of the cabinet next to a pair of nail clippers and two emery boards.

I've taken more supplies on my early camping trips with Nick, Sam thought, as she reached for the Tylenol. Ula was either the proverbial Scrooge, or old habits from a deprived childhood had not eased as her brother's wealth accumulated. She must have been given some financial remuneration for all the work she did in this house. Surely, Ula could have afforded more than what Sam had seen thus far. Much more.

Sam stepped back into the bedroom.

Now, to get myself back to Charlie and try not look in that closet. Not one peek. Really…

If she shouldered the closet door open just two more inches, she could easily slide inside. What was the harm? She wouldn't touch anything. And she *had* been hired by Katherine to clear her name. On the other hand—God! Now she sounded like Nick. But, snooping into peoples' closets was not right.

Where are you ethics, Sam?

After a quick glance down the hall, she flicked on the light in Ula's closet, and slipped inside, the Tylenol bottle clutched in her sweaty left hand. This time, the heat generated from her palms wasn't from so-called hot flashes.

She eyed the racks. She hadn't seen this much black since JFK's funeral.

She stuck the Tylenol bottle in the pocket of her new skirt, and clasped her hands behind her back, stilling the urge to reach out and finger the fabrics. On a single pole to her left were three black dresses and six pairs of black slacks, plus one garment bag with the sales tag still attached to the hanger; on the right, double poles supported five black skirts and eight black blouses. A cream-colored blouse and one pair of brown slacks had somehow found their way into the closet.

Must have been on sale, Sam reasoned.

On the floor in a neat row sat four pairs of black shoes and one pair of black sneakers, the latter probably worn while playing Maid-For-Hire.

Even more curious than the color selection (or lack of it) in Ula's closet was a free-standing clothes rack covered with a white sheet. Rills in the rug at the rubber feet suggested it had been moved recently.

Sam hesitated, then stepped toward the ghostly metal frame as if she expected the *floating dead man* to rise up from under the sheet and call her name. The air in the closed space felt oppressive and stale and carried a faint trace of lilac.

Her heartbeat sounded hollow in her ears.

Calm down. Breathe.

Sam peeked under the sheet. No ghostly limbs, just wire hangers. Joan Crawford would not have approved. Odd, though. Why would Ula have an empty clothes rack in her closet covered by a sheet?

That's when she noticed the table.

Sam was really sweating now. What if Ula walked in and found her in the closet? What possible excuse could she offer? She was cold and thought she'd borrow a sweater? Something in black, perhaps?

Sam dashed to the bedroom door and once again glanced down the hallway. Nick was still standing in their bedroom doorway, motioning her to come. She shook her head, held up a forefinger signaling one more minute, then returned to the closet.

No hands behind her back now. Carefully, she slid the clothes rack forward. That's when she saw the display! Silver candlesticks, a deck of Tarot cards, a gold ring, and the implements spoken of in the Tarot book: the wand, the cup, a coin and...*a freshly polished shiny knife.*

CHAPTER 25

❀

The *festivities* were going to be a success.

Cool sun glinted off BMW's, Lexuses, and Mercedes, which were being parked next to pick-up trucks and Hondas by black-suited young men. Young women in crisp white tuxedo shirts and black slacks wove through the already assembled guests with silver platters brimming with hors d'oeuvres and champagne.

For the time being, Katherine Vandalay buried worries about her missing rock under layers of rationalization. Ula was most likely responsible, and after the festivities, Katherine would lay her out in lavender. Ula would never violate her private space again.

Katherine stood tall and refrained from beaming as she surveyed the gathering. After all, as the grieving widow, a modicum of sobriety was called for. Her guests, however, were here to enjoy the day—and to write out five-figure checks.

At first, most of the attendees struggled to remain somber. That is, until Katherine Vandalay, with a tear in her eye, announced that today was a celebration of Henry's life, not his death, and that he would want everyone to eat, drink, have a good time, and be *very* generous to his favorite charities. The young woman behind the table at the front of the tent would be happy to help them lighten their wallets. That brought a few conservative chuckles. Soon, with the champagne, iced shrimp and caviar, chamber music and intoxicating ocean air, contagious laughter erupted above the cacophony of voices.

Dozens of bodies queued in front of the bar and the spotless, white-clad chef at the banquet table. Newspeople, smelling a potentially salacious scoop about the widow of the murdered magnate, snapped photos of Katherine at every opportunity: with state and local officials, with CEOs of major corporations, with celebrities of one sort and another, and with members of the Seacoast's established families.

The reporters had been asking for Ula Vandalay. Katherine assured them that her sister-in-law would be out shortly. No photographs were taken of Katherine with Tony Vernelli, Berma Battles, Kenny Ash, or any of the lower caste of attendees—although the cameras snapped in the employees' direction in case any of them would be implicated in the murder. The sole purpose of Katherine's invitation to the media (to bolster her image in the community) was a far cry from the motivating force behind the media's enthusiasm.

Katherine was stunning in an elegant gray silk pantsuit with a string of simple white pearls at her throat. Her slender shoulders held stiffly, she smiled as her photo was snapped beside a State Representative, but her mind was elsewhere.

Katherine was again thinking about last night when Ula said she had an announcement to make today at the festivities. What could the woman possibly have to say? Katherine shuddered. She had to keep Ula under control. She could feel the corner of her left eye quivering as she thought, *Ula must have written KATY on the list and taken my stone from the nightstand. If she does anything to spoil my day…*

Even as fear gripped her heart, a murderous thought found its way into her mind.

"A penny for your thoughts, Mrs. Vandalay."

Katherine swung around to find a slim, silver-haired Boston financier who summered in Rye.

"Oh, Mr. Wiecock." She almost stammered, but managed to take a breath, then cast him a dazzling smile. "I'd rather you contributed a bit more than that." She offered her hand.

He laughed as he took it and held it a few seconds too long. "I'm sorry about Hank. He was a good man."

"Yes, he was. Thank you." She lowered her lashes demurely while retrieving her hand. After a pause, she said, "Please, have a glass of champagne." She snapped her fingers at a passing serving person. "Enjoy yourself. Henry would have wanted that."

She turned away and mentally checked off her list of things to monitor. Earlier, to Samantha, she had pointed out all but two of the faces behind the names on her suspect list. In return, Samantha told her that Charles was feeling much better and would be down shortly. The serving people were doing their jobs, contributions were being collected at the charity table, people were smiling and conversing, and food and drink were plentiful. Katherine thought the chamber music complemented the service—restrained, but with a touch of gaiety.

As she moved off to greet Agatha Coldbath, President of Coldbath Industries (who had just been delivered by her driver from a vintage black Chrysler New Yorker), a server stepped up and said, "Mrs. Vandalay?" The young woman looked a bit perplexed.

"Yes? What is it?"

The server cleared her throat. "A man asked me to give this to you." In her outstretched hand was Katherine's polished beach stone.

Katherine gasped and took a step back as if the stone were an asp ready to strike a death blow at her breast. All her blood seemed to drain to her feet. She started to sway. "A man? What man?"

The young woman turned and pointed toward the side of the house. "That man over there."

Katherine squinted and strained to see over the babbling heads. A man, partially concealed by the rhododendron bushes, held up a hand with the forefinger extended. From that distance, she couldn't make out who it was. She managed to steady herself and dismissed the serving person with a "Thank you. That's all."

Katherine swallowed dryly, and felt what little saliva there was in her throat catch halfway down. She lowered her chin and worked at swallowing again.

Who the hell is that? Did Ula set him up to this? What is going on?

Somewhere, in the mists of her mind, she suspected who it was, but her conscious mind fought off the thought.

With a sudden surge of courage born out of sublimated fear, Katherine wove through the crowd, automatically smiling and nodding as guests spoke to her. She then strode toward the figure who had stepped back into the shadow of the bushes, against the clapboards and out of the sight of prying eyes.

As Katherine rounded the corner of the house, ready to demand—"What's the meaning of…," she stopped dead in her tracks. The stone fell from her hand and made a soft thud on the ground.

"Katy, my Katy," the man cooed, a big smile spreading beneath his red-veined nose. "It's been a long time."

CHAPTER 26

✿

"I'm feeling a lot better. Thanks, Sam," Charlie said, keeping a keen eye on his plate of hors d'oeuvres while stuffing a tissue into the pocket of his sports jacket. His nose was rosy from abuse. He squinted into the sun. "What's been happening on the war front?"

"Everything seems under control at the moment," Sam said, "but I feel a storm coming on."

Charlie scanned the horizon. "Sky's clear as a bell."

"Not a literal storm. Something's going on here, on the Vandalay estate. I can just feel it. A sort of heaviness in the air. I don't know how to explain it."

Charlie scarfed down a shrimp from his well-laden plate and mumbled, "Maybe Tony the Tiger has something to do with your mood."

Nick agreed, sliding a surreptitious glance at the dark, wedge-shaped man. "That one eyebrow's been at half-mast since he got here. I wonder if he ever smiles."

"The one I'm curious about is Ula." Sam craned her neck and looked out over the crowd. "Have you seen her?"

"Just look for someone draped in black from head to toe," Nick said, following Sam's lead and scoping out the guests.

"I haven't seen her," Charlie said, too intent on the baby shrimp and goose paté on his plate to play watchdog.

"I see you've regained your appetite," Sam said.

"Can't let good food go to waste, whatever this stuff is."

After all Charlie's lean years, it made Sam happy to see him enjoying his food. "Ula was going to make an announcement today at the service," she said. "Remember?"

"After her dramatic exit last night, who could forget?" Nick added, cocking an eyebrow at his wife.

"It wasn't my fault!" Sam cried.

Nick smiled down at her, his silence more condemning than anything he could have said.

Then a pungent odor assaulted Sam's nostrils. Chemicals of some kind.

"Miss Samantha. How are you today?"

Even before Sam turned around, she knew who it was. Poised behind her with a champagne glass in his hand, was Clarence Tuttle wearing his wide, lizard smile.

"Clarence!" she said, her smile genuine.

He took her hand and kissed it. The men shook hands.

"Did you know Henry Vandalay?" Sam asked. She was surprised to see him at the services and curious about his connection to the Vandalay family.

"No, no, Miss Samantha. I didn't have the pleasure. Actually, I know Miss Vandalay." He sipped at his champagne.

Even Charlie stopped eating.

"Katherine?" Sam prodded.

Over the lip of his glass, Clarence's huge watery eyes blinked once, then again. He took a quick sip, then said, "No. Not Mrs. Vandalay. *Miss* Vandalay." With Clarence, it was hard to decipher salutations.

"You mean Ula?" Nick offered. Startled, Sam glanced at her husband. It wasn't like him to help with interrogations.

As a breeze stirred, Clarence smoothed the few strands of hair that circled the front of his forehead. Sam watched flakes fall from his dry skin and hoped their descent was outside the range of his champagne glass.

Clarence was wearing his traditional starched white shirt with sharp creases down the front. His uniform, Sam thought. The only time he changed out of it, as far as she knew, was at 4:35 every afternoon when he closed Clean As A Hound's Tooth Cleaners, climbed the outside stairs to his apartment, slipped into his red-striped seersucker robe, and settled in with a chipped bank-issue coffee mug to watch the evening news. She knew this because she had been invited up one evening last year, during the Cowberry Necklace Murders.

Idly observing Clarence's crisp white front, Sam wondered if the shirt was an odd statement about his abandonment by his wife, an unconscious need for sympathy from the community. Clarence repeatedly told his customers how Harriet had run off with the previous owner and left him with only a note and one over-starched shirt. It was a wonder the news wasn't engraved over his doorway or bannered across *Publick Occurrences*, the town's only newspaper.

"So you know Ula?"

"Why, yes, Miss Samantha. Miss Vandalay is a customer. A very nice lady. She requested my presence at today's services. I am here to acknowledge her loss. Poor woman." He paused. "Amazingly, she's turned quite colorful this past week."

Charlie and Sam exchanged glances. Earlier, Sam had told Charlie about the closet chapel in Ula's bedroom, about the Tarot cards, and the widow's weeds. 'Colorful' was a stretch even for Clarence who, by unanimous (if unspoken) consent, was allowed poetic license.

Nick, slipping back into his tactful mode, frowned at Sam as he saw her getting ready to speak. She noticed his frown, but said what was on her mind anyway. "How has Ula turned colorful, Clarence? Do you mean her personality or the way she dresses?"

"Well, both, really, Miss Samantha." Clarence, anticipating the attention of an audience, would have rubbed his hands in glee if he hadn't been holding a champagne glass. "I am rather curious about her transformation."

As the chamber music started up once more, Sam stepped closer to Clarence so as not to miss one syllable. Nick shifted from one leg to the other; Charlie hovered over his plate like a dragonfly over a bog.

"Henry Vandalay moved here I'd say…" Clarence's eyes rolled up toward his flaky forehead "…about two years ago. Miss Vandalay stayed behind for a few months to take care of her dying mother. She moved here after Mr. Vandalay married Mrs. Vandalay.

"Miss Vandalay came into my establishment one morning, after checking many other cleaners in the area, so she told me, and found I had the most reasonable prices. She is a thrifty lady." He hesitated, but only briefly.

Sam wondered where the rambling discourse was going, but she wasn't about to pull a hoof-in-the-mouth act now.

"What I find most curious is that Miss Vandalay, who has an almost exclusively black wardrobe, suddenly showed up with a lime-colored dress. It needed alterations." He leaned toward Sam. "I do that, too, you know."

As Clarence began to pontificate, he stood a little straighter, his eyes twinkled a bit brighter. "One can tell a great deal about personalities through clothing, as well as the stains upon those clothes. Take Mr. Nick, for instance." His watery eyes washed over Nick. "The tomato stains tell me he likes Italian food." Clarence's eyes crinkled. After all, stains were his bread and butter. "The outdoor clothing from L.L. Bean, EMS, and Timberland suggests that, even though he works in an office all week, he'd rather be outdoors in his canoe or hiking a mountain."

Even if Clarence hadn't known Nicholas Bennett for over twenty years, he would have made the same assessment. Sam had heard him do it before.

"Yes, you are so right, Clarence." She angled in even closer, stifling the impulse to say 'I haven't had my V-8 today.' "You were saying about Ula Vandalay?"

Charlie had stopped chewing, a sure sign that he realized something important was about to be said and he didn't want to miss a word because of the crunching and sloshing inside his head.

"Well…" He stopped, as if searching his memory banks for the exact sequence of events. For some reason, a vision of a cow chewing her cud materialized behind Sam's eyes. She wanted to scream 'Get to the point!', but she wouldn't hurt Clarence's feelings for the world. After all, this *was* his world. Center stage, circulating information. What else did he have besides that one over-starched white shirt?

After an interminable pause, he went on. "For the past two years, the clothing that Miss Vandalay has brought to me has been very dark, black mostly. Good quality, but almost exclusively black." He paused, and nodded at his accurate assessment.

Sam was about to throttle him.

"Then a strange thing happened last week, after Mr. Vandalay's death," Clarence said, his brow furrowing. "Miss Vandalay brought in that stunning lime-colored dress for alterations. It's a size five, Miss Vandalay's size, so I know it isn't for Mrs. Vandalay. Now." He set his eyes upon Sam. "Don't you think that's a bit odd? It's as if she has suddenly gone through a personality change."

Ula? The Italian mourner in luscious lime?

Sam looked at Charlie who raised his brows. She was getting ready to ask another question when Agatha Coldbath approached with a purposeful stride.

"Samantha. Nicholas. Charles. Clarence. Good afternoon."

The group of four practically bowed, giving the dowager her due. Diminutive and barely ninety-eight pounds soaking wet, Agatha Coldbath dominated any space she occupied. (Sam knew it was the A's in Agatha, which added up to a three, which explained the magnetic aura surrounding the elderly woman. The vowels in her full name added up to another three. Agatha Beatrice Coldbath was not a woman to be ignored.)

Dressed in her double-breasted woolen Chesterfield coat with the black velvet collar and sturdy black shoes and clutching her worn but expensive black leather bag firmly under one arm, Agatha Coldbath said, "I expect to see you at the meeting tomorrow night, Samantha."

The Keep Our Berry Bogs Clean Committee was meeting for one last time before the Cowberry Fall Fair, and Sam, appointed to the Presidency by the doyenne herself, was expected to attend the KOBBCC (although Agatha would never stoop to using the abbreviation). Sam knew there was no need to answer, so she nodded dutifully. Now that she had been chosen by the childless Agatha to one day receive the Coldbath Cowberry Chutney secret recipe, Sam's appearance was a command performance. This was the recipe that supported Georgetown's economy by providing jobs at the state-of-the-art chutney plant, from which jars of chutney were shipped around the world. The plant also supplied Georgetown's tourist trade; every day of the year, garlands of cowberries festooned every fence, lamp post, and store front in town. One day, Georgetown's future would rest on Sam's reluctant shoulders. Sam knew her responsibilities.

Ever the diplomat, Nick offered his hand. "You're looking very well, Agatha."

Agatha took his strong hand in her arthritic one. She lifted her chin and said, "Thank you, Nicholas. I am just fine."

May you live forever, Sam prayed, thinking that that sentiment was prompted by her fear of running Coldbath Industries. In reality, even though Agatha was troublesome, hard-headed, stubborn, and opinionated, the woman meant more to Sam than she wanted to admit.

Two peas in a pod, Nick had said half-jokingly when Sam, in an exasperated mood, had related her feelings about the elderly Ms. Coldbath. Sam's denial did not cloud the truth however, and she finally had to admit to owning some of Agatha's traits herself. She often told clients that we (the generic 'we' so as not to cast aspersions) often dislike in others what we sublimate within ourselves. Perhaps that's what was meant by the saying, "bless your enemies," Sam reasoned, for these troublesome individuals are a mirror reflection of our own inner worlds, exhibiting traits we need to examine.

The more Sam had pondered the concept of her own weaknesses over the years, the less irritating Agatha had become. But still…

"Where is Mrs. Vandalay?" Agatha inquired. "I want to offer my condolences." She never bothered to look around because her view of the crowd was at most people's chest and shoulder blade levels.

"The last I saw of her," Nick offered, "she was headed for the house."

"Would you excuse me, please?" Clarence said. "I see our Selectman over there, and I wanted to speak with him about a troublesome stain on his good suit." He bowed out and left.

Giving Nick a quick look, Sam also excused herself and slipped away before Nick, Charlie, or Agatha had time to respond. She wended her way through knots of bodies, following Clarence's trail, when a reporter sidelined her. When the aggressive young woman realized she would get nothing from the taciturn Samantha Blackwell, she flitted off to find easier prey.

Sam then sidled past a glowering Tony Vernelli and his large-chested, bird-like wife. At the edge of the tent, Sam stood partially concealed behind some potted fronds, most likely brought by the caterers. The fronds reminded her of the classic movie, *Casablanca*.

Clarence was nowhere in sight. But Sam could see Katherine Vandalay leading a large, rather rumpled, man around the front of the house and up the wide verandah steps.

CHAPTER 27

If Berma had to listen to any more drivel, she would scream. Candy had been bubbling on about the food, the size of the mansion, the grounds, what the women were wearing—all the while tugging at her thigh-high black skirt with her left hand and balancing a third glass of champagne with her right. Her hemline had not escaped the eyes of most of the men present as well as the women, albeit for different reasons.

"Do I look alright, Berma? Really?"

"Really, Candy. You look fine. Relax and enjoy yourself." She nudged her son's arm and said, "Kenny, why don't you get Candy a plate of food?"

Before she gets drunk and makes fools of us all, she wanted to add. Berma had plans other than standing around discussing her daughter-in-law's wardrobe—what there was of it. She reached into the pocket of her jacket to reassure herself the photographs were still there, then ran her hands over the smooth fabric on her hips. She was pleased with the cranberry sweater and black suit she had picked up yesterday at the mall.

Just then, Berma noticed Anthony Vernelli standing behind his wife at the food table. One of the worker's wives was passing when Tony turned slightly, and with a hand lowered and hidden from view (or so he thought), pinched the young woman's rear. The woman flinched, then straightened up as a little smile curled her pale tinted lips.

Berma smiled. Tony and his latest paramour should have been more discreet. Lipstick-coated cigarette butts were a dangerous thing for a married man to leave in his office ashtray. The suspicions Berma had thrown at Tony in the office were proven true when he verbally accosted her at the mall parking lot. Berma had Tony by the tail and was loving it.

But today, Tony wasn't the object of her mission. She was going to have a woman-to-woman talk with the mistress of the mansion, Katherine Anne Vandalay, and finally get balm for old wounds.

"Candy," Berma said, smiling at her daughter-in-law, "I'm going to mingle a little."

Candy mumbled something into her champagne as Berma barreled into the crowd. Kenny returned with two plates of food and handed one to his wife. While Candy tottered with her food plate and champagne glass, Kenny, his arm tightly around his wife's waist, ushered her to one of the linen-covered tables set up around the perimeter of the tent. He hadn't liked the looks Tony was throwing at Candy, and if Tony didn't quit it, well…he'd take the guy out if he had to.

Kenny set his plate down, eased his wife onto a chair and dropped into the seat next to her. He pulled a pack of cigarettes from his shirt pocket, and said, "Honey, maybe you should take it easy on the champagne." He hesitated, his heart thumping in his ears. "What if you're pregnant?"

Some of the sparkling liquid spilled over the rim of Candy's glass as she plopped it on the table. With a slightly slurred voice, she said, "Pregnant? What ever gave you that idea, Kenny? I'm not pregnant, and I'm fine. Isn't this a great party?" She blinked and gave Kenny a cock-eyed smile. "Do I look alright, honey? Really?"

Kenny started breathing again. He lit his cigarette, took a deep drag, blew out the smoke, and leaned in toward her. "You're beautiful. You're the most beautiful woman here." He dropped the match on the corner of his dinner plate.

Candy giggled. "You always say that."

"Because it's true," he said. Filled with relief at the good news, Kenny leaned back as his eyes move nervously over the crowd. His right knee was jiggling involuntarily. The movement sent vibrations through the table, causing the champagne to dance in its glass.

Candy reached into the slim purse slung on a narrow strap over her shoulder and pulled out a compact. She stared at her reflection for many minutes, her mouth partially open. Then she flipped the compact shut, put it back in her purse, and took another mouthful of champagne.

A sudden burst of wind off the ocean ruffled Kenny's straw-colored hair. Candy's hand flew to her head where she patted at the blonde spikes.

Kenny laid his cigarette on the corner of his plate, then took both his wife's hands in his. "Candy, sweetheart, relax. You look fine. If you keep worrying, you're going to miss all the fun. How often do we get to go to something like this?"

At that thought, a dark cloud passed over his face. He loosened her hands and sat back in his chair. "I could never give you anything like this."

Candy stared hard at Kenny for a full minute.

Then she reached out, took his hand, and pulled him closer to her. Her eyes filled with tears. "Kenny," she said, "don't you know how much I love you? Don't you know there will never be another guy for me besides you? You and the kids are my life, and if we have to live in that trailer for the rest of our lives, I'll be happy because I'm with you. All I ever wanted was you, from the first time I saw you in high school. I've been crazy about you since our first date, and I'll love you 'til the day I die."

Kenny was stunned. He had never heard such an outpouring from his wife. He had always thought she wanted more—more clothes, expensive jewelry, better furniture, a bigger house and car, a handsome husband she could show off.

Unable to control the flood of emotions sweeping over him, his eyes filled to overflowing. He bent his head and covered her hands with kisses. When, finally, he looked up at the woman of his dreams, he saw a secretive little smile on her sweet face. "And Kenny," she added, "I've known from the beginning that you poked holes in those condoms back in high school."

A few steps away, camouflaged behind a table bearing an enormous vase of white lilies and ebony orchids, Berma Battles heard it all.

CHAPTER 28

✿

The cologne he wore seemed a stark contrast to his disheveled appearance.

Katherine stood in the large foyer of her home with her arms folded across her chest. She felt herself trembling. "What do you want?"

"What I've always wanted, Katy," Gene Meeker slobbered, stepping closer to his stepdaughter. He reached out with a coarse hand to stroke her cheek, but she pushed his arm away and stepped backward.

His face contorted, making his nose seem almost clown-like amidst the draping flesh of his cheeks. Alcohol and cruelty had left its imprint on that face. The sixteen years since Katherine had last seen her stepfather had not been kind to him.

"You'd better be nice to me, Katy. Not like the last time I saw you. You left a pretty big bump on my head that night." He snorted, sort of bemused, as his hand felt the spot. "And then you stole all my money. That wasn't nice."

"So it was you who took the stone from my bedroom," she accused.

"Yes, it was, my pretty girl. You looked so beautiful laying there in the moonlight, I wanted to take you right there. But I knew I had to be strong. I did get some good shots with my camera, though." He hesitated, as if savoring the moment. "I also wrote KATY on your clever little suspect list. I found that in the library. I wanted to get your attention. And I did. Pretty clever, huh, Katy Thayer?"

Katherine drew herself up. "My name is Katherine Vandalay!"

Gene's eyes became slits. "Don't put on airs with me, Katy Thayer. You and I are more alike than you think."

Katy wanted to smash his face in, but Katherine said evenly, "If it's money you want, I'll pay you back. Every cent. With interest."

Gene made a point of looking around the foyer, then he tilted his head to glance into the living room behind her. "I may want a lot more than that," he said, his gaze returning to slide over her silk suit. "You want to pay back the money you stole from me with *just* interest? Looks like you can afford a lot more than that, my *Katy.*" He emphasized the name. "Yeah. It's going to take a lot more than interest to satisfy me."

In the brief silence that followed, Katherine stared at the alcohol-ravaged face before her, wondering what to do. From outside, she could hear laughter and the clinking of dishes and glassware above the music.

…the front door was still open.

She went quickly and shut the door. For a moment, she just stood there, her hand still on the knob, her back against the heavy wood. Everything had been going exactly as she planned. Gene could spoil everything—everything she had worked so hard for, given up so much for. She would be ruined. She couldn't let that happen. She would do whatever was necessary to get rid of him.

In a surprisingly even voice, she said, "What exactly do you want?"

Gene Meeker shifted his weight onto one foot and stuck his hands into the pockets of his rumpled gabardine slacks. He looked gaunt under a navy polo shirt with a frayed collar.

"Now that's more like my Katy."

A quick smile revealed uneven yellow teeth; the right incisor was missing. Even after sixteen years, his breath still had the same sour smell. Katherine's loathing for him filled every cell of her body.

She didn't resist when he took her by the arm and led her into the living room. "We might as well be comfortable while we negotiate," he said.

Gene pushed her down on the white leather sofa. He sank onto the cushion right next to her, his knee touching her gray pants suit, then put his arm around her shoulders.

"Isn't this comfy?" he said, as he pulled her against his chest and nuzzled his scrubby chin into her hair.

Shaking off the revulsion that threatened to immobilize her, Katherine jerked herself away. She stood up, straightening her jacket as she rose.

"If you want to talk, we'll talk, but keep your hands off me."

She sat on the edge of the matching white leather chair, soldier straight, feet planted on the floor, hands knotted in her lap.

Gene gave her a look suggesting a coiled spring about to snap, but then settled back against the cushion. "Everything in good time," he said, as he leered at her, his gaze stopping pointedly at her breasts. Then he looked up into her violet eyes and shook his head. "The things I've done for you, Katy."

"Look," Katherine said. "I have guests to attend to. Can we discuss this after the service?"

Gene threw a look over his shoulder, out the front windows. "Hey. This is a great party. How come I wasn't invited? Not good enough for my Katy?"

Tired of his games, Katherine said, "How did you find me?" She was trying not to scream.

"A private investigator. It took a while but he finally traced you to this area. Then he happened to see you in Market Square. Wasn't he lucky? Well, then again, maybe he wasn't so lucky." He laughed. It was a cold, heartless sound that curdled Katherine's blood.

"You know, Katy. You haven't changed that much since you were a kid. You're still beautiful. And by the way, you're going to pay me back for the investigator's services, too. I spent a lot of time and money tracking you down."

With her body nearing collapse, Katherine had to find out one more thing before she settled this matter. "Where's my mother?"

The corners of Gene's mouth drooped in mock sadness. "Sweet Mary. She drowned in the bathtub, under her cherry bubbles, with a bottle of wine in her hand. I was watching a ball game and never heard a thing." His eyes told a different story. "The police ruled it an accidental drowning. But if you ask me, the bitch deserved it, whoring around with the store manager. She broke her marriage contract. You know how I feel about broken contracts, don't you, Katy?"

Katherine drew in a sharp breath and looked down at her white-knuckled hands. She knew Gene had murdered her mother, probably in a drunken rage, when he found her sleeping with another man.

What did Katherine feel? Loss? Sorrow? The need for retribution? Strangely enough, she felt nothing for the woman who had given her life. Her mother was a nonentity, letting a string of men like Gene dictate her life, allowing one of them to almost molest her daughter, and ultimately, becoming the victim of his rage.

Katherine couldn't hold back any longer. Something inside her snapped. She leaped up so violently, she knocked a shepherd figurine off the end table. It smashed onto the parquet floor, sending up a shower of porcelain splinters. Katy never noticed.

"Get out of my house, you filthy drunk! Get out and don't ever come back or I'll kill you!" The little vein over her eyebrow pulsed, the cords on her neck stood out in bas relief.

Gene Meeker tilted his head, giving her a lopsided, gummy smile. He deliberately waited a long minute before saying, "You don't want to do that, Katy. I have some revealing photos of you, safe and sound in a rental box. I'm staying at the Comfort Inn in Portsmouth. If you don't call by nine o'clock tonight, I'm calling the newspapers. I'm sure they'd love to know more about the fancy Mrs. Vandalay. I can just see those photos splashed over the front page of all the papers. What would your fancy friends think of Katy then, huh?"

Photos? My God! What kind of photos could he have? Katherine began to panic.

Gene's image became a blur. It was as if she couldn't see. Then her anger burst out in searing red waves. Blindly, she lashed out, some primal part of her brain screaming attack!.

"I said, get out!" She shook her fist at him. "I mean it! I'll kill you, you bastard! I have money, and money can buy anything! So you'd better get your filthy rotten self out of my house and out of this town."

Gene sat motionless for five seconds, then lunged for Katherine. He bumped his knee against the glass coffee table and fell, his head bouncing off the beveled corner.

His arm swiped ineffectually at her. "Come here, you little slut!" His voice broke with intensity. "You still owe me a roll in the hay."

Katherine screamed over her shoulder. "I'll see you in hell first!" And with that, she tore out of the room.

Gene sat on the floor, his back against the white sofa, and touched his forehead. He looked at the red smear on his shaking fingers as pinpoints of light jiggled before his eyes.

CHAPTER 29

✤

"Samantha! Why are you lurking in the shrubbery?"

Sam whirled around to find Agatha Coldbath on her heels. "What? Oh." She began to finger the little hollow at the base of her throat as a flush crept up her cheeks. "I wasn't lurking, Agatha. I was observing."

During her "observations," Samantha was visited once again by the vision of the *floating dead man*. He beckoned her with decomposing arms. Only this time, there was another figure in the background: a rumpled silhouette, waving a gun in a bony hand. Somehow the spectral figure reminded her of the man who had followed Katherine Vandalay into the house.

A chill wormed its way into Sam's spinal column and crept out through her back and arms. She hugged her chest, glad now that she had worn the long-sleeved black sweater. She was absolutely certain that someone in addition to Henry Vandalay had been murdered. It was someone linked to the crime, and she sensed that the act had taken place near water or that the body had been dumped into water. Sam didn't know why the dead man was reaching out to her, but she had learned not to question the visions that had come to her since childhood.

She was yanked back to the present by the sound of Agatha's voice.

The white hairs above the old woman's top lip quivered as she said, "We will not quibble about semantics today, Samantha." Even though

Agatha's voice seemed filled with disdain, a look that might be inter-
preted as concern, flitted across her wrinkled face. "You seem distracted.
Is something wrong?"

"No. Yes. I mean…" Sam looked around to be sure no one was listening. The gaggle of voices competing with the chamber music ensured
that no one could hear what they were saying. Sam and Agatha stood
several feet away from the nearest guests.

"Well, girl, what do you mean?"

Sam felt beads of moisture under her fingertips as she brushed a
loose strand of hair off her forehead and tucked it into the scrunchie. If
anyone could keep information locked "in the vault," it was Agatha
Beatrice Coldbath.

Sam leaned in. The clean smell of Agatha's perennial aloe soap
drifted into her nostrils. "I'd appreciate it if you wouldn't say anything
about this…" She took a big breath. "Katherine Vandalay hired me to
prove she didn't kill her husband."

Agatha's wispy brows raised in unison and her thin lips tightened
before she said, "I see. I hope this will not interfere with the Cowberry
Festival."

Sam's jaw muscles tightened. "No, of course not, Agatha. I have that
under control."

The old woman stared at her for a moment, looked her up and down
as if she were observing a store mannequin, then appeared satisfied.

Knowing that Agatha didn't approve of her usual wardrobe of sweat-
shirts, Sam thought she must have passed the dress code muster. She
silently thanked Caroline for the shopping excursion to the mall.
Surprised when a tiny curl of pleasure graced the corner of her lip, she
felt like a five-year old basking in her mother's approval.

Agatha said, "I take it you were…observing that rather disheveled
gentleman Mrs. Vandalay ushered into her home."

Sam nodded. She was beyond wondering how diminutive Agatha had seen through the clumps of bodies and shrubbery to observe a scene that only lasted about two minutes.

Agatha finally said, "How can I help?"

Sam felt herself relaxing. "What do you know about Henry Vandalay?"

Before she spoke, Agatha appeared to sort through her mental files. "As you probably know, I hired Mr. Vandalay two years ago to add an addition onto the Coldbath Chutney plant. The man had impeccable credentials. He was a meticulous craftsman and he monitored his work-men carefully. I knew his shortcomings, but I felt that I could handle any improprieties. I do not wish to speak ill of the dead. Suffice it to say, I would not have hired him again."

"You would not be speaking ill of the dead, Agatha," Sam said, "You would be speaking the truth about your experience with Henry Vandalay. A woman's life may hang in the balance here. If you know something that could help with this investigation, please tell me."

Agatha looked down at the glass in her arthritic hand. "I am not sure I have anything to offer that would aid in your investigation. Mr. Vandalay did his job and was paid."

"Please..." Sam said.

Agatha took in a breath, her frail shoulders lifting and settling with the effort. After a brief pause, she relented. "I believe Mr. Vandalay tried to cheat me out of many thousands of dollars for that contract. If it had not been for his secretary..."

Sam interrupted. "You mean Berma Battles?"

"Yes. Mrs. Battles. She caught the error. In fact, I was about to call Mr. Vandalay's office when the phone rang and it was Mrs. Battles. She explained they had made an error and she would send me a corrected bill. Now that I think of it, she said Mr. Vandalay had made the error. He seemed very angry the next day, and he avoided me for the rest of the week."

"And you think that Mr. Vandalay was angry at Berma for revealing the error?"

"That thought did cross my mind."

"And you think the error was intentional?"

"I am afraid I do." Agatha took a sip of her champagne, then dabbed at her whiskered top lip with a small napkin. "I understand that Mr. Vandalay and Mrs. Battles had a number of disagreements over the years."

Agatha paused for a moment. Sam was sure the CIA had installed a red phone in Miss Coldbath's private study for easier access to her vast reaches of information.

"From what I have heard," Agatha took up her story again, "Mrs. Battles is very efficient, but given the dislike she and Mr. Vandalay seemed to have for each other, I was never sure why he kept her on as an employee or why she stayed."

Sam wondered that, too. She also wondered what Berma and her employer argued about, and if Berma could have gotten angry enough with Henry Vandalay to kill him.

CHAPTER 30

✿

"I just love your books!" Maria Vernelli gushed at Sam. "I've read all of them."

"Thank you, Maria," Sam said. Her mind was elsewhere. Right then, she would have loved to be eavesdropping under the Vandalay living room window. "That's always wonderful to hear."

Agatha had been bundled off by one of the Selectmen, leaving Sam behind the potted fronds staring at the mansion. Sam was wondering what Katherine and the odd-looking stranger were doing inside. The man certainly wasn't dressed for this occasion.

Undeterred, Maria went on, her small hands working like those of an interpreter for the deaf. "Understanding the numbers, plus your columns, has helped me tremendously with my Tarot classes."

Sam swung her full attention on the diminutive woman. Maria was pretty. Her dark hair fell in soft short curls around an oval face. Rosy cheeks were complimented by rose-colored lips.

"I'm sorry," Sam said. "I was deep in thought. I do appreciate your interest in my work. Umm…did you say Tarot classes?"

Pleased, Maria bobbed her head.

"By any chance, does Ula Vandalay attend your class?" Sam asked.

"Why, yes!" Maria said. "She's been coming to class for about two years, right after she moved here." Her hands were getting a workout now. "She's a quiet sort. She hasn't said more than two words since I met her. She comes to class, listens, and leaves. I don't know anyone who's heard her speak more than a sentence since she moved here. I hear she never leaves the house, except for our classes."

And visits to the dry cleaners, Sam thought. *She is fastidious.*

"She's quite the recluse," Maria added.

Sam's mental wheels were spinning. "It would appear so." She struggled for a way to introduce her next thought, then said, "The Tarot is a fascinating study."

Maria's eyes lit up. "Yes, it is." Her hand flew to her ample bosom. "I'm the Queen of Cups, and my Life Lesson card is the Three of Wands. What do you think that means?"

Sam laid a hand on the woman's slim arm. "I'm sure, with your years of study, you know more about that than I do. My forte is numerology."

She paused, took a breath, then said, "Isn't it a shame that the Tarot cards were placed at the scene of Mr. Vandalay's death. It seems such a sacrilege to use the Tarot in such a way."

Maria didn't miss a beat. "Oh, I agree. I was horrified when I heard about that." Both hands were now clutched against her chest. "Who would do such a thing?"

Who, indeed?

"Does your husband support your study of the Tarot?" Sam asked.

"Oh, you know men," Maria said, with a quick wave of her hand. "Tony is all muscle and hard work. He said he doesn't have time for such foolishness." She sort of laughed. "But he lets me go, so I should be grateful for that."

Lets her go? Sam wasn't going to get into that one. "So, Maria, I hope you're feeling better. I heard you were quite ill."

Maria looked perplexed.

"Did I hear wrong?" Sam said. "I heard Tony was late for work the morning Mr. Vandalay died because you were ill."

"Oh, that." Maria tossed her head and laughed. "No. I wasn't ill. I had a hangover." She seemed embarrassed. "I don't usually drink, but Tony was quite amorous the night before." Her face reddened. "He called me from work and told me to cook a good meal because he had a surprise. He brought home a bottle of wine and a beautiful bouquet of flowers. Red and white carnations, my favorite. We had a wonderful romantic evening, just like when we first met. He rarely does anything like that. It *was* quite a surprise."

A shiver went through Sam as she thought about Tony Vernelli in a romantic embrace.

"Are you cold?" Maria asked, a concerned look on her face.

"Oh, no. Thank you, Maria. I was just thinking…"

She was thinking about Tony bringing that bottle of wine home. Did he deliberately get his wife drunk so he could slip out during the night undetected? Did he plan to meet Henry Vandalay on some pretext and then knife him in the back? Tony had access to Maria's Tarot cards and books. He was an intelligent man, she had to give him that. It wouldn't have taken much for him to learn about the Keltic Cross, then select specific cards to get his message across. But why would Tony Vernelli kill Henry Vandalay? Tony had a good job. You don't kill the goose that supplies you with golden eggs.

CHAPTER 31

Ula ran her hand over the dress.

The candlelight from her closet altar sent iridescent streams over the material as it moved under her touch. Soon, she would slip into this new garment, just as she would slip into a new life.

Her new life. She could hardly believe how things had turned out. She was finally free!

She dropped her hands to her sides and turned toward the altar. The two white candles flickered, as if her emotions had stirred them. A smile welled up behind her eyes.

Her Tarot cards.

A defiant gesture against the father who had told her these pursuits were evil and ordered her never to speak of such things again. She remembered the beating she got shortly after the trip to the Red Sox game in Boston, when he found her paperback on psychic development under her mattress. Because of that incident, she had totally closed down during her teenage years.

And then, seven years later, when her father was thrown from a horse and lay dying in the hospital, she had thought she was free. But Hank, who had the same domineering personality as her father, had stepped into his shoes. Ula found it easier to snuff out the light that had begun to stir within her and revert to her old ways. The submissive female.

Many years later, when her mother had become so ill and was confined to her shabby bedroom on their farm, Hank had left to come east to start his business. He promised to send for Ula. That's when she had made the life-altering decision.

She had marched into the only bookstore in the small town, headed straight for the occult section, and plunked the Tarot book and deck of cards on the counter in front of Mr. Simmons. He slid his round spectacles up on his balding forehead and tented his brows. Her reading material up to this point had been mysteries. Mr. Simmons knew her father. But when he had seen the look on her face, he never said a word. Ula kind of regretted that. For the first time in her life, she had been ready to do battle, and no one took up the call.

Ula had immersed herself in the cards, spending days at a time studying just one. Those months had been her happiest since that trip years ago to the Boston Red Sox game.

Ula shook her shoulders. She had finally beaten her father. Her Tarot cards were a symbol of her freedom from the years of repression and fear. She had won, after all. She threw her head back and laughed.

Now it was time to get dressed for the ceremony.

As she slipped out of her black skirt, that uneasy feeling she'd been having came over her again, the sense that Katherine had been snooping in her closet. It wasn't that anything had been disturbed. It was an awareness of someone else's energy in her space.

Ula's eyes narrowed as she clipped her skirt to a metal hanger. She hoped Katherine didn't think she could set her up for Hank's murder because, if she did, she had another think coming. Ula's cards told her she didn't have to worry about her closet altar. She felt confidant about that. But, she hadn't thought to consult the cards about Katherine's role in the events of the last few weeks. She'd do that after the services and before the reading of the will.

Ula could hear the muted strains of music and conversation from the gathering on the front lawn. She had to get down there soon. She'd make a dramatic entrance, and when she had their attention, she had something to tell them. Something that would shatter the poised *Mrs. Vandalay.*

*   *   *   *   *

Sam was telling Nick about her latest scoop and its ensuing implications when Ula emerged from the mansion.

Ula stood at the top of the wide verandah steps surveying the gathering. She never even noticed the man on the living room floor as she strode through the foyer on her way out the front door. She was too focused on her mission.

She inhaled the salty air as her black hair, now loose, lifted in the ocean breeze. Her lips were ruby, her cheeks a pink blush. Pale green highlights accentuated her sable eyes and complemented her lime hip-hugging dress with its low-cut V-neckline. Diamonds sparkled at her ears and a gold ring shone from her finger. Ula patted the small beaded bag hanging at her side. She felt wonderful.

It had been two years since Ula had gone into mourning. At that time, in a purple but silent rage, she had buried her mother in Utah, then packed up her clothes and dropped them off at a Salvation Army receptacle before moving to Rye. She had arrived at the mansion with an exclusively black wardrobe. This act was a statement of rebellion against Hank, underscoring her unspoken anger at his audacity in bringing another woman into their home. Hank knew her all too well back then, knew she wouldn't leave him no matter what he did.

But the past two years of Tarot classes, the hours spent studying the cards and performing the rituals in her closet, had given Ula the confidence to face the world on her own terms. She had proven to herself that she could take anything Hank Vandalay threw her way. Like the Charioteer in the Tarot, she had triumphed over her enemies. It was time to victoriously enter the city that now lay at her feet.

Her feet. The new heels she had picked up at Macy's felt tight and uncomfortable, but she'd endure the pain because it would elevate her another three inches when she stood before Katherine. Her feet were practically wedged into the damned things—like Cinderella's stepsisters trying on the tiny glass slipper.

As Ula tried to wiggle her cramped toes, tried to get her mind off the temporary discomfort, she thought about the ancient Chinese practice of binding the feet of girl babies, how the men left the women to the distasteful job of enduring their babies' tormented screams. Ula doubted that small feet as a sign of beauty was the only motivating force behind that barbaric ritual. It was more about keeping the women at home. You can't run when your feet are crippled and twisted.

Ula pressed her upper arms against her sides so her breasts were more prominent, pasted on a smile, silently rehearsed her short speech one more time, then began her descent into the crowd.

*   *   *   *   *

Sam grabbed Nick's arm.

"Nick! Look! I can't believe it." Sam's eyes resembled Little Orphan Annie's as her voice rose above the music and the din of voices around them.

Nick, ever the diplomat, lowered his head and said in a quiet but restrained voice, "Please, Sam, keep your voice down. What is it?"

Sam, speechless for one of the few times in her life, could only point.

Nick needn't have worried about his wife's reaction because all heads were now turned toward the front of the Vandalay mansion. As the last conversations died out, the musicians, realizing something was going on, stopped mid-measure and looked quizzically at one another.

As if Moses were approaching, the throngs parted. Ula Vandalay glided through on her way to the dais upon which the musical ensemble sat frozen.

Sam's eyes swung toward Katherine Vandalay who hadn't moved a false eyelash. A small hors d'oeuvre plate hung in her hand, her sentence to an admiring Senator stuck in her throat.

Ula stepped up onto the raised platform and reached for the microphone. She was stunning.

A palpable silence fell over the crowd—a silence broken only by a passing car, a gull croaking in the distance as it swooped down toward the white-capped waves, and the sloshing of the ocean as it met the shore in a wet embrace.

As Ula's small hands wrapped around the microphone, it seemed as if everyone's breath hung in abeyance, awaiting the words about to issue from this enigma of a woman.

"Good afternoon," she said in her sweet, childlike voice. She cleared her throat. "Thank you for coming. I hope you will be very generous with your contributions in my husband's memory."

CHAPTER 32

Husband!

The woman had finally lost her mind!

Katherine Vandalay's fury was red-hot, even as a cold chill pounded down her spine. She felt assailed from all sides: Gene in the house threatening to reveal her past, Ula in some outrageous costume, making ridiculous announcements just to embarrass her, the press waiting for her slightest mistake. A scarlet flush crept up her cheeks as all eyes swung toward her.

Her successful celebration teetered on the brink of a precipice, threatening to fall into a chasm of ridicule and failure. If Katherine let that happen, she would be the butt of jokes for years. She couldn't, no, she *wouldn't* let that happen. She would take care of Gene later. More urgent was Ula. She had to be dealt with immediately...but gently.

Katherine's brain cells went into overdrive.

Gently.

If Katherine expressed compassion and support for Henry's unstable and grieving sister, she would be the heroine. The community would accept her as the gracious and understanding wife of a prominent businessman who had to deal not only with her own grief, but handle her loopy sister-in-law as well.

Slowly, Katherine Vandalay moved toward the platform, following Ula's same path through the sea of people. Her face registered compassion and understanding. "Ula, dear, come with me. You must be tired. We'll go into the house and you can lie down for a while."

Ula, now eye level with Katherine because of her position on the small platform—and her three-inch heels—cocked a crooked smile. "But I'm not the least bit tired, Katherine, dear. In fact, I have never felt more energized in my life."

Katherine's eyes moved briefly over the motionless audience as she tried to assess their reaction. Reaching for Ula's hand, Katherine's voice was liquid silk. "Please, Ula. Come with me. Your brother's death has been far too much for you to handle."

Ula's knuckles, on the stem of the microphone, seemed about to break through the skin. She refused to take Katherine's hand. "Thank you, Katherine, for your concern," Ula said sweetly. "But you see, Henry was not my brother. Henry was my husband. And I have our marriage license right here in my handbag." She loosened her grip on the microphone and patted the small beaded bag at her side. "And this," she wiggled her ring finger bearing the simple gold band, "is the inscribed ring given me by my husband twenty-five years ago. So, you see, dear Katherine, you were never legally married to Henry Vandalay. You were merely his mistress."

* * * * *

Berma Battles felt like laughing...hysterically. It really shouldn't be funny, but somehow it was. Here she was with a document in her jacket pocket, a document that would expose Henry Vandalay for the man he truly was, and along comes Ula with another document that just knocked the socks off the congregation. The man really was a piece of work!

Too many emotions played in Berma's head. She wanted public retribution, wanted it badly…but at whose expense? Was she willing to hurt
the ones she loved, make laughingstocks out of them because of her
own selfish pride? She didn't think so. Especially now. After hearing
Candy's proclamation of love for her son, Berma's heart had melted like
chocolate in the August sun.

And that thing about poking holes in the condoms. The sudden realization that *Kenny* thought he had tricked Candy into marrying him
and that Candy kept his secret was Berma's moment of epiphany. Candy
was a perfect mate for Kenny. She adored her husband and she was a
good mother. And she deserved better treatment than Berma had given
her over the years. Berma vowed to herself that Candy would get better
from now on. There was a lot of making up to do.

The document in Berma's pocket proving that Kenny was Henry
Vandalay's son—the result of a summer fling many years ago between a
trusting young girl and a worldly man—would stay where it was. Berma
would feel out Ula Vandalay and see where things were going from
there. But she would not embarrass her son and his family in public.

Suddenly, her shoulders slumped. What had she become? As her need
for revenge ebbed, she thought about her years of anger, and how that
anger could have destroyed her family. Berma decided that when she got
home tonight, she would dump the contents of the secret box hidden
under the sofa in her living room. She was through hurting others.

CHAPTER 33

❀

"You bitch!" Gene Meeker bellowed.

He waved his gun in the air as he battered his way through the star-tled crowd. A woman screamed. People fell back. "You're not going to get away with breaking our contract! I'll have you and your money, too."

Katherine gasped. Her world was falling apart. The sea of faces around her blurred into one gigantic wave of stunned looks as she stared straight into the mad eyes of her attacker.

Gene grabbed her, spun her around, and pulled her hard against his body, his purple-veined nose and foul breath just inches from her ear. Sweeping the gun over the crowd, he yelled, "Don't anyone move!"

No one did.

Katherine tried to catch her breath as Gene's arm tightened against her chest "You slut," he growled into her ear. "You took my fifteen hun-dred dollars and left me with a knob on my skull. It took me sixteen years to find you and I'm cashing in. I didn't kill that bastard for noth-ing. You owe me."

Without warning, Katherine threw back her head, smashing it into Meeker's nose. He yowled, let her go, and stumbled back, his free hand clutching at his nose.

Katherine had gone only two steps when he ordered, "Stop!"

She turned, as if in slow motion, her heart flapping like a wild caged thing. She said in a voice that sounded far away, "Look, Gene. We can settle this peacefully." She saw her arms spread open, her palms facing up. "You don't have to use that gun."

Gene wiped blood from his nose, looked at his hand, then held his palm up, facing Katherine. His eyes grew narrow as he said, "Three strikes and you're out." Then he laughed, his eyes reflecting years of rage and hate. "I realize now that you're nothing but trailer trash like your old lady. And you're gonna die just like her." He leveled the gun at Katherine. "So, get set to meet your mommy. On the count of three. One...two..."

It was then that Charlie, who had steadily slipped behind the terrified guests, leaped out and took Gene Meeker to the ground. As if awakened from a long sleep, the crowd screamed and scattered in all directions.

Nick grabbed Sam's arm, pulled her behind a potted urn, and threw her to the grass. He covered her with his body.

Gene still had hold of the gun. As Gene and Charlie wrestled on the ground, the gun went off between them. Sam, peering around the base of the urn, felt her heart stop. She held her breath.

The two men slumped over and fell silent.

That's when Sam screamed.

CHAPTER 34

❀

"What the hell is going on!" Nick said, as Sam flopped on the sleigh bed in the Vandalay mansion. "We have a crazy man attempting to kill Katherine, Ula claiming she is not Henry Vandalay's sister, but his wife, another dead body, and we still don't know who killed Vandalay."

"I have no clue," Sam said, spread-eagled and staring at the ceiling. Nick plunked himself into the stuffed chair by the window and scowled. "Thank God Charlie wasn't hurt," Sam added. She had almost recovered from the horror of that possibility.

Gene Meeker was dead.

His body had been carted off. The local police had taken Charlie's statement, as well as those of hundreds of corroborating witnesses. Katherine claimed she had no idea who the man was. He had crashed the celebration; he must have been crazy.

It was now hours later. Katherine and Ula were in their respective rooms. Charlie had retired to his bedroom to call Brun on his cell phone. He didn't want her hearing some distorted version of what had just happened. They were all awaiting Attorney Herman T. Lawlor's arrival for the reading of Henry Vandalay's will.

"Even though Katherine claims she didn't know this Meeker guy," Nick continued, "she must have. He was raving about her mother being trailer trash and something about breaking contracts."

"It must be something from her past that she doesn't want anyone to know," Sam said. "And these events certainly put a new light on things. Like, why did this guy suddenly turn up now? Katherine's had money these past two years. Why didn't he come forward two years ago?"

"Maybe he just found out," Nick said.

"Possible." Sam tossed her shoes on the floor and wiggled her toes. "Do you suppose Meeker had help? Maybe that's where my vision of the floating dead man comes from. Maybe he's connected to Meeker."

"We may never know now," Nick said, as he followed Sam's lead and pulled off his shoes. He crossed his ankles on the hassock before him.

Sam said, "Do you suppose Katherine hired Meeker to kill her husband—that's if she was legally married to Vandalay?"

Nick shook his head, and stared out the window.

"And then," Sam continued, "there's Ula. Do you suppose she really is Henry's wife? If she is or was, do you suppose she killed Henry for his money? And what about Tony? Do you suppose he drugged his wife the night of the murder?"

"That's a lot of supposes, Sam."

Her mind swirled with questions. She folded her hands over her chest.

After a moment, Nick said, "If Ula is Henry's wife, and her claim is not the product of a demented mind, she has to be a sick puppy to endure that kind of treatment. I can't imagine a woman doing that."

"No, you couldn't, Nick. Look who you're married to."

Nick half smiled. "There is something in that."

"Believe me, Nick. There are women in this world who will take a lot from a man, especially if their security is threatened. And Ula is very security conscious. Remember the four in her first name. Her first unconscious reaction will always be self-preservation."

"Well," Nick said, "the reading of the will tonight should clear up the confusion around who the real Mrs. Vandalay is."

Sam nodded. "By the way, you cut quite the figure out there on the front lawn this afternoon. Have I told you lately you're my hero?"

Nick grinned. "That sounds like a good title for a song."

Sam blew him a kiss, and said, "However, you owe me a pair of panty hose."

Nick's dimple deepened. "Small price to pay for a little roll on the lawn."

But Sam didn't hear him. Her mind had already turned down another path of thinking. "Why do you suppose we say a pair of panty hose? We don't say a pair of sweaters. They both have two extensions."

Nick rolled his eyes toward the ceiling and leaned his head against the back of the chair.

When no enlightenment was forthcoming, Sam reached for the Tarot cards on the night stand.

"What are you doing now?" Nick asked.

"I don't know. I just want to lay out the Keltic Cross again, the same cards that were left next to Henry Vandalay. Now that things have changed, maybe I'll look at this in a different light. The killer must have left a clue in that layout. It's almost a compulsion with some of them to leave their signature. And the pictures on the Tarot cards evoke so much from the subconscious, I think it would be hard not to reveal something of yourself. That is, unless the killer just took the top eleven cards off the deck without any thought. But I don't think that happened. The cards that were left beside Vandalay tell a story, just as if they were pages in a small book."

Nick got up and crossed over to the bed. "Whatever. I'm going to take a nap." He dropped onto the bed and crossed his arms over his chest. "Call me if anyone else gets murdered." Seconds later, he was snoring softly.

Sam would never know how he did it.

Trying to get into the mind of the killer, Sam laid out the cards as he, or she, must have done beside the cold body of Henry Vandalay—with premeditation and precision. She studied each card as she placed them in the spread.

She leaned back into the pillows propped behind her and stared at the Keltic cross for many minutes.

"Talk to me," she said. She closed her eyes.

Her mind was so full of images and questions that for a moment she couldn't get a clear picture behind her lids. Then *he* emerged. The floating dead man. And he was pointing at two Tarot cards.

Sam's eyes snapped open! Could it be?

For the next half hour, she mulled over the images she had seen. A plan formulated in her mind. Could it work? She wasn't sure. But it was worthy trying.

Slipping quietly out of bed, she left her bedroom and crossed the hallway to Charlie's room.

When Charlie saw who it was, he ran a hand through his hair. "What is it, Sam? Another body?"

Sam ignored him. "Listen, Charlie. I've got an idea. I know it's a long shot but it's worth trying. Are you willing to play along?"

A glint appeared in Charlie's eye. "What do you have in mind, Sam?"

CHAPTER 35

❀

Katherine had escaped to her room after the police and guests left. Ula had then taken over, instructing the caterers to lay out the remaining food on the dining room table for the evening buffet. She requested that two servers return to clean up after 9:00.

Berma, Kenny, and Candy arrived first, followed ten minutes later by the ever-glowering Tony Vernelli and his wife, Maria.

Ula, seeming to relish her new-found role as mistress of the manor, greeted them graciously. She was still stunning in her lime dress. *What else would she be wearing?* Sam thought. *The rest of her wardrobe is black.*

Candy Ash was awestruck by the elegance of the old mansion. She kept tugging at Kenny's sleeve, pointing out one expensive item after another. Berma and Kenny seemed more interested in the buffet than the bibelots surrounding them.

Tony sat stiffly in a brocade chair by the front window, waiting and watching while his wife flitted from one invited guest to another. Maria kept voicing her wonder about why they were there in the first place. She seemed nervous and kept glancing at her husband.

Katherine had yet to show herself.

Sam noticed that Charlie had outdone himself with three helpings from the buffet. He was definitely feeling better, she thought happily, as she and Nick stood by the fireplace, each with a glass of wine in their hands.

As the clock chimed 7:00, the front door bell rang. A silence settled over the group as all eyes swung toward the foyer. Sam took advantage of the distraction to slip into the adjoining library.

Attorney Herman Lawlor was ushered into the room where he nodded greetings to the group, made a circuit of the room, and shook everyone's hand. Sam later told Nick she thought Lawlor was the spitting image of Teddy Roosevelt, albeit a bit thinner and minus the monocle. He was about forty, tanned, robust and bursting with energy.

"Please, everyone," Ula said, as Sam slipped unobtrusively back into the dining room. "Let's gather in the library. I'll get Katherine, and we'll join you shortly."

Like a scene from an Agatha Christie mystery, Sam thought, as the flutterbys attacked her stomach. She hoped that, as in Christie's often repeated plot lines, the killer of Henry Vandalay would be revealed this evening. The theatrical part of her wanted to stand in the middle of the library and say, "The killer is someone in this room."

Maybe she would. She grinned to herself. Unpredictability made life exciting.

The library smelled of leather and fresh flowers. Dark wooden floor-to-ceiling bookcases lined the four walls. Pristine volumes of the classics filled the shelves with surgical precision, interrupted only by small white busts of Plato, Shakespeare, the Pietà, and other notable figures. A gleaming walnut desk sat at the far end of the room. In front of the desk, comfortable dark green leather chairs and a sofa were arranged in a horseshoe pattern around a large coffee table, a slab cut from a huge tree and finished to a high gloss. From the end tables, fresh flowers punctuated the room.

But all eyes were drawn to the coffee table. It was bare except for a group of eleven Tarot cards laid out in the form of a Keltic Cross.

Sam watched as everyone silently took a seat. Berma, Kenny, and Candy sat to the left of the desk; Tony and Maria to the right. Sam and Nick seated themselves next to the Vernellis, while Charlie pulled a chair in from the dining room to sit a foot or so behind Sam and Nick. That left the leather sofa opposite the desk free for Ula and Katherine.

Sam knew the group had all seen the Tarot cards, but no one had said a word.

Lawlor positioned himself behind the desk in an impressive high-backed black leather chair, opened his briefcase, and pulled out a folder. From it, he drew out a sheaf of papers with a light blue outer cover. Then he sat back in the chair and folded his hands across his stomach. A somewhat restrained smile spread across his ruddy face. It seemed hard for him to reign in his natural exuberance.

"Relax, folks," he said. "This won't take long." He looked toward the doorway. "As soon as Katherine and Ula get here, we'll begin."

Maria fidgeted with the hem of her dress, tugging it down over her shapely knees. Tony hadn't moved a muscle since he'd lowered his wedge-shaped body into the chair closest to the desk. Under his one long black eyebrow, his eyes circled the room, appearing to assess everyone, but always coming back to the Tarot cards.

Candy had a death grip on Kenny's hand, while Berma avoided looking at the coffee table.

Sam felt her palms sweating. Something was going to happen. The suspense was almost palpable. She knew what the first half of that "something" was, but the second half was anybody's guess.

She looked around the room at the collection of unlikely guests: stolid, seemingly unruffable Berma; anemic, chain-smoking Kenny, who cradled the hand of his wide-eyed, star-struck wife; and the black eye-browed Tony the Tiger, who sat stonelike, seeming to take pleasure in ignoring his wife. Maybe Maria was used to being invisible in her husband's eyes, but, Sam thought, she did seem as nervous as a long-tailed cat in a room full of rockers.

Yup, Sam thought. *As eclectic a group of suspects as one could imagine.*

She had to wonder why Henry Vandalay would request these particular people be present at the reading of his will. Clearly, he wasn't enamored of his secretary. And for what possible reason would he ask two of his hired help and their wives to be present? Answers to these questions flickered at the back of her mind but they were all suppositions. She would just have to wait like all the others.

She knew that everyone in the room was hyped by the shooting on the front lawn a few hours earlier, and none of them would feel the residual effects until after the will had been read and they all went home to let the incredible events of the day sink in.

At that moment, Ula entered the room and seated herself in one corner of the wide leather sofa. Ula's breath caught in her throat when she saw the Tarot cards, but she never said a word.

A theatrical few moments later, Katherine swept into the room. Without speaking, she arranged herself at the far corner of the sofa from Ula and began turning her gold cigarette case in her hand. She never once looked at the woman whom she still believed to be her sister-in-law. Katherine's attention was fastened on Herman Lawlor.

Sam didn't see Katherine glance down at the coffee table. But Katherine might have seen the Tarot cards from the doorway and chose to ignore the spread.

Sam was counting on that kind of reaction from the group. They were all in sensory overload. The accumulation of tension from the death of Gene Meeker before their eyes hours earlier, and now the reading of a will that could change their lives forever, was all they could process. They couldn't handle any more surprises.

Besides, Sam reasoned, the only person who would care about the layout would be the killer. Sam would see to that. At least, that's what she hoped would happen.

Lawlor stirred in his seat, cleared his throat a few times, and said in a deep baritone, "I assume everyone is here." He looked up questioningly. Ula and Katherine nodded in assent.

"Well, then. Let's begin. I won't bore you with a lot of legalese. Just let it be known that this is the last will and testament of Henry Kenneth Vandalay and that he was of sound mind when he signed it. The document was legally witnessed and signed."

Tony's foot began to jiggle. Maria became as still as death. Ula and Katherine fixed their eyes on Lawlor, the space between the two women generating enough wattage to energize Boston for a day. Sam could almost feel the sparks.

Candy started to cough.

"Are you alright, honey?" Kenny asked, his brow furrowed.

"Yes," she said, trying to swallow. "I just need a drink of water." She coughed again, her hand over her mouth.

Out of habit, Katherine turned toward Ula and said, "Would you get our guest a glass of water?"

Ula glanced over her left shoulder, one dark eyebrow lifted. "Get it yourself, Katherine, dear."

Charlie jumped up. "I'll get it." He disappeared through the doorway.

The electricity in the room was now lifting the hairs on the back of Sam's neck. They all sat in crypt-like silence.

All eyes now seemed focussed on the Keltic Cross. The Tarot cards lay like an offering on a pagan sacrificial altar. But no one spoke.

Lilac perfume and Hypnotic Poison mingled with the cool, sweet smell of cut flowers. Sam felt heady. The prickles started. She pulled at the neck of her black sweater, praying to the powers that be that she didn't spontaneously combust.

Charlie returned and handed Candy the water. She thanked him, took a few sips, then wiped the bottom of the glass on her skirt before placing it on the end table beside her.

"There now," Lawlor said. "I guess we're ready."

There was a general rustling and intake of breath as the assembled group waited. Sam pulled a tissue from her skirt pocket, and trying to remain inconspicuous, dabbed at the rivulets starting down her forehead. She needn't have worried. The heartbeat of the room halted as every eye fastened on the lawyer.

"I'll get right to the nitty-gritty," Lawlor continued. "Please remember. These are Henry Vandalay's words, not mine." He took a breath, then said, "To Anthony Vernelli, I leave the sum of one dollar for the use of his wife."

Tony blanched. As the meaning sunk in, his eyes cut to his wife with such hate that she shrunk back as if he had physically struck her.

"Let it be known," Lawlor continued, "That if Maria Vernelli is assaulted in any manner, my attorney, Herman T. Lawlor, is to release to the press a letter I left in his possession concerning certain events in Mr. Vernelli's past. I am not a man who believes in violence against women."

A pin-stuck balloon couldn't have deflated more visibly than Tony, as he dissolved back into his chair.

My God, Sam thought. *So Maria was one of Henry's conquests. Surprises never cease.*

"Secondly," Lawlor read on, "to my son and only child, Kenneth Ash, I leave the sum of five hundred thousand dollars. In addition, to each of my grandchildren, I leave the sum of one hundred thousand dollars, to be used only for their education."

Kenny's mouth dropped open. Candy stared at the lawyer. Her skin paled. She looked about ready to pass out.

A frown wrinkled Lawlor's brow as he struggled to continue. He obviously found the will distasteful. "Upon the day that Kenneth divorces his wife, Candace Ploski, he will receive an additional two million dollars."

Kenny appeared comatose. His father was Henry Vandalay? Two million dollars to divorce his wife? If Sam was having a hard time processing this, she could only imagine what Kenny was going through. But

Berma seemed to have filtered it without a problem. She took Kenny's other hand and held it firmly.

"To Berma Battles," Lawlor read, "the mother of my only child, I leave the sum of five hundred thousand dollars."

The unflappable Berma Battles flinched.

At this point, Lawlor cleared his throat one time too many. He was more than a bit uncomfortable with what he was about to read, but he took another deep breath and plunged ahead.

"To my mistress, Katherine Thayer, I leave the sum of two hundred thousand dollars. One hundred thousand dollars for each of her two years of service."

At first, Katherine didn't move. The cigarette case fell still in her hand. Then, her body began to quiver. Her face, a mask of confidence to this point, flushed red with rage. She seemed unable to speak.

"And finally, to my wife, Ula, I leave the property in Rye and a monthly trust fund of twenty-five thousand dollars beginning with the month of my death.

"Vandalay Enterprises is to be sold, and the proceeds are to be distributed equally amongst the charities I have listed below."

"That is the bulk of it, folks," Lawlor said, folding the document and sitting back in his chair.

The catacombs of the Vatican could not have been more silent.

Strike while the iron's hot, Sam told herself.

With her heart in her throat, she leaned forward and said, "This is the Tarot spread that was left beside Mr. Vandalay's body."

Incredulous, disbelieving, shocked eyes locked on her. Even though he was privy to the game, Nick tensed beside her.

"I've been studying this layout for some time," she said, "and I found, hidden in the spread of these cards, a clue to the killer of Mr. Vandalay."

Taking advantage of the disoriented silence, she waded in deeper. "You see, the killer has a brilliant mind. At a subconscious level, this brilliant mind wants recognition. This is shown by the specific cards chosen for this spread."

Pop psychology, Sam thought. But, in some cases, it was true. At least, according to the books she had read. "So, you see…" Sam hesitated for the effect "she left us a message in these cards."

"She?" Tony exclaimed hoarsely, then cast a glance at his wife. Berma scratched the side of her neck.

"Yes. She," Sam said.

Katherine's left eye began quivering. Ula remained motionless except for restless fingers that twisted at her wedding band.

Herman Lawlor leaned forward, his hands folded on the desk before him. He was straining to see the cards. Curiosity had overcome propriety.

Sam pointed at one of the cards. "When I first saw the Queen of Cups here in the layout, I thought only of the literal meaning of the card. Then it dawned on me that the card can also describe the physical characteristics of a person. In this case, the Queen of Cups represents a blond woman who is the recipient of riches."

Ula stared at Katherine. Katherine lifted her chin defiantly. Candy patted her bleached tufted hair.

"Yes," Sam said. "A blond woman with a brilliant mind, a woman who plays the good wife, a woman who is superior to all those around her. I was very impressed by the way this blond woman cleverly concealed her message. Yet, underlying the complexity here, this blond wanted the world to know how she felt about being betrayed. She wanted the world to know that she was intellectually above the common herd, above those who are mere servants."

Katherine could stand it no longer. She leaned forward and slammed her cigarette case on the coffee table. "What the hell are you doing? How dare you accuse me!"

Sam's heart was thumping so hard she could barely get her breath. She forced herself to say, "You are a brilliant woman, Katherine. But you couldn't help revealing yourself through your selection of the cards. Especially this one." Sam held up the Queen of Cups.

Without warning, Ula leaped up. She snatched the card from Sam's hand, screaming, "You've got it all wrong, you stupid bitch!"

Ula tore the Queen of Cups into small ragged pieces and threw them in Katherine's face. From the end table next to the sofa, she grabbed the remaining deck of cards in which Sam had earlier placed the Queen of Pentacles on top. Ula slid the cards out of the box.

"Katherine hasn't got the brains God gave a goose," she said, with a wobbly laugh. "She can't think past her manicures and massages. The card I left was the Queen of Pentacles. Here…see!"

She tossed the deck and box on the couch and held up the Queen of Pentacles. "The Queen of Pentacles! I'm the Queen of Pentacles! I'm the one who selected the cards! I'm the one with the brilliant mind! Me! Ula Vandalay!"

Ula bent over the coffee table. She placed the Queen of Pentacles in position nine. She stared at the card, tipped her head, and then adjusted the Queen so it would align with the cards above and below it.

When she was satisfied, Ula Vandalay sank into the corner of the sofa. She curled into a ball and began to laugh uncontrollably.

CHAPTER 36

❀

"It really was a long shot," Sam said.

"You can say that again," Nick agreed. They had been having the same conversation for the past nine days.

Dressed in gray slacks, a white shirt and light blue pullover, Nick stood behind Sam's chair and massaged her shoulders. She was still in her redplaid nightshirt and had been at her computer since 5:00 A.M., trying to get her brain cells to obey the command to concentrate. Behind schedule, her columns were due like, right now.

She groaned as Nick's fingers dug into a tender spot. "What do you want for breakfast?" she asked.

Nick stopped, glanced at his watch. "It's Tuesday. I've got to leave for Hampton Rotary in about twenty minutes."

"Oh, yeah." She tilted her head and kissed his strong hand, then stood up, rubbing her rump.

"Sam, you've got to get a timer or something. You need to get up from your desk every half hour or so. It isn't good to sit for so long."

Sam wandered over to the couch and flopped down. The sun was making a weak attempt to break through the trees. She rubbed her third eye spot as a light sheen broke out on her forehead.

"Charlie called when you were in the shower."

"Oh, yeah," Nick said. "What did he have to say?"

Nick took up the rocker opposite her and stretched out his long legs.

"A lot. First, the police obtained a search warrant for the Vandalay home. Seems they found a stiletto hidden in Ula's bathroom curtain rod."

Sam squinted in thought. She thought she had seen that very thing on an episode of *Murder She Wrote*.

"Anyway, traces of blood on the blade match Henry Vandalay's blood type.

"Then, some smart detective linked a missing person's call to Gene Meeker. It seems this investigator—Carl Gleason—is missing. He was registered at the Port Grande Hotel in Portsmouth, and his secretary, Glenda somebody, called the hotel manager because Gleason hadn't checked in like he was supposed to.

"When the manager couldn't find him, Glenda called the Portsmouth police. When Gleason didn't return to his room to pick up his things, a detective ended up calling Gleason's secretary back. He found out that Gleason was on a case looking for a Katherine Thayer. That set the detective to wondering if there could be a link between Katherine Thayer and the widow of Henry Vandalay. There was, and further investigation revealed that Katherine's stepfather, Gene Meeker, had hired Gleason to find his stepdaughter. Seems he had heard she married into money, and he wanted his share."

As Nick nodded, pale sunlight played with his curls. He tented his fingers as he said, "Jeez, Sam. That must have been your vision of the man floating in the water, calling out to you."

"I'm sure of it." Sam patted her forehead, then examined her palm. "The media had a ball with this one. Kind of makes last year's debacle with the Cowberry Necklace Murders seem mild."

"I know," Nick said. "I keep thinking about Ula. Imagine a woman living with her husband for two years while he pretends she's his *sister* and he brings another woman into the house."

Sam clucked. "One can only marvel at the lengths a person will go to hang onto what they want. Ula's Soul Number four sure came through with flying colors. She wanted that security and was willing to endure the humiliation. Of course, she hardly ever left the house or spoke to anyone anyway."

"Maybe Ula kept to herself to avoid playing the role of Henry's sister," Nick said. For a moment, he gazed up at the Siamese angel hanging from the ceiling.

"I heard she got herself a high-priced criminal lawyer from Boston," Sam said, "and is, as they say, remaining silent upon the advice of counsel. It'll be interesting to see what angle she uses. She did make quite an entrance during Henry's service. That lime dress, makeup, jewelry, flowing raven hair. She really is a beautiful woman."

"Explain again about the Queens in the Tarot spread," Nick said.

"Well," Sam said, "the only Queen Ula originally placed in the spread was the Queen of Pentacles. One of that card's definitions is security. When you were taking your nap before the reading of the will Sunday afternoon at the mansion, I was looking at the cards, and I kind of vegged out. That's when the floating dead man came to me in a vision. He pointed toward the Queen of Cups and the Queen of Pentacles. Made me think of the dark and the light, the yin and the yang, Ula and Katherine. The thought had gone through my mind when we arrived that Saturday for the weekend.

"Anyway, that's when I remembered that the face cards can represent people. Besides security issues, the Queen of Pentacles also signifies a dark-haired woman. So, I naturally thought of Ula. I also figured, if Ula was really Henry's wife, she had to be terribly jealous of Katherine. So, I figured I would try that little ruse with the layout to see if it would flush out a killer. I replaced the Queen of Pentacles with the Queen of Cups, and played up a blond as the killer. Then I suggested this blond woman was brilliant, hoping that the misplaced glory would push Ula over the edge."

"And it did," Nick said.

"Did you know that the letters in USA add up to a four, like in Ula's first name?" Sam added. "And this country is also security conscious."

Nick executed a jaw-breaking yawn then rubbed his eyes with his palms. "She didn't look too security conscious to me in that green dress she wore Sunday," Nick noted. "She almost fell out of it."

Sam sighed. She frowned at the ceiling as she thought about the thirty pounds that she wanted to lose. She felt like a beached whale.

Quickly shifting gears, she looked over at Nick. "That reminds me. The check Katherine gave me. Since Katherine was not legally married to Henry Vandalay, I doubt if it's any good."

"Better check with Charlie."

"Is that a pun?"

"Sure. Why not?" Nick grinned.

"You know," Sam said, "what I don't understand is why Ula left the Tarot cards at the crime scene. I mean, surely the police would have eventually searched the house and found that hidden altar of hers."

"Like you said," Nick said, rubbing the back of his neck, "at some level, she must have wanted the world to know."

"Of course," Sam reasoned, "Maria was also into the Tarot. Maybe Ula knew about her husband's affair with Maria and thought she could implicate her. And then again, Ula could have said that Katherine knew about her altar to try to shift the blame on her."

"Who knows what went on in Ula's past," Nick said. "Maybe the cards were some kind of statement."

Sam tossed a throw pillow toward her feet and maneuvered it into a foot rest position. She wiggled her toes and thought about pulling off the ragg socks. Was it possible to have claustrophobic feet? The toes on her right foot were not happy with the seam on the ragg sock. She recrossed her feet.

They each followed their own thoughts for several moments. Then Nick said, "I heard Katherine was seen on the arm of that Boston financier, Wiecock."

"Katherine will do okay," Sam said. "She must have had something for Vandalay to have kept her around for two years."

"Probably boosted his ego to have a beautiful young blond on his arm."

Sam grunted, then pulled off her socks and tossed them playfully at Nick. "Don't *you* get any ideas, big boy."

Nick dodged. One sock fell behind his chair, the other one landed in the wicker basket with the girls' stuffed animals. He held his hands up. "I surrender. I can hardly handle you. And by the way, your basketball days are over, my girl." He laughed.

"Hey! I was the leading scorer for two years in high school."

"That was thirty years ago."

"Thirty-one," Sam grumbled. "And thank you for reminding me." She wiggled her toes. Her feet were the best-looking part of her, and no one ever saw them.

Nick gazed at his wife with a smile on his face. "You're still the best looking broad in town."

Sam returned the smile. "And you're the best looking narrow."

Nick shook his head with that you-never-give-up look on his face. A rebellious lock fell over his eyes. He brushed it back.

Sam settled deeper into the cushions, her finger unconsciously tracing the fleshy scar on her left side beneath the plaid nightshirt. "It seems Kenny Ash is acting foreman at Vandalay Enterprises. I also heard that he and Candy are looking for a house. If Ula is convicted, he may have some claim to the Vandalay fortune. I wouldn't be surprised if Ms. Berma Battles has some cards up her sleeve on that issue."

Nick chuckled. "Let's hope they aren't Tarot cards."

They let the silence spin out. Then Sam said, "I'm glad for Kenny and Candy. They lived on the poverty line for so long. Did you know he's vowed to give up cigarettes?"

"Yeah. I heard that. I also heard he was fighting mad when the shock of the whole affair wore off. Imagine asking a man to divorce the woman he loves." It was beyond Nick's scope of understanding. "Want some hot chocolate before I go, babe?"

"No thanks, honey. I think I'll go to The Bog for breakfast. Pick up some scuttlebutt. See how the squirrels are running."

"'The news like squirrels ran.'"

"You've been reading Emily Dickinson," Sam said, pleased.

"No. I've learned by osmosis. You've quoted her before. Like a thousand times." Once again, Nick yawned, then stood up. "You ready for the Cowberry Fair?"

Sam stifled a matching yawn. "As ready as I'll ever be. Agatha will be proud of me."

Nick laughed and bent down to kiss her good-bye. "Hope springs eternal." As he straightened up, his eye fell on the large plant by the doorway. "Oh, by the way, the ficus is dry. You'd better water your little friends."

Sam reached over her head and fingered the spider plant on the table behind her. "Dry as the Sahara desert."

Sam heard the breezeway door open and close as Nick left for his drive to Rotary. She lay on the couch, eyes closed, relishing the quiet. Her body felt warm, cocooned in the safety of her home. The baseboard heat made crinkly noises. She drifted. Life was good.

Finally, the thirsty cries of her leafy friends got to her, and guilt pulled her off the sofa. She headed toward the kitchen with the green plastic watering pot in hand, but her attention was really focused on that last package of Ring Dings in the refrigerator.

Appendix

❀

Your Soul Number

I want the whole nine yards.

Things happen in threes.

I'm at sixes and sevens.

I've got the seven year itch.

Someone once wrote that numbers are the "ultimate reduction of philosophic thought." It's obvious from our common expressions that we have an intuitive understanding of the meaning of numbers. Figures are used for measuring how much, how far, how heavy; numbers represent qualities, characteristics, and predictable cycles.

We find numbers embedded in metaphysical literature throughout the world, including the Christian Bible. Number-coded messages were hidden behind names through a language called Gematria.

In ages past, the precise measurements used for the construction of sacred buildings were meant to bring about a desired result beyond the obvious. The ancient wisdom teaches that the Great Pyramid is a numerical, celestial, and terrestrial accounting in stone.

Numerology is the study of numbers: numerus (Latin), number; -logia (Latin), the study of. Numerology teaches that your basic birth numbers indicate character and predictable progressive cycles.

My husband listened politely one day, many years ago, while I expounded on such subjects, including where we come from and where we're going. He'd been quiet for some time when he suddenly cocked his head, smiled at me and said, "We're just temporary manifestations of solidified light."

That one sentence blew my socks off! Because he is right. We are composed of the material of exploded stars. We are "temporary manifestations of light", star children. He is so smart!

Science teaches that energy—i.e., light—cannot be destroyed; it changes form. So, when we die, our energy is transformed. If we go somewhere after we die, perhaps we were somewhere before we were born.

Like Samantha Blackwell, I don't believe we are born with a blank slate, the *tabula rasa*. I believe we came from somewhere when we were born into this existence, and we will go somewhere when we die. The "we" of which I speak is our souls.

Your Soul Number indicates the qualities you brought in with you at birth. The Soul Number is the depository of all your past light manifestations—much like a computer where every facet of your experience is stored. This depository has also been called the Akashic Records, that great library in the sky where your every thought, word, and deed is catalogued.

When you are faced with the unexpected events that life throws your way, you react instinctively through your Soul Number. Therein lies your past memories, experiences, and abilities. The Soul Number represents the qualities you already possess.

YOUR NAME

Your spoken name creates a sound.

Sound has the ability to create or destroy: sand on a piece of glass will form into beautiful patterns when a violin bow is drawn over the edge of the glass; a soprano's high voice can shatter that same glass. In the Christian Bible, Joshua blew the trumpet and the sound caused the walls of Jericho to tumble down.

The ancient adepts knew the power of sound. They believed that the vowels were sacred sounds. Metaphysical literature abounds with phrases like "the word of God" and "God spoke". There are stories about Egyptian priests whose trained voices could open secret doors in the Great Pyramid.

Words create sounds; sounds produce vibrations; vibrations can create or destroy.

Our names resonate to specific vibratory rhythms. Each time our name is spoken, we absorb a portion of the sound wave that flows over us. Eventually we become our names.

To find your Soul Number, use the number-letter code below. Remember, our language, including our alphabet, is embedded in our consciousness from the moment we are born.

Many of us remember the alphabet song from grade school days— "A, B, C, D, E, F, G,…Now I know my ABCs. Tell me what you think of me." That song placed the letters of the alphabet in numerical order in our subconscious minds. Therefore, we consciously interpret the letters in a numerically sequential fashion.

In the number-letter Code, numbers over 9 have been reduced to a digit. To reduce a number in numerology, add the single numbers to arrive at the base number. For example:

$$20 = 2 + 0 = 2;$$
$$13 = 1 + 3 = 4;$$
$$19 = 1 + 9 = 10, \text{then } 10 = 1 + 0 = 1.$$

Notice that A, J, and S all reduce to a 1; B, K, and T reduce to a 2; and so on.

NUMBER-LETTER CODE

A = 1	J = 10/1	S = 19/10/1
B = 2	K = 11/2	T = 20/2
C = 3	L = 12/3	U = 21/3
D = 4	M = 13/4	V = 22/4
E = 5	N = 14/5	W = 23/5
F = 6	O = 15/6	X = 24/6
G = 7	P = 16/7	Y = 25/7
H = 8	Q = 17/8	Z = 26/8
I = 9	R = 18/9	

Find your Soul Number by adding the numerical value of the vowels in your *full name at birth* using the number-letter Code above.

Example:

> 1 1 1 51 9 5 6   1   = 30
>
> Agatha Beatrice Coldbath
>
> 30 = 3 + 0 = 3
>
> Agatha's Soul Number is a 3

(No wonder she's always the center of attention!)

You can also work out other name changes you have experienced, but remember, the name at birth is the foundation upon which all the other names rest. You might equate this to the foundation of your home: you may renovate, paint, and refurbish your home but you seldom change the cement foundation.

Traditional numerology teaches that the vowels are the letters A—E—I—O—U and sometimes Y (when Y sounds like or stands for a vowel, as in the name Lynn).

Personally, I use the letter 'Y' as both a vowel and a consonant. Even the construction of the letter 'Y', with its diverging arms, suggests two paths. Individuals with Y's in their names may have led two separate lives in a prior existence. That inner diversity prompts them to look for separate paths in this life.

For instance, a conservative banker may secretly give palmistry readings through the classifieds. The banker's clients may know nothing about her palmistry, and her palmistry clients are not cognizant of her banking connections.

Work out the vowels in your name by first adding the 'Y' (or 'Y's'), then drop the 'Y' (or Y's') and add again. These two numbers indicate the diversity within you.

Example 1:

Add the Y (7):
1 1 639 5 6(7)
Sandra Louise Coby
1+1+6+3+9+6+7=38
$$38 = 3 + 8 = 11$$
$$11 = 1 + 1 = 2$$
(Also written as 11/2)

Example 2:

Add again, without the Y (7):
1+1+6+3+9+5+6=31
$$31 = 4$$
(Also written as 31/4)

Sandra Louise Coby has a double Soul Number: 2 and 4. When you find your Soul Number, read the delineation below.

Please note: The nine number categories below are the basic nine families to which all double numbers belong. For instance, Soul Number five includes 14 (1+4) and 23 (2+3) and 32 (3+2) and so on. The double numbers further refine your personality within the basic number family.

Your Soul Number

Your Soul Number indicates the qualities you possessed when you were born. These are the qualities you can rely on when the need arises. They are the spiritual credits in your bank book. Your Soul Number is your harbor of safety and comfort; it's the place where you feel most at home.

For more on this subject, please refer to my numerology books listed at the front of this book.

Soul Number One

You are an independent personality with an inner core of focus that sets you apart from others. People may look to you for leadership; however, you don't want to be burdened with the responsibilities that come with running an organization. You need the freedom to just get up and go.

In past lives, you were the pioneer, setting off on uncharted paths, seeking new vistas to conquer and new ideas to explore. You still have the urge to be first and best at what you do, which is why you don't like to take orders or work as a subordinate.

Because of your inner strength, you can alienate those who are emotionally insecure. You react instinctively by surging forward and taking over. It seems effortless on your part, and that is why some would try to appoint you the leader. But you prefer to go off on your own to figure things out.

You are comfortable as the loner, whether in positions of leadership or in a tucked-away nest of solitude. In these places, you have no restrictions; you have the freedom to do it your way, without interference from others.

Rely upon your inner core of strength and individuality. You are different. Treasure that difference.

Soul Number Two

You are the power behind the throne. You want to stay quietly in the background to observe, absorb, and assimilate the experiences around you. Therefore, you are the peacemaker.

You may find that loud noises, dissension, and trouble are unnerving for you. As a result, you draw upon your natural ability to see both sides of a situation to bring about a peaceful solution. Balance and harmony are important.

Your ability to consider both sides may make it difficult at times to make a decision. But this same ability will put you in the judge's seat as the arbitrator. Others will sense your fairness. You may find that you go through life straightening picture frames and realigning figurines because of this innate need for symmetry in your environment.

Your sensitivity and refinement show through your love of music and the arts.

The hidden, unseen side of life may fascinate you. You are tuned in to the patterns and rhythms in nature and life. You have a natural ability for psychic and intuitive development.

Your strengths are your tact, depth of understanding, and ability to reflect. Use your all-seeing eye to help others acquire self-knowledge. And draw upon your earned abilities as the diplomat to create peace in the lives of those you touch.

Soul Number Three

You are talented. You have a natural ability to perform and entertain. Life is a stage, and you are the central player. You are like Annie, singing, "The sun will come out tomorrow." By letting your inner optimism shine through, you draw others to you like the sun on the first warm days of spring.

You believe that your thoughts create your reality. Share this optimistic philosophy with others. You will bask in their admiration. Your innate sense is that if you help others, you will also help yourself.

One of the outlets for your vast imagination and for the beauty and happiness you seek is self-expression: art, public speaking, writing, acting, creative pursuits, and positive thinking.

You know that travel broadens your horizons, bringing you into contact with different peoples and cultures. Use your immeasurable social skills in the service of others. This is where you feel comfortable. It's the stage for your many creative abilities.

Soul Number Four

You have a strong need for security. That's why you need land, a bank account, and tangible objects around you. You are also the conservative builder with a well-developed sense of form and structure. You feel comfortable in disciplined environments where you can use your practical and analytical abilities.

Tradition is important to you, and you crave an orderly environment with everything in its place. Inborn tenacity makes detailed, routine work natural for you. You like to feel a sense of accomplishment when you're done, something concrete from your efforts.

You like to figure out how things work, often by taking them apart and putting them back together. Your sense of order and organization sets a standard for others, and they depend on your solid, trustworthy nature.

You have a methodical and logical approach to life, sort of an "I'm from Missouri, show me" attitude. You are a patient planner, with a practical eye for saving and an aptitude with finances or numbers. Your ability to look to the past establishes a foundation from which you make sound judgments about the future.

Land and ecology may interest you, for you are the master builder, the architect, the cog that keeps the wheels of society running.

Soul Number Five

Your five senses are always on high alert.

You want to know, experience, taste, feel. You don't want life to pass you by. Your restless and curious nature results from your inner need to accumulate information. Freedom is the most important ingredient in your life because it allows you the latitude for experience, travel, change, and multiple contacts, all of which add to your storehouse of knowledge.

As the communication center, you are the matrix to which all lines of inquiry lead. Your mind is an encyclopedia of disparate facts that you can pull up when anyone asks a question or needs directions. Like the flitting butterfly that ensures reproduction of the flowers it brushes, you spread creative information and excitement wherever you go. Your urge is to constantly search for experiences that will stimulate your five senses.

You are a natural detective with inexhaustible energy and a quick, clever mind. You have above average intelligence. This, coupled with access to your vast storehouse of information, reinforces your ability to adapt to any situation.

You dislike routine. In order to dissipate your nervous energy, you need changing scenery, new horizons, the freedom to travel and explore. This will provide you with the variety in life you crave. You want to live life to the fullest.

Soul Number Six

You are the lover of home, family, children, and community. You are sympathetic and patient, willing to listen to the problems of others. You have a natural ability to solve problems, so wear a thick towel on your shoulder because many will cry there.

Balance and harmony are an integral part of your life, therefore you are the artist, peacemaker, tolerant arbitrator, charming hostess—all key words for Mother. You tend to "Mother" others, and you need a pleasant home environment. Domesticity is important to you.

You want to bring beauty into the world through your love of the arts and other avenues that create harmony. You are the cosmic teacher, parent, nurse, or community volunteer. You are here to teach others what you have learned in past lives about sympathy, tolerance, loyalty, and affection.

The happiness and well-being of those in your care is paramount in your life. Since love, beauty, and harmony are your soul urges, your voice may have a soothing effect on others.

Soul Number Seven

In past lives, you may have been a priestess in a temple where you sought knowledge and wisdom above all other things. You have a tendency toward introspection and study. At times, you prefer your own thoughts to the conversations and company of others. Your own feelings and emotions are private.

You may find that you need to get away to the mountains or the seashore or the forests to renew your connections to nature and the universe. Listen to these urges. They feed your soul.

You live in a philosophical world of your own making where you seek silence and meditation. Your mind is your greatest asset. Noise and confusion disturb you. Nature and mysteries inspire you as you seek to understand the scientific, philosophical, and spiritual laws of life.

You are highly sensitive and intuitive, and may have powers of clairvoyance and extrasensory perception. You may not have always been understood by popular society in your search perfection. This deep need for truth still motivates you today. Use your finely tuned sensitivity to inspire others toward that perfection which you seek.

Soul Number Eight

You, above most others, understand Byron's line from *The Corsair*: "Ah, the weight of these splendid chains."

In your past, you were very much in the world of commerce and business where you were called on to use your executive abilities to handle large scale enterprises. You handle problems with vision, confidence, and good judgment, and you have the ability to organize major undertakings.

You have an innate ambition that stems from the past. Because you have the perseverance and strength to succeed, you are a natural leader. You may feel the desire to control situations because you feel you are the best equipped to handle any problems.

Your analytical acumen and sense of values stands you well in any business situation. You have an inborn desire to reach the top, and the confidence and courage to stay there. Your imagination is geared toward the material world where power, wealth, and success are possible. You were a steward of the resources of the earth, whether in finances, ecology, or land use. Use your wise, practical abilities to honor the earth, and bring order and material comfort into the world around you.

Soul Number Nine

You were the humanitarian with a desire to help the world, and you still carry these urges within you. Intuitive and sensitive, you feel a deep love for the weak, helpless, and less fortunate beings in the world.

You sought to find the balance between the material and spiritual sides of life. You understood that others looked to you for truth. Your influence was broad in a field where you served others. You may have shared your wisdom as a teacher or healer, giving freely of your abilities without expecting reward.

You had to learn to let go of the material side of life. In letting go, you found that you gained. Part of your wisdom was your understanding that you own your possessions; they do not own you.

Your vivid imagination may at times place you in a self-absorbed world of your own making; therefore, to some you may seem distant. However, you understand that we are all one. What we do to one affects all of us. This deep love for humanity may draw to you those who need to drink of your wisdom and open-heartedness.

Share your knowledge, for you are the humanitarian whose life should be an example for others.

*   *   *   *   *

Thank you for spending this time with me. May your life be blessed with Love and Light.

dusty bunker

About the Author

...dusty bunker, internationally recognized author of several books on the metaphysical and symbolic nature of numbers and dreams, brings her knowledge of the arcane into The Number Mystery Series. Her many credits include a segment in the Time-Life Books Series: Mysteries of the Unknown, columns for Mademoiselle Magazine, a dream column which ran for five years in the Manchester Union Leader, a humorous shopping column, as well as Tree Line, a cartoon strip for a New Hampshire publication.

One Deadly Rhyme is the first title in her new series: The Number Mysteries. The second title is *The Two-Timing Corpse.*

dusty grew up in a Navy family and has lived in the four corners of the United States—Maine, Florida, California, and Washington State, and some of the states in between. She graduated from Saugus High School in Massachusetts, and attended the University of New Hampshire. She now resides in a small New Hampshire town with her husband. Her grown family lives nearby.

0-595-21621-8

Printed in the United States
24368LVS00001B/93

9 780595 216215